Books by Jonathan Kellerman

FICTION

ALEX DELAWARE NOVELS

Deception (2010)
Evidence (2009)
Bones (2008)
Compulsion (2008)
Obsession (2007)
Gone (2006)
Rage (2005)
Therapy (2004)
A Cold Heart (2003)
The Murder Book (2002)
Flesh and Blood (2001)
Dr. Death (2000)
Monster (1999)

Survival of the Fittest (1997)
The Clinic (1997)
The Web (1996)
Self-Defense (1995)
Bad Love (1994)
Devil's Waltz (1993)
Private Eyes (1992)
Time Bomb (1990)
Silent Partner (1989)
Over the Edge (1987)
Blood Test (1986)
When the Bough Breaks (1985)

OTHER NOVELS

True Detectives (2009)
Capital Crimes (with Faye Kellerman, 2006)
Twisted (2004)
Double Homicide (with Faye Kellerman, 2004)
The Conspiracy Club (2003)
Billy Straight (1998)
The Butcher's Theater (1988)

NONFICTION

With Strings Attached: The Art and Beauty of Vintage Guitars (2008)
Savage Spawn: Reflections on Violent Children (1999)
Helping the Fearful Child (1981)
Psychological Aspects of Childhood Cancer (1980)

FOR CHILDREN, WRITTEN AND ILLUSTRATED

Jonathan Kellerman's ABC of Weird Creatures (1995)
Daddy, Daddy, Can You Touch the Sky? (1994)

DECEPTION

JONATHAN KELLERMAN

DECEPTION

AN ALEX DELAWARE NOVEL

BALLANTINE BOOKS

NEW YORK

Published in the United States by Ballantine Books,
an imprint of The Random House Publishing Group,
a division of Random House, Inc., New York.

BALLANTINE and colophon are registered trademarks
of Random House, Inc.

Library of Congress Cataloging-in-Publication Data
Kellerman, Jonathan.
Deception: an Alex Delaware novel / Jonathan Kellerman.
p. cm.
ISBN 978-0-345-50567-5
eBook ISBN 978-0-345-51923-8
1. Delaware, Alex (Fictitious character)—Fiction.   2. Sturgis, Milo (Fictitious
character)—Fiction.   3. Psychologists—Fiction.   4. Police—California—Los
Angeles—Fiction.   5. Sexual abuse victims—Fiction.   6. Women teachers—Crimes
against—Fiction.   7. Preparatory schools—Fiction.   8. Brentwood (Los Angeles,
Calif.)—Fiction.   I. Title.
PS3561.E3865D43 2010
813'.54—dc22   2010000507

Printed in the United States of America on acid-free paper

www.ballantinebooks.com

2   4   6   8   9   7   5   3   1

First Edition

To Oscar

DECEPTION

1

The woman had haunted eyes.

Pale, drooping at the outer edges, they stared into the unseen camera with an odd combination of defiance and defeat.

She didn't move. Neither did the camera. The wall behind her was brown-blue, the color of an old bruise. The couch on which she perched was gray. She was a pretty woman, made less so by fear. Her shoulders were bunched high, her neck tendons taut as bridge cables. A black, sleeveless dress showcased soft white arms. Too-blond hair fell limply to her shoulders.

Moments passed. Nothing happened. In another situation I might've cracked wise about it being one of Andy Warhol's old anti-films: interminable, static studies of the Empire State Building, a man sleeping.

When a homicide lieutenant brings you something to watch, you keep your mouth shut.

Milo stood behind me. His black hair and raincoat were rumpled. The coat was cheap, green, wrinkled past the point of salvation. It gave off a not unpleasant vegetative odor. He'd placed a massive breakfast burrito in a take-out box on my desk, hadn't touched it.

When he drops in, he usually beelines for the fridge, empties a quart of something, raids the shelves for bad carbs. This morning, he'd marched to my office, loaded the DVD with a flourish.

"For your consideration."

Blanche, my little French bulldog, sat next to me, uncharacteristically serious. She'd tried her usual smile, had figured out something was different when Milo didn't stoop to pet her.

I rubbed her knobby head. She looked up at me, returned her attention to the monitor.

The woman's lips moved.

Milo said, "Here we go."

More silence on the screen.

"So I lied."

The woman said, "My name is Elise Freeman. I'm a teacher and tutor at Windsor Preparatory Academy in Brentwood." Her voice was throaty. She knotted her fingers, flopped them onto her lap. "I'm making this recording to document sustained abuse I have received at the hands of faculty members at Windsor Preparatory Academy in Brentwood. Which I will hereon refer to as Prep."

Deep breath. "For the past two years at Prep, I have been subjected to repeated, unwarranted, aggressive, and distressing sexual harassment from three individuals. Their names are." Her right hand rose. A finger pointed upward. "Enrico Hauer. H-A-U-E-R." Two fingers: "James Winterthorn." More slow, enunciated spelling, then a trio of digits. "Pat Skaggs."

The hand dropped. "For the past two years Enrico Hauer, James Winterthorn, and Pat Skaggs have made my life a living hell by engaging in brutal, unsolicited, and threatening sexual behavior.

I am making this recording so that in the event something violent happens to me, the authorities will know where to look. I do not know what else to do as I feel trapped and frightened and have nowhere to turn. I hope this recording never needs to come to light but if it does, I am glad that I made it."

Her eyes clenched shut. Her lips moved soundlessly and she slumped. Suddenly her jaw jutted and she was sitting up straight. More defiance than defeat.

Staring hard at the camera. "Thanks for listening."

The screen went blue. Milo said, "Talk about a D-movie plot device."

I said, "But you're here. She was murdered?"

"Maybe. She's on ice."

"Backlog at the coroner?"

His laughter was harsh. "Nope, this morning I'm Mr. Literal. Ice of the dry sort. Frozen CO_2. She was found in her home, lying in a bathtub full of the stuff."

I tried to picture the blond woman as a frozen corpse, didn't like the image that flashed in my head, and reverted to Doctor Helpful. "Someone trying to mess up the time-of-death estimate? Or maybe a psychopath coming up with a new way to showcase his handiwork."

He winced, as if all contingencies were painful. Removing the disc, he slipped it back into a clear plastic jewel box. Not bothering to glove up; the DVD had already been printed, matched only to Elise Freeman.

I said, "Where are you going with this?"

He rotated his neck. "Got coffee? Maybe some toast?"

CHAPTER

2

We left my house with black coffee in travel-cups and six slices of lavishly buttered sesame-rye.

When Milo wants to think, phone, text, or sleep he sometimes asks me to do the driving. It's against LAPD regs but so are lots of things. He makes up for my mileage cost with bar tabs and such.

The toast was occupying his attention so I offered to take my Seville. He shook his head, scattering crumbs, continued to his latest unmarked, a bronze Chevy Malibu with a phlegmy ignition. Heading north on Beverly Glen, he steered with one hand, stuffed rye bread into his mouth with the other.

The police radio was switched off. The burrito rested in the backseat and filled the car with *eau de frijole*.

He said, "In answer to your question, too messy."

"That was low on my list of questions. Where are we going?"

"Where she died, Studio City."

"Not a West L.A. case but you're on it."

"Not an official homicide but I'm on it."

The difference between an experienced psychologist and a novice is knowing when not to speak.

I sat back and drank coffee.

Milo said, "Maybe there'll be a microwave and I can heat up the burrito."

Elise Freeman had resided in a green-sided, tar-roofed bungalow on a spidery, tree-shaded lane east of Laurel Canyon and north of Ventura Boulevard. Close enough to the thoroughfare to hear Valley traffic, but mature vegetation and larger houses blocked any urban visuals.

The little green box sat at the terminus of a long dirt driveway split by a strip of concrete. A gray sedan was parked near the front door. Full-sized car but not big enough to hide the bungalow's blemishes as we drew close: worn and ragged siding eroded to raw wood in patches, curling shingles, a noticeable listing to the right due to a sinking foundation.

No crime scene tape that I could see, no uniforms on watch.

I said, "When was she found?"

"Last night by her boyfriend. He says he talked to her on the phone three days ago but after that, she stopped returning his calls. A forty-eight-hour time frame fits the coroner's TOD guesstimate. Probably at the tail end—early morning. Apparently, dry ice doesn't melt, it sublimates—goes straight into the atmosphere—so there's no water residue for estimating degradation. In an ice chest, the rate of sublimation is five to ten pounds every twenty-four hours, but it's faster under normal room temperature."

"Any empty ice bags left behind?"

"Nope. Exactly."

Someone had cleaned up.

"The scene's still intact?"

He scowled. "I never got a chance to see the scene because my involvement began at five thirty a.m. today when Deputy Chief Weinberg woke me from a rare good dream. The DVD, the key to the house, and what's passing for a file were messengered to my house ten minutes later."

"High intrigue and an egregious break in procedure," I said. "Sounds like orders from on high."

He continued slowly up the drive, checking out the surroundings. Layers of greenery to the left, a two-story Colonial mansion to the right. The big house was wood-sided like the bungalow, but what I could see of it was painted white and adorned with black shutters. It sat on a generous lot partitioned from Freeman's skimpy ribbon of real estate by a ten-foot stucco fence topped with used brick. Bougainvillea topped areas of brick, amping up the privacy quotient on both sides.

The smaller structure might've begun life as an outbuilding of the manse, back when multi-acre estates spread across Valley hillsides. A guesthouse, servant's quarters, maybe tack storage for one of the cowboy actors wanting proximity to the Burbank film-lots that passed for Wild West badlands.

Milo rolled to a stop inches from the Crown Vic. No one at the wheel, but a man in a cream-colored suit emerged from behind the bungalow.

A hair over Milo's six three, he was broad, black, bespectacled. The suit was double-breasted and tailored to nearly conceal a gun bulge.

He gave a cursory nod. "Milo."

"Stan."

"And this is . . ."

"Dr. Delaware."

"Your psychologist."

"That makes it sound like I'm in therapy, Stan."

"Therapy's in fashion now, Milo. The department looks kindly on self-awareness and insight."

"Must have missed that memo."

A big hand extended. "Stanley Creighton, Doctor."

We shook.

Milo said, "What brings you down from Olympus, Stan?"

"More like Bunker Hill," said Creighton. "I'm here to keep an eye out."

"New clause in the captain's job description?"

Creighton said, "One does what one is told." He turned to me. "Speaking of which, Doctor, I appreciate what you do but you shouldn't be here."

"He's cleared for takeoff, Stan."

Creighton frowned. Cool morning but the back of his neck was moist ebony. "I must've missed *that* memo."

"Probably buried under a pile of wisdom from His Munificence."

Creighton flashed beautiful teeth. "Why don't you call him that to his face? Doctor, you really need to absent yourself."

"Stan, he really doesn't."

Creighton's smile degraded to something cold and menacing. "You're telling me you got papal dispensation for his presence at this specific crime scene?"

"Why would I improvise about that, Stan?"

"Why indeed," said Creighton. "Except for the fact that rationality doesn't always figure into human behavior. Which is why my wife, who has an M.D., still smokes a pack and a half a day."

"Feel free to call the Vatican to verify, Stan."

Creighton studied me. "Can I assume that Lieutenant Sturgis has informed you of the need for exceptional discretion here, Doctor?"

"Absolutely."

"Exceptional," he repeated.

"I love exceptions," I said.

"Why's that, Doctor?"

"They're a lot more interesting than rules."

Creighton tried to smile again. The result fit him like panty hose on a mastiff. "I respect what you do, Doctor. My wife's a neurologist, works with psychologists all the time. But now I'm wondering if Lieutenant Sturgis relies on you so not because of your professional skills, maybe it's more of a personality thing." Expanding his chest. "As in wiseass loves company."

Before I could answer he wheeled on Milo. "How much time are you going to need here?"

"Hard to say."

"I'm after a little more precision."

"C'mon, Stan—"

"You've already seen the crime scene pix, the body's long gone, the prints and fluid swabs are at the lab, and your vic's computer was lifted, so what do you expect to accomplish?"

No mention of the DVD.

Milo said, "Hell, Stan, why even bother to work when we can go on detective.com?"

"Yuk yuk yuk, ka-ching, rim shot," said Creighton. "Bottom line: There's nothing this place can tell you. Unless you're one of those paranormals, think you can feel vibrations."

"You were in my place you wouldn't do a walk-through?"

"Sure, cover your ass. But walk quickly. I've been here since six a.m., which is an hour after Weinberg woke me up and gave me my orders. Morning's aren't my fun time. This particular morning, my knee's being a nasty bitch. So what I'm gonna do right now is go for a nice, loose walk and when I get back, I strongly prefer to see you the hell out of here so *I* can get the hell out of here and do the job they officially pay me for."

Favoring me with a contemptuous glance. "Be careful, Doctor."

We watched him stride off, limping slightly.

I said, "Who'd he play for?"

"U. Nevada, didn't make the big-time."

"What do they officially pay him for?"

"He used to work Sex Crimes. Now he pushes paper and attends meetings."

"And occasionally plays watchman."

"Funny 'bout that."

We continued toward the green house.

I said, "If it's all so hush-hush how'd you get the chief to approve me?"

"I'll answer that once you're approved."

The bungalow's front porch creaked under our weight. A hummingbird feeder dangling from the overhang was empty and dry. Milo pulled out a tagged key and unlocked the door and we stepped into a small, dim living room. Blank space atop a TV table.

I said, "Her video gear's at the lab?"

Nod.

"Where was the DVD found?"

"Stuck in the middle of a stack of her favorite movies. Or so the file claims."

"Creighton didn't mention it."

"Like I said, it got messengered."

"By who?"

"Guy in a suit."

"And a badge?"

"That, too."

I said, "Any explanation?"

"A note in the envelope said it was found in a stack of the victim's DVDs."

"But not cataloged as evidence."

"Funny 'bout that."

"Who took the initial call?"

"Two North Hollywood D's who have absolutely nothing to say to me."

"Are you planning to tell me what got the gears grinding?"

"It wasn't her," he said. "They couldn't care less about her. *That's* the point, Alex."

I said, "The suspects are the point. Where they're employed."

"You never heard that from me."

"A school has that much clout?"

"It does when the right people's kids are enrolled. You ever have patients from Windsor Prep?"

"A few."

"Any pattern you'd care to share?"

"Affluent, attractive kids. For the most part, bright, but under lots of pressure academically, athletically, and socially. In other words, no different from any other prep school."

"This case makes it real different."

"Because of one student in particular."

Silence.

"College applications go in soon," I said. "Here's a wild guess: The chief has a kid aiming for the Ivy League."

He shoved a coarse shock of hair off his brow. Fuzzy light advertised every pock and knot on his face. "*I* never heard that from *you.*"

"Son or daughter?"

"Son," he said. "Only child. Another Einstein, according to his mommy, the Virgin Mary."

"Talk about a mixed metaphor."

"What the hell, they were both nice Jewish boys."

"Graduating senior?"

"Graduating with honors and aiming for Yale."

I said, "It's the toughest year ever, huge upsurge of applications, lots of honor students are going to be disappointed. A couple of patients I saw as little kids have come back for moral support and they say the most trivial factor can nudge the scales. A big-time scandal would energize the Rejection Gods."

He bowed. "O Great Swami of the East, your wisdom has pierced the miasma." He began circling the room. "Ol' Stanley was wrong. Why I *rely* upon you has nothing to do with personality."

Creighton might've been off about that but to my eye he was right about the house yielding nothing of value.

The miserly space had already taken on an abandoned feel. The front room, carelessly and cheaply furnished, sported a U-build bookshelf full of high school texts, SAT and ACT practice manuals, a few photography volumes featuring pretty shots of faraway places, paperbacks by Jane Austen, Aphra Behn, and George Eliot.

The plywood-and-Formica kitchenette was a sixties bootleg. Wilting fruit and vegetables moldered in the mini-fridge; a couple of Lean Cuisine boxes sat in the freezer compartment. A kitchen cabinet was crammed full of liquor mini-bottles and some full-sized quarts. Budget gin but Grey Goose vodka, no mixers prettying up intentions.

The sole bedroom was a nine-by-nine cave set up with a twin bed and IKEA trimmings.

Gloomy because a single window looked out to a wall of creeping ivy. Hillside close enough to touch but the frame was painted shut. A cheap fan in the corner pretended to circulate air. No match for faint overtones of decomposition.

Faint because dry ice had slowed down the inevitable. But we all rot, it's just a matter of time.

I said, "Any maggots?"

"A sprinkle in her nose and ears, mommy flies probably got in under the door. Little bastards were frozen stiff, dumb vermin."

He searched the room. A limited, drab wardrobe filled a makeshift closet. Oppressively sensible down to white cotton, full-cut underwear.

Crowding the bed was a space-saving, nearly wood desk. Vase of dry flowers on top, next to a pale rectangle where the computer had sat. A photo in a white wood frame showed Elise Freeman and a red-bearded bald man around her age standing near a bank of slot machines in an excruciatingly bright, garish room. Both of them in T-shirts and shorts, glazed around the eyes, beaming. The man held up a sheaf of paper money. Elise Freeman snaked an arm around his waist and flashed a victory sign.

On the bottom frame panel, cursive in red marker read: *Sal strikes it big in Reno!* Adorning the boast were hand-drawn pink hearts and green daisies.

Milo said, "Nice to be lucky once in a while," and continued to have his way with drawers and shelves.

The final stop was the bathroom. Modular fiberglass prefab unit; another aftermarket.

The medicine cabinet had been emptied by the crime scene techs. The tub was grubby but unhelpful.

Milo kept staring at it. If he was feeling vibrations, he wasn't showing it.

Finally, he turned away. "Boyfriend's a guy not surprisingly named Sal, last name Fidella. He let himself in with his own key.

Her car was here, no sign of forced entry or disarray. He found her in the tub immersed in dry ice, naked and blue. Accounting for sublimation, someone bought bags of the stuff, maybe twenty, thirty pounds. Because of no blood, the initial assumption was an O.D. Even though she hadn't vomited and Fidella claims she didn't use drugs and there were no pill bottles nearby. Fidella called 911. The tape's in the file and I've listened to it three times. He sounds totally freaked. But I haven't met him and I know nothing about him except what North Hollywood wrote. Which is no more than his driver's license says, so I'm reserving judgment."

"Where does he live?"

"Not far from here, Sherman Oaks."

"A couple but they live apart."

"Sometimes that works better."

"Sometimes it means domestic drama."

"You'll have a chance to meet the guy. Any other insights?"

"On the DVD she doesn't come across theatrical. Just the opposite: When she had good reason to dramatize, she played herself down."

"Depressed. You're thinking suicide?"

"Was she on top of the ice or submerged?"

"Partially submerged."

"That would've meant severe cold-pressor pain within seconds. Skin burns, as well."

"She was burned, all right."

"Most suicides avoid pain," I said. "And displaying yourself that way is flamboyant and exhibitionistic, nothing like the woman on that disc."

"Maybe she was trying to draw attention to those three teachers."

"In that case, she would've left a note and made sure the DVD was out in the open, not in the middle of a stack. Better yet, she'd have mailed it. There's also the matter of no empty ice bags."

"Those could be out in the trash, soon as we're out of here, I'll check." He took another look at the bathtub. Sagged. "Yeah, it's murder. You know it, I know it, His Grace knows it."

"But he'd love it if you could say otherwise."

"No signature on the note that came with the disc, but I know his handwriting. Even when he prints."

"Thought he had integrity."

"Everything's relative."

I said, "Who sells frozen CO_2 around here?"

"Let's find out."

3

Two plastic garbage cans at the rear of the house were empty. Milo phoned the sanitation department, found out pickup wasn't for three days. Ten minutes of bureaucratic-maze-running got him talking to a lab supervisor downtown. Yes, all trash and other items from the crime scene had been taken for analysis; not a clue on when that would start, the case had been marked non-emergency.

When Milo asked if empty dry ice bags and Elise Freeman's computer were part of the haul, he got put on hold. The answer, several minutes later, raised lumps on his jaw.

He clicked off, strode toward the unmarked. "No access to that information at this time."

We got in just as Captain Stan Creighton returned, necktie loose, jacket flapping, talking on a cell phone.

As we drove away, he was still on the phone. Talking faster.

◆

A trio of ice-rental outfits were situated within five miles of the murder scene. At the closest two, no one had purchased any frozen CO_2 for weeks. Both clerks said, "We do that mostly in the summer."

At Gary's Ice House and Party Rentals on Fulton and Saticoy, in Van Nuys, a muscular, puffy-faced kid with three eyebrow rings and a barbed-wire biceps tattoo studied Milo's card and said, "Yeah, dude bought a whole bunch." Staring closer. "Homicide? He's like a killer?"

"When did this happen?"

"I'd have to say Monday."

"What time of day?"

"I'd have to say seven."

"Morning or evening?"

"Evening, I close at eight."

"You sell a lot of dry ice?"

"Tailgate parties, long trips, not that much. Most places don't sell nuggets, just block. I asked Dude which one he wanted, he's like dry ice, thirty pound, in this Spanish accent. I gave him nuggets because we don't sell so many of those, why not get rid of 'em."

Out came Milo's pad. "Latino guy."

"Yeah."

"How old?"

"I dunno, thirty, forty? Looked like one of them dudes waits for day jobs outside the paint store over there." Pointing west.

"How'd he pay?"

"Three tens."

"How much dry ice did that buy him?"

"Thirty pounds of nuggets. They come in special bags, slows down the sublimation a little. That means the stuff turns to gas. Even with bags and an ice chest, you're gonna lose ten percent a day."

"This guy have an ice chest?"

"Not that I saw, he just carried the bags away."

"What was his demeanor?"

"His what?"

"His mood. Was he nervous, friendly?"

"I'd have to say kinda confused. And in a hurry."

"Confused how?"

"Didn't know squat about what he was buying," said the kid. "Took nuggets when most people like blocks and we even trim to size."

"How many bags of nuggets are we talking about?"

"Three ten-pounders. Dude really killed someone with D.I.? What, like froze someone to death? Or burned 'em? You gotta be careful with it, it touches you, it burns bad."

"How else could you hurt someone with it?"

"What do you mean?"

"Is there anything besides freezing or burning that makes it dangerous?"

"Well," said the kid, "I use it to kill ants. You get something in a closed-off space, you put a piece of D.I. in and they get so cold their bodies stop working and also they breathe in the sublimation and die. It's carbon dioxide, that's the global warming gas."

"Plants breathe carbon dioxide," said Milo.

"They do? Well, ants ain't plants." Laughter. "My sister had an ant problem in her basement and I stuck in a piece of D.I. block, taped off everywhere, couple days later millions of dead ants all over, she had to vacuum them, it was gross. So what did the dude do?"

"We're not sure. Do you still have the bills he paid you with?"

"Nope. Armored car came yesterday, collected everything from the register and the safe."

"Can you describe this guy a little more?"

"Mexican, like I said. Like thirty, forty. Little guy."

"Facial hair?"

"Like a beard? Nope, clean."

"What makes you think he was one of the day laborers?"

"He was wearing those white painter's pants." Nodding in appreciation of his own insight. The eyebrow rings jangled.

"Remember his shirt?"

"Um, let's see . . . T-shirt, like too big for him . . . um—oh, yeah, white, from a college, UC something . . . had a weird-looking animal on it, like a big rat with a long tongue."

"Oversized," said Milo. "Like a gangbanger might wear?"

"Dude was no gangbanger. No tats, no attitude, just a confused little dude in painter's pants. I figured he wanted the D.I. for a job. Killing ants or something."

"Wearing a college shirt but not a college guy."

The kid laughed. "Dude's waiting for day labor he probably didn't even get a GED."

As we left, I said, "The UC Irvine mascot is an anteater."

"And here I was thinking skunks were finally getting some respect."

We walked the two blocks to the paint store. Lots of boarded-up businesses punctuated the journey, with others on the brink. Five day laborers idled by the curb, looking bored and defeated. When times are bad, the trickle-down switches to misery.

All five men wore baggy white painter's pants, two had on white tees. One shirt was printed with the Disneyland logo, the other was paint-specked but blank. The first man who spotted us tried to walk away. Milo bellowed: "Stop."

When that didn't work: *"Policia, no La Migra."*

He talked to each worker, using LAPD Spanish and a relatively soft, detached approach. No one admitted to buying dry ice. Most of the men claimed not to know what it was.

One guy's eyes moved a lot and Milo asked for his I.D. first. Close to fifty, tall, thin, balding, droopy mustache. A California driver's license was handed over with shaking hands. Milo's request for backup paper brought a shrug. Handing the man his business card, he said, "Amigo, you help me, I help you."

Downcast eyes.

"Anything you wanna tell me now about a guy wears a UC Irvine shirt?"

"No, boss."

Milo pointed to the card. "See that? Lieutenant. That means big boss—*gran patrón. Muy importante.*"

"Okay."

"Okay what?"

"You *gran patrón.*"

Elise Freeman's DMV picture elicited a blank stare. Same for the other men. Milo handed out five cards, told the men cooperating would bring good luck. Five blank faces stared back.

Heading back to the car, Milo re-read the jumpy guy's stats. "Hector Ruiz, lives in Beverly Hills north of the boulevard where the estates are. Some forger's got a sense of humor."

"Maybe he was a live-in employee."

"Oh, sure, they dress him in livery and call him Jeeves. So . . . you see any obvious reason for a day laborer to need thirty pounds of ice? And the quantity's damn close to the techies' estimate."

"Unless Anteater picked his shirt with significance, my bet's on a paid buy to muddy the trail."

"Or nervous little dude's our killer." Laughing. "Like I believe that."

His cell played Beethoven's "Für Elise." Dark joke? No sense asking.

A twenty-second conversation ensued. Milo's part consisted of several "yessirs." Each one lowered his posture.

He pocketed the phone. "Summoned to the mount, A-sap."

"Have fun."

"We, not me."

"I'm invited?"

"You're demanded."

CHAPTER

4

In dream traffic, the police chief's office at Parker Center is a twenty-minute eastbound glide from Van Nuys.

Change of venue and bad traffic turned the drive into a seventy-minute, westbound stop-and-fume.

The Stagecoach Bistro abutted the ninth hole of a Calabasas country club built to look exclusive but open to anyone who could come up with the monthly.

As we drove toward the restaurant's gravel lot, perfect lawns and barbered pepper trees ill suited for the climate gave way to dust and rustic fencing. The sprinkle of cars out front included a navy Lincoln Town Car that Milo identified as the chief's civilian ride. No bodyguard, no auxiliary vehicle in sight.

The building was logs and shingles. A posted menu listed a French chef and described the fare as "nouveau-Tex-Mex-Thai comfort cuisine."

A perky ponytailed hostess guided us to a redwood picnic table tucked in a corner of a patio shaded by vegetation that fit: ancient California oaks, twisted by centuries of Santa Ana winds. The chief had concealed himself behind the rhino-thick trunk of the grand-daddy tree.

He continued chopsticking as we sat, pointed to two menus.

Comfort cuisine translated to heroic portions and headache-inducing prose.

The chief's rectangular platter was two feet wide.

"What're you having, sir?"

"Number Six."

Thirty-two spicy Mekong shrimp swimming in asparagus coulis and tinctured by a lemongrass-oregano reduction nestled in a terroir of goat-cheese livened by refried black beans and guarded by palace walls of home-cured porkbelly.

The chief said, "Seeing as you're a gourmet, Sturgis."

"Appreciate that, sir."

The chief lowered the brim of a gray suede baseball cap. Instead of the usual black suit and five-hundred-dollar tie, he wore jeans and a brown leather bomber jacket. The hat and mirrored aviator shades obscured a healthy portion of his mercilessly pitted, oddly triangular face. Additional tortured flesh was shielded by a bushy white mustache.

He's one of the few people who make Milo looked unscathed.

Another ponytailed girl came over, lofting a handheld computer. "What're you guys having today?"

Milo said, "Number Six."

I scanned the menu and ordered an elk burger with bison bacon.

The chief said, "Watching your cholesterol, Dr. Delaware?"

"I like bison."

"You and Buffalo Bill. And the Plains Indians. You have Native American in your background, right?"

"Along with a lot of other stuff."

"Mongrel, just like me."

I'd never heard he was anything but Irish.

He said, "Got some Seneca in there. Or so my paternal grandmother claimed. Can't be sure of that, though. Woman was a serious drinker." Twirling his chopstick. "Just like your father."

I didn't respond.

He removed the sunglasses. Small black eyes scanned my face like a dermatologist probing for lesions. "Clouds the judgment, serious drinking."

I said, "It's a problem in some families."

He turned to Milo. "What the hell were you thinking taking him along to the Freeman scene without authorization, then bullshitting Creighton about it? Didn't you figure he'd check with me?"

"I assumed he would, sir."

Down went the chopstick. "It was a *Fuck you*?"

"No, sir. It was a *Doing my job as best I can given the constraints.*"

"You can't do your job without him? We're talking some kind of psychological dependency here?"

"We're talking preference based on past experience, sir."

"You need a shrink on board to function?"

"When cases are unusual and Dr. Delaware has time, I find his input helpful. I thought you agreed, so I didn't foresee any objection."

"And Creighton?"

"Creighton's a bureaucrat."

The chief retrieved the stick, rolled it impressively from finger to finger. The black eyes divided their time between Milo and me. "You didn't foresee any objection."

"Based on—"

"I get it. But it's still bullshit. Amazing the doctor still puts up with you."

Twice, the chief had offered me important-sounding jobs with the department that I'd turned down.

"I can see the value of shrinkery for weird cases, Sturgis, but I'm not sensing any psychosexual horror on this one."

Milo said, "A body packed in dry ice, no obvious cause of death, and a total disregard for proper procedure made it unusual to me."

"You think it's unusual, Doctor?"

"It's different."

"Sturgis explain to you why discretion is paramount?"

"He did."

"What exactly did he tell you?"

"That your son attends Windsor Tech and has applied to Yale."

"What do you think about Yale?"

"Top school."

"Great reputation," he said. "Just like the hedge-fund wizards and the cretins at Fannie Mae had until they got their britches yanked and guess what was underneath? Empty space."

"You don't like Yale?"

"I don't care enough about the place to like or dislike, Doctor. They're all the same, holding pens for spoiled rich brats and kids who aspire to be spoiled richer brats. A few years ago, the geniuses on Yale's admissions committee rejected thousands of smart, quali-fied American kids but accepted some Afghan who'd served as the Taliban's spokesman. Want to take odds the guy ever took AP cal-culus and served as captain of his Model U.N. debate team? Then those same geniuses let in an alleged art student, her idea of creativity is getting knocked up, aborting the fetus, and videotaping the mess. After which she repeated the freak show over and over or maybe she was faking. We're living in Bizarro World, Rembrandt's writhing in his grave."

"No doubt," I said.

"I have nothing against Yale more than any other Ivy League resort. What I can't figure out is why Charlie wants to go there when my wife went to Columbia and Penn law school and I got that ridiculous master's degree at Harvard—two years commuting to Boston every week, my reward was listening to puffed-up fools yakking about nothing. I made the mistake of attending graduation, brought my wife and my mother, Charlie wasn't born yet. They do the ceremony in Harvard Yard, which was fine back in the seventeen hundreds when it was a little divinity school for rich twits. Now there's space for maybe a quarter of the people who show up, they give you a predetermined seat number with preferences for rich assholes who endow buildings. My wife and my eighty-seven-year-old mother stood for two hours in ninety-degree weather, finally they get to their seats and end up not seeing a damn thing because inconsiderate twits stood in front of them the whole time. A bunch of nice black ladies from the Bronx were in the row behind, their niece was the first person in the family to attend college, they had no clue what the hell was going on. My wife turned around and said, 'These are the geniuses who ran the Vietnam War.' They're all the same, Doctor. Arrogant, thoughtless, impractical."

"Ivy League schools."

"Any elite institution. It's like junior high: Insecure assholes can't feel popular unless everyone else is an outcast." Head shake. "My kid's got legacy status at Columbia, Penn, and Harvard, he obsesses on Yale."

"Kids will do that," I said.

"Be stupid and obnoxious?"

"Try to differentiate themselves."

"Psych-talk," he said. "Yeah, yeah, that's what my wife says. Supposedly Charlie's got a tough row to hoe being under the alleged shadow of his father so he needs to find himself as an *individual*. Which is ridiculous, you see me as intimidating? Not to him, trust me. He's twice as smart as me and plays the fucking cello."

Milo's smile was fleeting but the chief saw it.

"You're just loving this, aren't you? I'm in a spot where I can't kick your ass with my customary aim and fervor." To me: "I told Charlie apply to Harvard for early acceptance, it's nonbinding, he'll have a fallback. No, he said, that wouldn't be fair to kids who really want to go to Harvard. Guess what the average acceptance rate was last year at the big three—H, Y, and Princeton? Six fucking percent and this year's going to be worse because of the baby boom. Charlie's got over a 4.0 when you factor in APs and honors courses and he scored 1540 on the SAT, only took it once. Sounds like a shoo-in, right? Forget *that* fairy tale."

I said, "Sounds like he's a strong applicant on his own and being your kid—and your wife's—should help him."

"Why?"

"You're famous."

He jabbed his chest. "If I was a brain-dead actor with a brain-dead kid, I'd be famous. To those twits I'm a right-wing social climber—and don't think politics doesn't play into it. Yeah, Charlie's brilliant but I'm not booking advance flights to New Haven under the best of circumstances. Now I've got *this*. That stupid DVD, then she actually goes and gets herself killed. Give the twits an excuse to pass over my kid for some ▬▬▬ Hamas engineering whiz from Gaza who they can teach to build better fucking bombs and they'll jump at it."

I said, "So you don't see it as a suicide?"

"Body's packed in ice but no bags on the scene, vic's computer's missing, she's already given advance warning people are out to get her? Why the hell would I see it as a suicide—oh, Jesus." Sharp laughter. "You geniuses actually thought I was gonna push suicide on you? Turn this into some fucking Ice-Gate? Give me a break, I went to fucking Harvard."

He resumed eating. When Milo said, "Sir," he was waved into silence.

Milo tried again, two bites later: "So I'll be able to do my job as I see fit?"

"Now," said the chief, "you're sounding paranoid. Maybe you're the wrong guy for this case, seeing as it has psychological overtones."

"Even paranoiacs have enemies," said Milo.

"If they're assholes, they have a whole bunch." The chief's face flushed but a tirade was cut short by the arrival of our food.

My burger was dry and I put it aside.

Milo feasted.

When he'd cleared half his platter, he inhaled and put his fork down. "Sir, apologies for any offense, but I'm still not clear what's expected of me."

"Close the damn *case* is what's expected of you, but do it with discretion. What does that mean? Fine, I'll tell you: Do not go public on anything prior to my approval. No unnecessary ruffling of feathers, no loose talk about Windsor Prep being a den of iniquity, no stomping into the place like a storm trooper, no intimidation of administration, faculty, students, janitors, the squirrels that scurry up their damn trees, the birds that fly in their damn airspace."

"What about the three teachers Freeman named?"

"They will be made available to you. Have you checked out Freeman's boyfriend yet, the Italian guy?"

"All I've done so far is visit the scene and read the file, sir. What there is of it."

"What there is of it is enough for you to start on. Begin with the boyfriend. Who kills women? Men they're involved with. The Italian turns up absolutely clean, you'll have access to the teachers. Don't pester me until then. And no emails about the case to me or anyone else, the same goes for recording phone calls. The sole chronicle will be the murder book, you will chart strictly in accordance with the regs. That means no speculating in print. Or verbally to any civilian or any member of the department other than me. Got it?"

"Yes, sir."

"Furthermore, when you are not writing or consulting said murder book, you will keep it locked in your desk. The same goes for your daily notes and your message slips. Even your damn Post-its will be locked up. And don't photocopy anything until I've reviewed the material." Spearing a shrimp. "Other than that, it's business as usual."

"What about Dr. Delaware?"

"Now that you've made him a fait accompli, I might as well take advantage of him. I'm sure there'll be no problem because he knows that indiscreet psychologists get bitten hard by the medical board."

Tipping the brim of his suede cap, he winked. "Not that it would ever come to that, Doctor."

5

We left the chief mulling flan versus flourless chocolate cake.

As the unmarked idled, Milo found Sal Fidella's cell number in his pad and called.

"Helpful fellow, ready to meet us right now, onward to Sherman Oaks." He looked up the address in his Thomas Guide. "Hmm . . . this says it's Van Nuys. Maybe ol' Sal's a little pretentious. Be nice if he turns out to be a degenerate psychopath and lies about everything?"

I said, "Be nicer if the chief's kid had a low IQ."

The house was a Spanish one-story on Burdette Court just north of Burbank Boulevard, turned mangy by flaking gray spray-coat.

A brown seventies Corvette occupied the driveway. The neighborhood ranged from spotless cottages sporting pride-of-ownership gardens to dumps with paved-over frontage hosting trailers and junkers.

Fidella's place was somewhere in the middle, with a neatly edged lawn but no landscaping other than a struggling banana plant inches from the sidewalk. The picture window was draped with what looked like a bedsheet. The Corvette was dirt-streaked, the concrete beneath its well-worn tires cracked and crumbling.

Milo said, "He didn't spend his casino dough on décor."

Fidella came out the door, unlit cigar in hand, and gave a small wave. Five six with a low center of gravity, he wore a whiskey-colored velour sweat suit and yellow flip-flops. He'd traded the red beard for a soul patch and let it go white. A hunk of something shiny gleamed from one earlobe.

"Play-ah," mumbled Milo. "What's your guess, diamond or zircon?"

Fidella studied us but didn't approach. Licking the tip of the cigar, he folded an arm across his chest.

"He look grief-stricken to you?"

"Wouldn't that be nice," I said.

"What?"

"He really is a murderous psychopath, you close it quick, Charlie gets into Yale and becomes president of the United States."

"Dare to dream." He got out of the car.

Sal Fidella extended a hand to Milo, then to me. "Hey. This stinks."

He had deep blue eyes, pudgy, oversized fingers, and a back-slanted gait that made his upper body look as if it were hurrying to catch up with his feet. A smooth basso radio-announcer voice could sell you things you didn't need.

The living room he led us into was Bachelor Cliché Central: black leather couches fitted with built-in head pillows and cup holders, matching ottoman in lieu of a coffee table set up with ashtrays, cigarette packs, a cigar box, a collection of remote controls. A wet bar favored tequila and rum. A stack of audiovisual gizmos took up most of the hearth. The sixty-inch flat-screen above the mantel was tuned to ESPN Classic, no sound. Lakers-Celtics play-off from back when giants were okay wearing short-shorts.

The adjoining dining room was unfurnished. An open doorway flashed a glimpse of bare kitchen counters. The window cover wasn't a bedsheet; a frayed, beige curtain had come loose from its rod, was held in place by duct tape and clothespins. The place smelled like a cocktail lounge after closing.

Fidella said, "Beer, guys? Something else?"

"No, thanks," said Milo.

"Mind if I do?"

"Suit yourself."

Fidella slouched to the bar, poured himself a double shot of Silver Patrón, selected a lime wedge from a bowl of mixed citrus segments, and squirted the tequila.

Half the drink was gone by the time he sat facing us. "Can't believe Elise is gone. Crazy."

"Must've been tough discovering her," said Milo.

"Oh, man, it was out of a movie." Fidella sucked on his cigar and sipped. "I mean the moment I saw her, wow, it was . . . I knew she was gone. But I guess I didn't wanna accept it so I kept telling myself she'd be okay. It wasn't till later that it started sinking in." A meaty hand slashed air. "Permanent."

Fidella began rooting inside an eyelid with a fingertip, pulled something out, studied, flicked. "Guess she wasn't being paranoid."

"About what?"

"Bastards at Prep—the school she worked at. She told me they were out to get her."

"Which bastards?" said Milo.

Fidella shook his head. "That's the thing, she wouldn't mention names. I tried to get it out of her but she changed the subject."

"All she said was someone was out to get her."

"Yeah."

"Not how or why?"

"Uh-uh."

"When did this conversation take place, Mr. Fidella?"

"Maybe . . . a month ago? Three weeks? To be honest, guys, I figured she was being a drama queen. Elise could get like that. 'Specially that time of the month, know what I mean? Hormonal, almost kinda bipolar?"

"She could be moody."

"One day she's sweetness and light, next day it's like a dark cloud's over her, she's all closed up. When she gets like that, she doesn't answer her phone. What I used to do was come over, try to work things out, you know? But she never answered the door. And if I used my key, she'd freak out. Even though she was the one gave it to me in the first place. Tell the truth, that's what I kinda assumed when she didn't return calls for three days. That she was in one of those closed-up situations. But I went over anyway. 'Cause it wasn't that time of the month, know what I mean?"

"You keep tabs on that kind of thing," said Milo.

"Huh? No, it's just that when you're with a girl you get to know her rhythm."

"So you knew Elise wasn't premenstrual and you went over."

"Because she didn't answer the phone."

"You let yourself in with your key."

"I call out her name, no answer, figure maybe she's sick, in the bedroom, whatever. I'm worried, so yeah, I go in. She's not in the front, not in the bedroom, I go into the bathroom, the door's closed. I call her name, she doesn't answer, that's when I get this weird feeling. I open the door." Wince. "See her. I was gonna pull

her out but she was clearly gone, you know? Blue, not moving. I figured moving her wouldn't be a good thing. For you guys' sake."

"Preserving the scene."

"If I'd moved her and messed things up, you'd be pissed, right?
'Cause she was obviously . . . don't think I wouldn'ta helped her if
I could."

"You did the right thing, Sal."

"That was my intention."

"So," said Milo, "a month or so ago she told you people at Prep
were out to get her. She definitely used the plural?"

"Huh?"

"*They* were out to get her. More than one person."

"Hmm. Yeah, I'm pretty sure . . . yeah, yeah, definitely *they* not
him. That's another reason I thought she was being dramatic."

"What do you mean?"

"Everyone's against her? Like a conspiracy?"

"Was Elise into conspiracies?"

"Like Kennedy stuff, UFOs? Nah. But you know what I
mean."

"You didn't take her seriously."

"I would've if she'd *told* me something," said Fidella. "Also, to
be honest, when Elise drank she could get that way."

"What way?"

"Feeling sorry for herself, maybe a little paranoid."

"About what?"

Fidella looked at the carpet. Twirled his cigar. Slugged back
tequila and put the glass down.

"To be honest, guys, mostly about me. Enough juice in Elise's
system, she'd start convincing herself I didn't like her no more, was
gonna find myself another girl, someone younger. Stuff like that.
But normally, she was a great girl, she could be fun. I'm nauseous-
sick over what happened to her, you gotta nail whoever did it."

He rubbed one fist with an open hand. "I know I'm not supposed to say stuff like this but you get this asshole, you just leave me alone with him. I used to box Golden Gloves back in Connecticut."

"Last I heard," said Milo, "Golden Gloves didn't use tag-teams."

"Huh?"

"*They,* Sal. More than one person."

"Oh, yeah. Well, whatever, leave me with all of them."

Milo crossed his legs and spread his arms along the back of the sofa. "Where'd you meet Elise?"

"A bar."

"Which one?"

"Not here, Santa Barbara. Place called Ship Ahoy, off South State. I was there on work—Santa Barbara, not the bar. Elise was on vacation. She was all by herself and I was all by myself, we got to talking, we hit it off."

"What kind of work do you do?"

"I'm in between right now. Back then, I was a sales executive."

"What'd you sell?"

"Used to rep band equipment to schools, for G.O.S.—Gerhardt Orchestral Supply. They're headquartered in Akron, Ohio, I was their West Coast guy. The state budget for music classes got cut, my contracts started drying up. For a while, Santa Barbara was still good, it's a rich town. But then even they started holding on to their old instruments longer. I tried to switch to guitars and amps because they're hotter than trumpets and tubas. But the schools don't buy them and the mega-stores have that buttoned up. I tried to work for Guitar Center or Sam Ash, figured my experience would be a big deal. They use guys in their twenties, got eight million tattoos, pierces, heavy-metal hair extensions."

Touching his own bald head. "Before that, I used to sell truck tires, airspace for office buildings, exercise equipment, you name it."

"So when you met Elise you were on a business trip," said Milo. "How long ago are we talking about?"

"Two years, give or take."

"You two ever move in together?"

"No reason to," said Fidella. "I was traveling a lot and Elise liked her own space. Plus she enjoyed going off on her own—girlie vacations, you know? That's what she was doing in Santa Barbara. Some spa, they had a special. Elise was good at finding bargains. We didn't get possessive, you get what I'm saying?"

"Everyone had their own life."

"When we were both in the mood, we enjoyed each other's company."

Milo said, "Like that time in Reno."

"Huh?"

"There was a picture in Elise's house, you and her having a great time."

"Oh, that," said Fidella. "Jackpot day, yeah that was a fantastic day, how often does that happen?"

"Never to me."

"Me, I've had some nice experiences but not like that. Elise and me were getting eaten alive at the blackjack table, left for the buffet and walked past a dollar slot. Just for the hell of it, I tossed in a token and boom, bells start ringing, lights start blinking. Five thousand bucks. I split it with Elise, told her she was my lucky charm."

"You both like to gamble?"

"We like our games, no harm in that if you keep it under control, right?"

"Elise keep it under control?"

"Absolutely."

"Unlike her drinking."

"Yeah, vodka was a problem for her," said Fidella. "Sometimes."

"Sometimes?"

"What I'm saying is she wasn't one of those drunks, sucks it back every day. But give her a long afternoon, she's not working, she could put away a bottle of Grey Goose. Doing it slowly, you know? You wouldn't even notice unless you were with her the entire time."

"How often did she do that?"

"It wasn't binging," said Fidella. "She could control whether or not she drank. But if she felt like being a fish, she had the capacity."

"Same question?"

"Huh?"

"How often did she polish off a bottle?"

"I dunno . . . maybe two, three times a month. Maybe other times when I wasn't there, I really can't tell you."

"She paced herself."

"What would happen was, she'd have spare time. Or one of those moody times. I'd say something innocent, she'd march out and lock herself in her bedroom with her Grey Goose, or sometimes it was gin. I learned to just leave 'cause when it happened talking to her was no use."

"Silent treatment," I said.

"Silenter than . . ." Fidella let out an odd laugh—girlish, squeaky—slapped his own mouth.

Milo said, "Something funny, Sal?"

"Something stupid, guys. As in me. I was gonna say Elise could get silenter than the dead."

We didn't reply.

Fidella picked up his glass, finished the tequila. "Sure you don't want nothing?"

"We're fine."

"I'm sure as hell not." He got up, poured more Patrón. "Guess I'm still in that denial stage. Like when my mother passed. I kept expecting to hear her voice, it went on for weeks. Last night, I dreamed about Elise, saw her walking through the door, like the whole ice thing was a stupid joke. What was the point of that? The ice?"

"That's what we're trying to find out, Sal."

"Well, I say it's weird. Elise didn't even like ice in her vodka. I don't want you to think she was some drunk, there was plenty of times, like out to dinner, she'd have a nice cocktail—a Stinger, a Manhattan, like anyone else. She could keep control, you know?"

"She'd pick the time and place to finish a bottle."

"The place was always her house."

"What about the time?"

"When she worked she needed to be sharp. Who's gonna hire a teacher stumbles in drunk as a skunk?"

"What subjects did she teach?"

"English. She substituted at that place, anytime a regular English teacher was out, she was on call. Like a doctor."

"Did she teach anywhere other than Windsor Prep?"

"Not since I knew her. She said they made her an offer she couldn't refuse."

"Do you know the details?"

"Something like thirty grand just to be on call, then thirty bucks for every hour over ten per week that she actually worked. She was putting away decent dough. Also, she did tutoring at night, for that she got eighty, ninety an hour, more if she sniffed out the family was filthy rich."

"How much tutoring did she do?"

"To be honest, I couldn't tell you. But she was busy, plenty of times I called to go out and got her machine. The pressure worked for her."

"The pressure?"

"On the kids. She didn't tutor just dumb kids, she had smart ones, too, parents pushing on them. She told me sometimes a kid would come in with an A-minus, parents wouldn't let up till the minus went away."

"These are students from Windsor Prep we're talking about."

"Yeah," said Fidella. "She did SAT tutoring. And that other test, I forget the name."

I said, "The ACT."

"That's the one. She said all those tests were stupid and meaningless but God bless whoever invented them because rich people were so insecure they needed their kids to be perfect, she could charge 'em big bucks for something they could do themselves."

"What was her training?"

"What do you mean?"

"To tutor SATs."

"She went to college."

"Where?"

"Somewhere in the East, I don't know. The thing about Elise, she didn't like to talk about herself." He spread his palms. "I'm the kind of guy, you want to know something about me, ask. Elise was just the opposite. 'We're not going there, Sal.' She said that a lot. 'We're not going there.' But I stuck with her, she was good-looking, could be a ton of fun."

Milo said, "The times she got moody and nursed the bottle, did things ever get unpleasant?"

"What do you mean?"

"She ever get aggressive?"

"Elise? You kidding? She was a pussycat. Like I said, she'd just go into her room."

"And you left."

"No point staying."

"Did things ever get argumentative?"

"How can you argue with someone who won't talk?"

"That musta been frustrating, Sal."

"I figured it out soon enough."

"Any idea what happened to Elise's computer?"

"Huh?"

"Her computer's gone."

"Really."

"You didn't notice?"

"I was looking for Elise, not some computer."

"What kind of computer was it?"

"I dunno."

"Laptop or desktop?"

"Laptop—a Dell, I think."

"When's the last time you saw it?"

Fidella's mouth screwed up. "Hell if I know. You're saying the killer took it? Makes sense if it was those bastards from the school."

"Why's that?"

"Maybe Elise learned something weird about some rich family, put it on her computer. That makes sense, right?"

"Anything's possible, Sal." Milo uncrossed his legs. "I need to ask this: What was your schedule the day before you discovered Elise?"

"The whole day?"

"As much of it as you can recall."

Fidella brushed his soul patch with the side of his thumb. "You're asking this because I was the one found her?"

"There are basic questions we always need to ask, Sal."

"Fine, I get it, no offense taken." But the blue eyes had narrowed and Fidella's thighs tightened, lifting his shoe-tips above the carpet. "Let me just say one thing: Sal Fidella loves women and respects them."

"Granted," said Milo. "We still need to ask."

"Where was I that day?" said Fidella. "I was at Star Toys and Novelties, San Pedro Street, the toy district. Why was I there? Trying to get a job repping crap from China. They had an ad on Craigslist for an opening. I show up, it's all bullshit, they had to run it to show they were being fair, know what I mean? They're all Chinese, every one of them, some of them didn't even speak no English. You'd think my speaking English would be a good thing, right? Wrong."

"They wanted someone Chinese."

"They didn't come out and say it but it was pretty damn obvious when they asked me if I spoke Mandarin. They couldn't put that in the ad? Must speak Mandarin?"

"What a hassle," said Milo. "So what time were you there?"

"Let's see . . . the appointment was for eleven. I showed up early, maybe a quarter to, they kept me waiting till noon, I'm in there maybe five minutes, sitting and listening to the guy behind the desk talk in Chinese over the phone. Then he smiles, walks me out, don't call us, we'll call you."

"So you were out of there shortly after twelve."

"Guess so."

"What about the early part of the morning? What time did you wake up?"

"You're kidding," said Fidella. "C'mon, guys, I loved Elise."

"We still need to ask, Sal."

"What you need to do is go to that fuckin' school and find out who was hassling Elise. She hated the place, called it a . . . hotbed of stupidity and pretentiousness. She only stayed there for the money."

"We'll be heading to the school soon as we finish talking to you. What time did you wake up?"

Fidella exhaled. "Maybe eight, eight thirty? I didn't have to get downtown until eleven, I wasn't exactly setting the alarm. What'd I do from then till I left at ten thirty? Real exciting, guys. I had some breakfast, watched some shows I TiVo'd—*Rides,* they made over a Chevy pickup, if you wanna know. And *Repo Men: Stealing for a Living,* some guy with a semi got his entire rig taken away, talk about pissed. Then I took a shower, got dressed, drove to Star Toys, and got shafted by the Chinese."

"What happened after you left Star Toys?"

"I ate lunch," said Fidella. "Philippe's, on Alameda. The French dip. Will they remember me? Hell, no, place was jammed like it always is, I waited in line, ate my sandwich, had a beer, got the hell outta there. Where'd I go next—by then it's probably one thirty, two. I drive back to San Pedro, looking for other places I can contact for a job interview, if the signs got no Chinese lettering just English. Did I follow up when I got home? Hell, yeah, with half a dozen. Did it make a difference? Hell, no. Oh, yeah, I also drove around the garment district a little. Never repped clothes before, but it's how you do it, not what you're doing that counts. Did that work out any better? Hell, no."

"Sorry," said Milo.

"For what?"

"Tough times."

"Hey," said Fidella, "it happens. You wanna cheer me up? Find out who killed Elise and leave me with 'em. Five minutes."

"You're sure she was killed?"

"What?"

"There's no official cause of death yet, Sal."

"You said you were Homicide."

"We look into suicides, as well."

"Suicide? Why would Elise commit suicide?"

"She was moody, Sal. Sometimes moods get the best of people."

"She wasn't moody like that," said Fidella.

"Like what?"

"Like suicidal. She never talked about ending it."

I said, "Those times she'd drink and lock herself into her room, there was no way to know how she felt."

"But she always came out of it. And got herself in a *good* mood."

"How long did she take to cheer up?"

"Like . . . a day. She'd call me, let's go out, Sal, have a nice dinner."

"Was it ever longer than a day?"

"I dunno . . . maybe sometimes it was two." Fidella cracked his knuckles. "Elise wasn't some nut-job, you guys are on the wrong path if you're thinking suicide. Lots of times, I saw her happy. Why would she kill herself? She did okay money-wise, was even talking about getting a bigger place."

"She own the house?"

"No, it's a rental, she was talking about renting a bigger place. And it's not like she was drinking the day I found her, there was no bottle in the bathroom. And why the hell would she put herself on ice, you answer me that."

Milo said, "At this point, Sal, we've got questions not answers. Let's get back to your schedule. After lunch, you drove around looking for possible employment. Then what?"

"Then like I said, I drove home and got on the phone and came up empty. You want my phone records?"

"If you don't mind."

Fidella stared. "You're serious."

"We need to be, Sal."

"Fine, look at my phone records, I got nothing to hide."

Milo had him sign a release form.

Fidella said, "You guys are unbelievable. You wanna bother,

suit yourselves, but I can tell you what you're gonna find: I made calls to a buncha places downtown. Real short calls, no one gave me the time of day."

"Frustrating," I said.

"Been through it before, something'll turn up."

Milo said, "What time did you finish making your calls?"

"Musta been fiveish, five thirty. Took a walk over to Van Nuys Boulevard, there's a bar, Arnie Joseph's. I had a coupla drinks, some shrimp and wasabi peas and hickory almonds, and watched TV. Over there, they'll remember me, they know me. Just do me a favor, don't tell them I'm a suspect or nothing. I don't need no one looking at me weird."

"No problem," said Milo.

Fidella studied him. "What're you gonna tell 'em?"

"That you're a witness. When did you leave Arnie Joseph's?"

"Musta been eightish, eight thirty. What'd I do then? Go home, fix myself a sandwich—anchovies, tomatoes, and mozzarella cheese. Then I called Elise because she still wasn't picking up. So I watched more TiVo, had a beer, brushed my teeth and used mouthwash for the cheese and the anchovies, just in case Elise answered. She didn't, I said forget about her, she'll call you like she always does. Then I got worried 'cause this was longer than usual and drove over. Musta been close to elevenish."

"You were home for most of the evening."

"Seeing as the yacht was out of commission and the Malibu Beach house was being borrowed by Brad and Angelina? Yeah, I was home. Where else should I go?"

Fidella slumped and his eyes grew sad. As if his question had turned metaphysical.

"Nowhere to go," he said.

We left him pouring a third tequila.

CHAPTER

6

Milo drove a block from Fidella's house, parked, and called in a search for current wants and warrants. Clean, but Fidella had paid a fine for a first-offense DUI eighteen months ago. "Time to verify his whereabouts, I'll drop you off first."

"You see him as a serious suspect?"

"I see him as someone whose whereabouts need to be verified."

"Planning on taking Van Nuys to the Glen?"

"Yup."

"You'll pass that bar on the way."

Arnie Joseph's Good Times Inn sat north of Riverside, your basic dim, tobacco-bitter, serious-drinker establishment. The octogenarian behind the bar verified Sal Fidella's account. So did bowls of dried shrimp that looked like fish food, hickory almonds, wasabi peas. Mention of Fidella's name elicited smirks from the other customers. A woman nursing a beer said, "Sal Fidella, the luckiest fella."

"Lucky, how?" said Milo.

"He won a jackpot in Reno. Didn't he tell you? He tells everyone."

"Claim to fame," said a man.

The woman put her beer down. Fifty, stout, gray-haired, wearing a pink waitress uniform created by the same sadist who designs bridesmaid's dresses. "So what's he a witness to?"

"A crime."

"Not some get-rich-quick thing?"

"Sal's into that?"

"Sal talks a lot."

"About what?"

"Coulda been, shoulda been. What's he a witness to?"

"A crime."

She shrugged, turned away.

Milo walked up to her. "Anything else I should know?"

"Not from me." She buried her face in her mug.

Another man said, "Hey, if Sal had enough money he could finance an infomercial, sell a million of something. You ask him what something is, he says it don't matter."

"That's 'cause money ain't the issue, smarts is," said a guy nursing a tall glass of something amber.

Milo said, "Sal's not smart?"

"Wins a ten-grand jackpot and blows it in a day? You tell me."

The guy next to him said, "Straight down the toilet, oughta work for the government."

Laughter slithered up and down the bar.

Milo distributed business cards like a Vegas dealer. A few people actually read them. "Anything else anyone wants to tell me about Sal?"

A man laughed. "We love Sal. Sometimes he even offers to pick up a tab."

Back in the car, Milo said, "Tells us five, tells them ten, even a bunch of alkies know he's a loser. Elise was an educated woman, smart enough to teach at Prep and tutor SATs. Why would she hang with someone like that?"

"Love," I said. "The ultimate mystery."

"Seriously, Alex. I'm trying to know my victim."

"People tend to select mates they think they deserve."

"Elise didn't like herself, so she aimed low?"

"I'm not saying she thought it through, but low self-esteem generally shoves you downhill. It's also a factor in depression— cause as well as effect. Fidella claims Elise withdrew only when she drank but who knows? On the DVD, her words weren't slurred, on the contrary, she seemed focused. So either she'd built up enough tolerance over time to maintain, or alcohol wasn't the only thing that laid her low."

"Sexual harassment could do that," he said.

"Any other situation, you'd already be talking to those teachers."

He frowned and drove south to Ventura Boulevard, headed west and connected to Beverly Glen. "People get what they think they deserve, huh? What's that say about Rick and me?"

"Rick's smart, affluent, handsome. Strip away all that morose Irish cop stuff and I'll bet you feel pretty nifty about yourself."

"Only on alternate Wednesdays," he said. "We won't get into Rick's psyche."

Robin's pickup was parked in front of the house. I found her in her studio at the back carving the top of a mandolin. Spruce shavings created a soft, creamy carpet at her feet. Blanche had found herself a warm spot and burrowed.

Cozy as Elise Freeman in her bed of frozen carbon dioxide.

The studio smelled like a conifer forest after a drizzle. That brought back autumns in Missouri.

Walking through the parkland behind the little sad house I grew up in. A kid with a head full of fear and confusion sneaking out when Mom escaped to her locked room and Dad raged at high-burn.

Hoping I'd get lost.

I smiled and kissed Robin. She put down her chisel, flexed her fingers. "Perfect timing, I'm ready to quit."

The mandolin top was smooth, curvy, with a subtly arched belly. Unmistakably female. "Nice."

Robin tapped the spruce. A musical tone rang out. "The music's already in the wood, my job is to not screw it up."

"Any serious job is like that."

We headed for the house, pausing by the fishpond to feed the koi. Blanche stuck by us, smiling in that strange but endearingly humanoid way.

Over coffee, I told Robin about the woman on ice.

She said, "Someone bragging *I'm a stone-cold killer?*"

"Interesting slant."

"Long days carving, I get symbolic."

I filled her in on the chief.

She said, "Politicians are a low life-form."

"The chief's appointed."

"His commodity's power, Alex. That puts him two notches below slime mold."

"My girlfriend the anarchist."

"If only," she said.

"If only you were an anarchist?"

"If only reality made anarchy a reasonable approach."

That evening, I was at my computer, keywording *windsor prep* and learning nothing beyond official P.R.

I switched to victimology. Eleven-year-old Elise Freeman from Great Neck, New York, had an artful MySpace page that showcased her pastel drawings and successful orthodonture. Ninety-six-year-old Elise Freeman had just celebrated her birthday in Pepper Pike, Ohio, and received a card from the Cleveland Cavaliers. No hits on Elise Freeman, deceased tutor.

When Milo rang in at nine forty, I said, "She's cyber-invisible, Fidella was right about her liking her privacy."

"Everything else Fidella told us is checking out, including his calls to Elise four hours before she died. The phone subpoena only covered one week of his account, I'm preparing another one for Elise's, we'll see how far back they'll let me go. For the time being, Sal's out of the spotlight."

"Had a beer and watched TV at home isn't much of an alibi."

"That's what His Augustness said. I asked him for alternative suspects and he responded with less-than-pristine language. Ten minutes later, his secretary calls back: We've got face time with Windsor Prep's president, guy named Edgar Helfgott."

"Saw his name on the website," I said. "A parent?"

"No, at Prep that's a paid job. Helfgott used to be the headmaster before they created the position for him and moved him into the Oval Office. His assistant is now the headmaster, a Dr. Rollins. Under her is an assistant headmaster and it keeps going, the place is structured like a Fortune 500 corporation. Anyway, Helfgott will grant us an audience tomorrow at eleven, you'll never guess where."

"Some manse the school lets him use as an official residence?"

"Even better."

7

Edgar Helfgott de-planed from the Gulfstream V.

A trim, rock-jawed uniformed pilot descended behind him lugging two burnished leather suitcases. The aircraft was sleek and white. The same could be said for Helfgott.

Pausing at the bottom of the stairs, he removed and pocketed a pair of earplugs, gazed up at the silver sky, rotated his neck.

Quiet time at Santa Monica Airport; lots of private jets parked on the tarmac but no other takeoffs or landings. After a bit of negotiation, Milo's badge had gained us access to the field. We stood five yards behind Helfgott's prearranged black Escalade. Moments before the Gulfstream's arrival, we'd made small talk with the chauffeur.

Yes, he'd driven Mr. Helfgott a few times but didn't really know him, the man didn't talk much, always read books in the car. Unlike the man who *owned* the plane and the car and paid the driver's salary.

"Mr. Wydette talks to you like a regular guy, lets you know what's on his mind."

"What's Mr. Wydette's first name?"

"Myron," said the chauffeur. "Not that I ever use it."

Milo said, "What did he do to afford a plane?"

"Fruit."

"Fruit?"

"Peaches, apricots, that kind of thing. He owns a lot of land, I don't know the details."

"He lend the plane out often?"

"Nah, mostly it's the family, sometimes it's Mr. Helfgott."

"Mr. Helfgott's a frequent flier?"

The driver frowned. "I don't keep a list." He headed back toward his SUV.

Milo and I followed. "Where's Mr. Helfgott flying in from this morning?"

The driver opened his door. "I just show up where they tell me."

He got inside the SUV. Up went the windows.

Milo looked back at the building behind us. A Fixed Base of Operations called Diamond Aviation. The pretty young female concierge in the marble-and-glass terminal had responded with the same level of protectiveness. "Unless you're Homeland Security, we're not allowed to give out flight information. Can I get you guys some coffee?"

One step from the bottom of the jet's stairs, Helfgott spotted us. Showing no sign of surprise or recognition, he snatched his bags from the pilot, toted them to the Escalade, and placed them in the trunk. Rotating his neck again, he shot his cuffs as he walked toward us, expressionless.

"Morning. I think. Ed Helfgott."

Six feet tall and somewhere in his sixties, Windsor Prep's president was thin and angular but slightly broad in the beam, with the kind of pale, waxy skin that shaves well and connotes long nights of scholarly study. Longish rusty hair streaked with silver swept back over a high brow and broke over his collar in waves. The glasses were owlish, framed in tortoiseshell. A gold watch chain hung from the vest of a whiskey-colored glen plaid suit tailored to give him more shoulder. His shirt was lime-green broadcloth, his tie a hugely knotted ocher foulard. A yellow handkerchief flecked with brown was stuffed haphazardly into a breast pocket, just short of tumbling.

"Thanks for meeting with us, sir."

Helfgott scanned Milo's card absently. "My pleasure, Lieutenant. I do hope this doesn't stretch on for too long." Sudden, incongruous smile. "I'm a bit tuckered."

"Long journey?"

"Journeys, plural," said Helfgott. "Monday was a conference in D.C., then on to New York to interface with some alums, followed by a jaunt over the pond to London and back for a stop in Cambridge, Mass. London, in particular, posed challenges. Scaffolding everywhere and despite the financial vicissitudes, the pace and magnitude of construction remain Promethean. Unfortunately, so does the volume of motor traffic. None of my destinations were in walking distance from my lodgings in Mayfair so a fair bit of ingeniousness was at play."

I said, "School business in London?"

Helfgott's thin lips turned up. What resulted was the initial knife-slice for a jack-o'-lantern mouth. "If you're asking was it a holiday, quite the opposite. I interfaced with my equal numbers at Oxbridge, Cambridge, and LSE—the London School of Economics."

A high school administrator with counterparts at three major universities.

I said, "Smoothing the way for your graduates."

"Most of my time was spent listening as *they* tried to attract *our* alums. In a world of growing globalism, Windsor Prep people are regarded as prime intellectual property. Creators rather than prisoners of destiny, if you will. One of our grads attended Oxford twenty years ago and ended up settling in Scotland. He's just been short-listed for the Booker Prize."

"Congrats," said Milo. "Sounds like ultra-prime property—kind of like Wagyu beef."

Helfgott squinted. "Sir?"

"Wagyu—"

"I know what Wagyu is, Lieutenant. What I'm failing to see is the crux of your analogy."

"The stuff comes from pampered cows, right? Back in Japan, they get to guzzle beer, snarf gourmet grub, have regular massages. All that to keep the meat tender. Then they're shipped off to dates with destiny."

Helfgott removed his specs. Ripped the silk handkerchief free, wiped both lenses energetically. Glancing at the Escalade, he pulled out his pocket watch. I was close enough to see it had stopped six hours ago. That didn't stop Helfgott from tsk-tsking.

"Later than I thought. How say we wend our way to the lounge, do whatever it is you feel is important. Then we can all be on our merry ways."

Diamond Aviation's waiting area was thirty feet high, walled in glass, with air spiced by cinnamon-flavored air-freshener. A man in a white jumpsuit dry-mopped the black marble floor. No jet-setters occupied the puce leather seating; off to the side, a couple of bored-looking pilots studied a computer terminal. One said something about weather in Roseville. The other said, "Maybe we'll get delayed enough to stick around and try that sushi place."

Without being asked, the same cute concierge addressed Helfgott by name as she set down a glass of soda water and lime.

"Change your mind about coffee, guys?"

"No, thanks."

"Anything else, Mr. Helfgott?"

"Not for the moment, Amy. Thank you."

"Anytime, Mr. Helfgott." She sashayed away. He drank, rotated his neck yet again.

Milo said, "Are you in pain, sir?"

"Chronic condition exacerbated by age and too-frequent air travel, Lieutenant. Yoga helped for a while, then some unfortunate personal training led to sprains precisely where I didn't need them."

He eyed Myron Wydette's jet through the glass, now being fueled by a tanker truck. Held his gaze and inhaled, as if yearning to be aloft.

"Nice piece of machinery, Mr. Helfgott."

"Work of art, Lieutenant. I won't pretend it's not immeasurably superior to commercial aviation, but in the last analysis, flying is flying. One strives to eat properly, stretch, hydrate oneself. Nevertheless, the hours of enforced immobility take their toll. As soon as we wrap up whatever it is you feel you need to do, I'm going to swim, then settle in a warm bath and pop off to sleep."

"Sounds good, sir. What have you been told about this meeting?"

"Mr. Wydette's office called me midflight to inform me that poor Elise Freeman had passed on and the police had requested to speak with me. I took that to assume an irregular death."

All the emotion of a Chia pet. He continued admiring the Gulfstream until his eyes lost focus. Somewhere else; maybe thinking about his bath.

Milo said, "If by irregular you mean other than old age, that's true, sir."

"How dreadful," said Helfgott. "May I ask when and where it occurred, and the particulars?"

"Several days ago, at her house, sir. The particulars remain the big question."

"I'm not sure I understand, Lieutenant."

"Mode of death hasn't been determined."

"So there's no obvious crime."

Milo didn't answer.

Helfgott finally swiveled away from the jet field. "And you requested to speak with me because . . ."

"Elise Freeman worked at Prep."

"Surely you can't imagine her passing has anything to do with her job."

"Was she happy at Prep?"

"Why wouldn't she be?"

"Any job can be stressful, sir."

Helfgott put his water glass down, removed his specs. His eyes were small, diminished further by heavy lids, with watery hazel irises. "I don't customarily deal with faculty issues but if there'd been a serious problem, I assume I'd have heard about it. In fact, she seemed quite pleased at the contract we offered her. After I received Mr. Wydette's call, I immediately phoned Headmaster Rollins and she confirmed that fact, as well as the fact that Ms. Freeman had been happily and uneventfully employed."

"Sounds like you wondered yourself if her death had anything to do with Prep."

Back went the glasses. "Not at all, Lieutenant. I am not a brilliant thinker and I attempt to compensate for my intellectual deficits with meticulousness. That's a lesson I try to pass on to our less inspired students. Rara avises though they are."

"Prep's website says you graduated cum laude from Brown."

Helfgott smiled. "You've researched me?"

"I read the website."

"Well, Lieutenant, that was a different Brown. Now, what else can I help you with?"

"When did you offer Ms. Freeman her contract?"

"She came on as a per diem temporary employee four years ago. A year later, we offered her more steady employment. I remain puzzled by that term—*mode of death*."

"She's being processed by the coroner as we speak."

"How grim sounding. So it could be a medical condition, one of those rough patches—an aneurysm."

"At this point, anything's possible, Mr. Helfgott."

"Then why, may I ask, am I talking to homicide detectives?"

"We investigate any unusual death."

Helfgott tucked his handkerchief tighter. "I see. When can we expect some definitive answers as to *mode of death*?"

"I really can't say, Mr. Helfgott."

"Are we talking days, weeks, an inordinate amount of time?"

"I really can't answer that, sir."

"Surely some kind of narrowing—"

Milo leaned in closer. "Sir, I know from your website that Prep's got a great mock-trial team. Maybe the best in the country, you guys took high national honors last year. All those big-time lawyers' kids, no surprise. But right now, it's best if I ask the questions."

Helfgott's manicured fingers grazed the tips of the handkerchief. "Mea culpa, Lieutenant, I didn't mean to upset your investigatory routine, I was simply thinking of our students and faculty. The news of Elise's death is going to be upsetting, particularly if the mode is . . . unusual. Ergo, the sooner we can offer accurate information, the sooner closure will arrive." Faint smile. "I should point out that the captain of that extraordinary debate team was the daughter of a neurosurgeon, not an attorney."

"I stand corrected, sir. So Ms. Freeman's employment was uneventful."

"We paid her handsomely, her duties were light, no reason for her to be unhappy."

"What was her salary?"

Helfgott's hand waved. "I don't get involved in that kind of thing, but typically, our salaries are the best in the preparatory school universe. Do you work regularly with the chief of police, Lieutenant?"

"We talk when necessary."

"I ask that because when Myron—Mr. Wydette—requested that I meet with you immediately as a favor to the chief of police, I was surprised."

"Why's that, sir?"

"Mr. Wydette emphasized the chief's affection for Prep and how it's benefited his son, Charlie. Who, if you weren't aware, is a graduating senior."

Milo remained silent.

Helfgott said, "Until now, the chief and Charlie's mother have been rather low-profile members of the Prep parent community."

No participation, no donations, no ass-kissing.

"Have you met Charlie, Lieutenant?"

"No, sir."

"Not a social boy, but bright."

We're not easily impressed, so tell your boss not to push it.

Milo pulled out his pad. "So, to your knowledge, Ms. Freeman never complained about any problems with students or faculty— with anyone at Prep."

"Lieutenant, we seem to be hovering over a single issue and not moving forward appreciably. Are you saying you're aware of a complaint—let me amend that to a statement. It sounds as if you doubt my word about Ms. Freeman's sanguine employment history." Hard glint behind the eyeglasses.

"Not at all, sir, and sorry for implying that. Like you said, you don't usually get involved in faculty issues. But unfortunately, we've become involved in just that."

Helfgott's waxy skin paled to cold tallow. "What, exactly, are you saying?"

"We're in possession of a communication from Ms. Freeman in which she claims she was sexually harassed by fellow teachers at Prep."

Spots of color splashed on Helfgott's sunken cheeks. His lips twitched. "Ludicrous."

Milo thumbed through his pad. "Three other teachers, to be exact: Enrico Hauer, James Winterthorn, Pat Skaggs. Are those individuals still employed at Prep?"

"This is beyond absurd." Helfgott had kept his tone low enough to discourage eavesdroppers but something in his body language caused one of the pilots to turn.

Milo said, "I'm sure you're right, but with Ms. Freeman deceased, we need to check it out."

"Enrico, Jim—no, that's not possible."

"So they are still working there."

"Of course they're still with us, no reason they shouldn't be." Helfgott rose to his feet, teetered, regained balance by clutching the arm of his chair. "I'm sorry, Lieutenant. I know you've got your job to do but so do I. Ergo, I cannot continue in this vein without benefit of legal counsel. Not because those outrageous accusations are anything but slanderous rubbish." Pausing to let that sink in. "Because my responsibility to Prep precludes me from exposing the school to untrammeled attack without prior . . . consultation."

"Institutions can't be slandered, sir, only individuals."

"Well, then, Enrico, Jim, and Pat have been slandered and I won't have it."

Milo stood. "No one's saying the accusations are true, Mr. Helfgott, but my responsibilities preclude *me* from ignoring them. And I'm sure all three of the individuals in question will appreciate the chance to clear their names."

"I don't see why they'd need to—"

"The point of today's meeting was extending a courtesy to you, sir, as well as to Prep. I need to have access to Enrico, Jim, and Pat and rather than disrupt your school during working hours, I'm giving you the opportunity to set up off-campus interviews at a discreet time and place." Stepping closer, he invaded Helfgott's personal space. His bulk turned Helfgott into a small man.

"Furthermore, it's essential that my courtesy doesn't lead to advance preparation on the part of Enrico, Jim, and Pat. Meaning, I expect you not to alert them as to the purpose of the interviews."

Helfgott backed away two steps, nostrils flaring, beads of moisture collecting under the rims of his eyeglasses. "The police chief has authorized this?"

"The police chief takes his responsibilities seriously."

"How . . . interesting." Suddenly Helfgott's hand landed on Milo's shoulder. Patted. "I'm sure you're a fine dedicated police lieutenant, sir. Merely doing your job. However, I must do mine. I cannot commit to a course of action without conferring with professionals. We'll chat in due time."

He headed toward the electric doors that opened to the tarmac. Before he got there, the concierge pushed a button and the doors swung open. Helfgott marched toward the Escalade. The driver popped out, hurried to open the passenger door.

Milo said, "Who says teaching's a thankless job."

As we passed the desk, the concierge looked up from her copy of *Elite Traveler.* Smiling and murmuring, "Bye, guys."

Her eyes said we'd soiled the furniture.

CHAPTER

8

s we passed from Santa Monica into West L.A., Milo placed a call to the chief's office, failed to get past the first secretarial rung, and hung up.

"So what do you think of Il Presidente?"

"Loves his job, will do anything to keep it."

"Perks like he's got, he'd probably kill to keep it, Alex." Tapping the wheel. "Too bad pomposity's not a felony."

"I thought your beef analogy was particularly astute."

"Yeah . . . my high school experience was ground chuck. You know what really irritated me, Alex? That patronizing false modesty—*I'm just a poor, dumb, hardworking mope who somehow managed to earn a cum laude at Brown.*"

"*A different Brown,*" I said. "But there might be some truth to that. Like the chief said, most of the Ivies began as divinity schools but they quickly became repositories for rich white boys. Later, when quotas were relaxed, they became meritocracies but Helf-gott's old enough for the pre-merit days."

"You were a whiz kid, how come you didn't go Ivy?"

"My high school was blue collar, same as yours. The guidance counselors directed kids to the trades, most of my friends never even thought about college. I aimed higher because I knew I needed to get away from my family. The night I left Missouri, I snuck out without saying good-bye, hit the road in a clunker I'd bought on the sly."

"Sixteen years old. Gutsy boy."

"It was a matter of survival," I said. "And here's something I've never told anyone: I enrolled at the U. under false pretenses. My mother had an old friend who'd made her own escape—moving to Oakland, becoming a teacher. She knew what I was contending with, lied about being my aunt and my guardian, claimed I'd been a California resident for years. Without that, I could've never afforded the out-of-state tuition. I stayed with her for two weeks, mowed her lawn, painted her gutters. Then I bought her some daisies, left a note and cut out again in the middle of the night, drove down to L.A. It wasn't until my postdoc at Langley Porter that I even saw Oakland again."

"My buddy the miscreant. Time to revoke your degrees."

I said, "Fraud's below your pay grade." A mile later: "If you add up the alumni contributions I've made, they exceed the difference."

He laughed. "Everything needs to be atoned for, huh?"

"You have to start somewhere."

Back at his office, Milo phoned Dr. Clarice Jernigan at the coroner's office.

Last year, he'd closed the murder of one of Jernigan's investigators, a man named Bobby Escobar, though the solve was officially recorded as a Sheriff's Homicide victory. Back when the case had looked hopeless, Jernigan flippantly offered to trade priority cutting for resolution on Bobby.

Woman of her word.

Milo switched his phone to conference as Jernigan's crisp voice filled his tiny office.

"Just sewed up your victim, Milo. Which demigod do you have inroads with besides me?"

"What do you mean, Doc?"

"Freeman's body comes in, leapfrogs immediately over our backlog, straight to the table, along with an unsigned message slip on different paper from the ones we use with orders for me to get to it stat and keep the findings to myself. When I call my boss, he's not in, even though I know he is. My C.I. is sure the slip wasn't with the body when it came in, our drivers say the same thing, so somehow, this body got tagged without our spotting it. I figure maybe it was you, you're pushing our arrangement a bit, but fine. Then moments after the body hits the table someone calls my private cell line—the ones my kids use—and warns me to be discreet on Elise Freeman. I think the exact phrase was 'This needs to be handled ultra-quietly.' When I try to ask why, she hangs up."

"Who's she?"

"Someone who identified herself as calling from Parker. Is it true?"

"Probably."

"What's going on, Milo? I Googled Freeman and she's not rich or famous or otherwise noteworthy."

"It's complicated, Doc."

"Meaning shut up and cut," said Jernigan. "Well, I put my irritation aside and did both and here's what I've got for you: Freeman's blood alcohol was over three times the legal limit, plus she'd ingested some kind of opiate. No needle marks, so she probably snorted. Precise metabolites will take time to analyze. There's also clear pulmonary evidence of an overdose. In a relatively healthy young woman."

"Relative to what?"

"She had a smidge of atherosclerosis and some hepatic scarring—the beginnings of cirrhosis. Meaning she could've been hitting the sauce pretty hard. Clogged arteries could also be booze-related, or she had bad genetics. Or both. But none of that would've proved problematic in the short run, she had years to go before she slept. There are no signs of violence to the body, no damage to the hyoid to indicate strangulation, same for ocular petechiae. No sexual assault and she's never been pregnant. Cause of death is overdose, mode of death is up for grabs."

"Could it be an accidental O.D.?"

"Or suicide. Or homicide. My C.I. didn't spot any vomitus at the scene, or other signs of a seizure. Same for empty liquor bottles or drug Baggies. That dry ice bath is bizarre, never seen that before. I suppose it could've been some sort of erotic game that she played by herself, though it's hard to see how she could've withstood the agony."

"Could she have O.D.'d herself into stupor, slipped into the ice just before losing consciousness?"

"I suppose it's theoretically possible—talk about feeling no pain. Any idea where the ice came from? My C.I. didn't see any bags, either."

"I just got the case, Doc."

"Given a drugged state," said Jernigan, "I'd expect her to plunge rather than slip and that would've caused a mess, maybe even a head bump. There was none of that. Dry ice doesn't melt, it sublimates, so you wouldn't expect puddles. But still, she was tucked in too perfectly and skin burns say she'd been in there for a while. We both know this is homicide, but I don't have enough to put that in writing."

"Any way to know if she was alive or dead when she got put in?"

"Rosiness in the burns suggests alive but on the stand my answer would be 'I don't know.' How come you caught it when it's a Valley case?"

"My silence is profound, Doc."

"Got it," said Jernigan. "Well, good luck."

"Thanks, Doc."

"If you really want to show your gratitude," said Jernigan, "continue to keep me out of the loop."

Milo phoned the lab, ate some double talk, engaged in a spirited conversation with someone named Bill, and said, "I don't get clarification right now, I'm coming over to do a hands-on. Instructions from above."

Bill said, "What do you mean, above?"

"Use your imagination."

"I don't get paid for that."

"See you in thirty."

"That's not going to work, Milo. Per our specific instructions."

"My instructions are as of five minutes ago and they trump your instructions."

"Who are yours from?" said Bill.

"From where you can't go higher."

"Just like that, you've got a direct line to God."

"Santa, too. Don't believe me, here's the number. Now tell me what I need to know. Were there dry ice bags at the scene, empty booze bottles, drugs, or drug paraphernalia?"

"Negative on the bags," said Bill. "One empty Grey Goose bottle in the kitchen, negative on the dope. And here's a freebie: The only prints throughout the house are the vic's and that's just on a corner of the bed. Which is not right. My guess? Someone wiped the place down. But I'm not allowed to guess on this one. Now do me a favor, okay?"

"What?"

"Don't call for a while."

9

The following noon, Milo phoned. "Ready for a DTA meeting?"

It took a moment to process that. "There's a detective-teacher association?"

"There is now. His Exaltedness just let me know three members of Windsor Prep's faculty will avail themselves to me at two p.m., three fifteen, and four thirty. Not at the school, God forbid. Some address in Beverly Hills. I said, 'Arbitrary time limits don't help, sir.' He said, 'Be thankful you're getting more than a forty-five-minute hour, ask Delaware.' That was his way of saying you can be there."

"Are they coming with lawyers?"

"Didn't get the chance to ask. Here's the place."

McCarty Drive, two blocks south of Wilshire.

I said, "Nice neighborhood. Who lives there?"

"Guess we'll find out when we get there."

◆

We got there twenty minutes early. The house was a white two-story Mediterranean with diamond mullion windows, a front courtyard teeming with flowers beginning to go to seed, a lawn greener than envy. A *For Sale* sign was staked to the left of a gracefully winding stone footpath.

The front door was unlocked. We stepped into a high, tiled entry. Clean, warm light filtered to the right of a sinuous staircase. In an otherwise empty living room, a woman sat reading in a folding chair. From what I could see, the entire house was vacant.

She put her book down. Ash blond, midforties, she wore a black pantsuit and a white silk blouse with ruffles that spilled over her lapels like whipped cream.

The book was a four-inch-thick bio of Lincoln. She placed it on the chair. "Lieutenant, Doctor, you're a little early."

"And you are . . ."

"Mary Jane Rollins." Her face was round, soft, and unlined. Pale eyes and lashes said the blond was probably a renewal of her childhood.

"Nice to meet you, Headmaster Rollins. Mr. Helfgott assigned you to me?"

"Dr. Helfgott," she said, standing. "He's got an Ed.D. in educational administration. And yes, he asked me to facilitate."

"Ed.D. from Brown?" said Milo.

Rollins cocked an eyebrow. "From the U."

"Going the public route, huh?"

"The U. runs a fine program in education, Lieutenant."

"You send many of your students there?"

"When appropriate. If you don't mind I've got some reading to do, we've set up a back room for your—"

"As long as you're here, let's chat—is it Dr. Rollins?"

Curt nod.

"What can you tell us about Elise Freeman?"

"Nothing Dr. Helfgott hasn't told you."

"Dr. Helfgott told me he doesn't get involved in faculty matters, so you'd be the person to ask."

"I can tell you about Elise's lesson plans but I'm sure that's not going to help you."

"Was she happy at Prep?"

"Of course."

"Of course?"

"Why wouldn't she be happy?" Smiling suddenly, jarringly. "As to her private life, that's a matter about which I have no information."

"No socializing with the help, huh?"

Rollins fingered the frothy blouse. "My knowledge of Elise is limited to the hours she worked at Prep. She was a diligent substitute teacher, unfailingly responsible."

"That's why you gave her a standing contract, whether or not she worked."

"We felt it was the best way to provide her a sense of security. Teaching, as I'm sure you're aware, is not a lucrative profession."

"Dr. Helfgott said you pay better than anyone."

"We certainly do. Even so, the life of a substitute is unpredictable and many people need to supplement. Which is how Elise came to our attention. She'd tutored several of our students, had produced excellent results."

"Raising SAT scores."

"Doing what was necessary."

"Meaning?"

"Correcting deficits and aiming people in the proper direction. Now, if you don't mind—"

"Who owns this house, Dr. Rollins?"

She licked her lips. "I do. More precisely, I own half."

"Divorce?"

Another abrupt smile. "Ergo the sale."

Another ergo. I wondered if the school offered a Latin course.

"Sorry," said Milo.

"Don't be, it's in everyone's best interest. My ex and I have both moved on. Literally and figuratively."

"Got yourself a nice condo?"

Mary Jane Rollins's mouth tightened. "My living circumstances are relevant?"

"My bad, Doctor. Sorry."

"As a matter of fact, I've acquired a condominium much more suitable to my current circumstances, leaving my ex to contend with his dogs, his fish, his children, and all the hideous furniture he brought with him from his previous marriage. Now, if you don't mind, I'll—"

"Doctor, did Elise Freeman have any conflict with anyone at Prep?"

"Not that I know of and certainly not with the three people you'll be interrogating shortly."

"We don't interrogate, ma'am, we interview."

"I stand corrected."

Milo said, "What about dissatisfied customers? Parents or students who didn't like her results."

Rollins tugged at her ruffles. "Lieutenant, you can't seriously be suggesting someone did harm to Elise because their SAT scores were below expectation."

"Impossible."

"Beyond impossible."

"Hmm—let's be hypothetical for a moment, Dr. Rollins. Say there's a student, ambitious, reasonably smart, comes from a long line of Ivy alums—say Harvard. His dad, granddad, bunch of great-granddads went to Harvard, say all the way back to . . . John Adams. One of those whatchamacallits . . ."

"Legacies," said Rollins.

"Exactly, a serious legacy. Maybe some of those ancestors weren't even that bright, back then places like Harvard were repositories for rich white boys. Unfortunately for our bright-but-no-genius applicant, now you've got to be super-smart. Like another student at the same prep school. I'm talking certified genius."

"Lieutenant, we send far more than two alums a year to Harvard—"

"Granted, but not everyone gets in, right? Even from a great place like Prep."

Silence.

Milo said, "So on top of the national competition, there's competition among your students. Okay, so what if the morning of the SAT, that legacy kid, smart but not as smart as the other kid, happens to find himself with access to an unpleasant chemical and the genius's can of soft drink is all by itself."

"This is absurd, Lieutenant."

"Is it? That's exactly what happened a few years ago at an elite East Coast school. The victim didn't die but he was sick for a long time."

Mary Jane Rollins's hand flew to pale lips. "I don't know where you learn these things, I've certainly never heard of this. And regardless, a Prep alum would never stoop to something so utterly . . . criminally repellent."

"I'm sure you're right, Dr. Rollins, but my point is high stakes can lead to desperate behavior. Now let me repeat my question: To your knowledge were any students or parents highly dissatisfied with Elise Freeman? Enough to complain to you."

A beat.

"No, Lieutenant."

"Did anyone complain to Dr. Helfgott, or to anyone else in administration?"

"No one." Mary Jane Rollins's hands relaxed. "Lieutenant, faced with a baffling case, I'm sure you need to hypothesize imaginatively. All I can tell you is you're way off the mark if you believe Elise's death had anything to do with our people. One of Prep's virtues is our ability to combine rigorous academic training with the instillation of solid moral values. We've gone so far as to adapt Vanlight's moral dilemma training into our curriculum. Our students wrestle with a variety of complex choices."

I said, "Vanlight committed suicide after being accused of sexually harassing his students."

Rollins studied me like a zoologist confronting a new species. "Be that as it may. Now I do need to return to President Lincoln. He's the topic of my upcoming chautauqua—that's a mini-seminar I'll be offering the graduating seniors next semester."

"Freeing the slaves," said Milo. "Good timing, Doctor."

"Pardon?"

"Graduating seniors are starting to see the light at the end of the tunnel. You could call it their own emancipation proclamation."

Before Rollins could reply, the doorbell rang.

10

The man at the door was young, sparely built, with an elfin face, cropped hair the color of muddy water, a scatter of freckles, and searching green eyes. He wore a white button-down shirt, blue slacks, brown loafers, might've passed for a Windsor Prep senior.

Mary Lou Rollins said, "Thanks for being punctual, Jim. Lieutenant, this is Mr. James Winterthorn, assistant head of our science department."

Winterthorn took our hands warily, offering limp, dampish fingers. "I wish I knew what this was about."

"Come on in, sir, and we'll educate you."

Rollins led us past the staircase to a rear space that looked out to a vest-pocket garden. Empty bookshelves, working fireplace, cable hookup for the flat-screen that once sat over the mantel.

The family room, back when Rollins had adapted to the life her husband had brought with him.

Two folding chairs faced a third, with seven or eight feet between them. Milo narrowed the gap by half, directed Winterthorn to the singleton, turned to Rollins.

"Enjoy your book, Doctor. Somewhere other than the house, please."

"I was instructed to remain here, Lieutenant Sturgis."

"I respect that, ma'am. However, you're being re-instructed."

"Lieutenant, please don't put me in an awkward situation—"

"Heaven forbid. You can stay close, just not inside. My suggestion is you take a stroll. Weather's good, Rodeo Drive's not far. Otherwise, we'll have to be the ones who leave. With Mr. Winterthorn."

Winterthorn followed the exchange with growing agitation.

Rollins said, "I'll have to report this."

Milo said, "Good idea. Nothing like open communication when it comes to inculcating solid moral values."

Rollins's footsteps on hardwood were followed by the thump of a closing door.

James Winterthorn sat with his hands in his lap. His bare forearms were pallid, hairless, prominently veined.

Milo said, "Thanks for coming, sir."

"I really didn't have a choice. Dr. Helfgott pulls me out of my chem class, he obviously feels it's important."

"Did he explain why it was important?"

"Actually, it was his office I spoke to. She—his secretary—said Elise Freeman had passed away and the police needed to talk to faculty members. I don't understand why."

"What was your relationship with Elise Freeman?"

"Relationship? We were colleagues. So to speak."

"So to speak?"

"She subbed English and history, I teach chem and physics."

"Never the twain shall meet?"

"Science faculty tends to stick with science faculty and so on. Maybe that kind of tribalism is embedded in our DNA."

"So not much socializing at work," said Milo. "What about after hours?"

"I wouldn't know about that, Lieutenant."

"You're not much for socializing?"

"I have a girlfriend, we plan to move in together at the end of the school year. Between work and hanging out with Emily, my days are pretty full."

"Emily's a teacher, too?"

"She's a medical student at the U."

"You both live by yourselves, at present?"

Winterthorn blushed. "We both live with our parents. It's not ideal but with the economic situation the way it is, we felt maximizing our savings will give us a leg up on ownership."

"Where do your parents live?"

"Encino."

"South or north of the boulevard?"

"South," said Winterthorn.

"Nice."

"My father's a neurosurgeon."

"Dad and girlfriend are both doctors," said Milo.

"My brother and sister, as well."

"You're the rebel."

Winterthorn smiled.

"Premed didn't work for you?"

The smile vanished. "Why is my educational history important to you?"

"Just trying to get to know you, Jim. How old are you?"

"Twenty-nine."

"How long have you been working at Prep?"

"Two years."

"What'd you do between college and work?"

Frown. "Got a master's and began work on a Ph.D."

"In . . ."

"Physics."

"Still working on the Ph.D.?"

"I'll finish the dissertation eventually."

"Where'd all this education take place?"

"M.I.T. undergrad, U. Mich for grad school."

Milo whistled. "You teach anything else at Prep?"

"Advanced Placement chem, AP physics, and a seminar in the biophysics of ecology offered to students who get A's in the AP classes."

"The lowdown on global warming?"

"We're a bit more complex than that."

Milo edged closer. Winterthorn's startled look said *What did I do?*

"Chemistry . . . you work with dry ice?"

Winterthorn giggled.

"Something funny, Jim?"

"My fifth-grade science teacher brought dry ice into class and did volcano tricks, trying to show us science could be cool. No, Lieutenant, we're a bit beyond that in AP. There's an emphasis on computation, it's basically a college-level curriculum."

"No volcanoes," said Milo. "Too bad. When my teacher did that I *was* convinced science was cool."

Winterthorn turned serious. "Are you saying dry ice had something to do with Elise's . . . with what happened?"

"What were your impressions of Elise, Jim?"

Winterthorn's thin frame pressed against his seat-back, as if trying to will the chair into reverse. "She seemed conscientous."

"Seemed?"

"I'm sure she was. Occasionally, I'd see her making herself available after hours."

"You noticed her after-hours because . . ."

"I do the same thing myself."

"Do the students appreciate that kind of dedication?"

"I would think so."

"Did Elise have any particular favorites—students she hung out with more than others?"

"I wouldn't know—can you tell me what this is about? I'm assuming there's something suspicious about her death, why else would we be talking to police detectives."

Milo handed Winterthorn his card.

The young man's eyes widened. "She was definitely murdered?"

"Definitely?"

"What I mean is . . . the immediacy," said Winterthorn. "Something so terrible hitting so close." He sounded more fascinated than horrified, might've been describing a complex molecule.

"So," said Milo, "no favorites you were aware of."

"I wasn't paying attention."

"What about conflict with anyone at Prep? Students, faculty, janitors?"

"Absolutely nothing like that," said Winterthorn.

"If she did have problems with someone, would you have known, Jim?"

"What do you mean?"

"Being in the math-science tribe."

"That demarcation applies to socializing," said Winterthorn, shifting his weight and scratching the bridge of his nose. "Prep's an intimate place, significant events can attain broad coverage. If Elise was experiencing significant conflict—something that would lead to . . . yes, I might know about that. But I never heard a thing."

"You're saying there's a well-oiled gossip mill operating."

"Not really, it's just . . . important facts travel."

"What did the mill have to say about Elise?"

Winterthorn bit his lip. "I'm not comfortable talking behind her back. Especially now."

"Now is when you need to talk behind her back, Jim. That back is currently resting on the cold steel surface of a coroner's dissection table."

Winterthorn shuddered. "Good Lord, you don't pull punches, do you?"

"I've found that unhelpful when dealing with murder."

"Murder . . . this is surreal."

"Let's get back to the gossip question, Jim. What did loose lips flap about concerning Elise?"

"Do I have to be quoted on this in your official document—your file, whatever you call it?"

"Not if you're forthcoming, Jim." Smooth lie.

Winterthorn rubbed his eyes. "I can't vouch for this firsthand but yes, there was talk to the effect that Elise had a drinking problem. I certainly never saw it, but people claimed they had."

"Which people?"

"Other teachers."

"Names, please."

"I . . ."

"Jim, this is important."

"Please don't say it came from me."

"Deal. Who, Jim?"

"Enrico Hauer, he teaches psychology and urban studies. He claimed he'd seen Elise drunk."

"At school?"

Head shake. "At a bar."

"Which one?"

"I didn't ask. He said she was pretty much wasted."

"Are we talking a single episode or a pattern?"

"He claimed he'd smelled it on her breath at work."

"And what did Mr. Hauer do with this information?"

"Nothing," said Winterthorn. "At least as far as I know. I didn't want to hear it. I try to remain above the fray."

"What fray is that?"

"It's an expression, Lieutenant. I don't like getting involved in other people's issues." Winterthorn's voice had taken on metal. Tightened posture brought out muscle in the thin, pale arms. Small man, but sinewy, with square shoulders, maybe stronger than he looked.

Milo said, "What about drugs?"

"That I never heard," said Winterthorn. "Are you saying drugs were somehow used in conjunction with dry ice? Because as a chemist I really can't come up with an obvious scenario—"

"So you never hung out with Elise."

"Never."

"So if someone else testified that you did hang out with her, they'd be lying."

Winterthorn's eyes raced from side to side. "Who told you that?"

"What would you say if I told you Elise did?"

"I'd say that's ridiculous."

Milo summarized the DVD.

Winterthorn gripped the sides of his chair. Burst into tears, lips churning.

Milo said, "That goes beyond hanging out, Jim."

Winterthorn rocked, clutched his hair, as his mouth continued to work soundlessly. Two strangled words finally escaped:

"Only. Once."

11

James Winterthorn kept shaking.

Milo said, "Tell us about the one time."

"You know already, why play games?"

"Know what, Jim?"

"It's your strategy," said Winterthorn. "Don't ask questions unless you already know the answer. Lawyers do that." Bitter smile. "Mom's a litigator."

"Tell us anyway, Jim."

"One damn time, okay? We were both working late and then we walked to our cars together and that's where it happened."

"In one of your cars."

"Hers. I walked her there. Being a gentleman and all that." Arid laugh. "She thanked me and kissed my cheek." Winterthorn's arms crossed his chest. "She turned her head, cheek turned into mouth, and then . . . what's the difference? It was one time, neither of us talked about it again and there was certainly no harassment and if she claimed different, she was obviously deranged."

Milo kept silent.

"In point of fact," Winterthorn went on, "she was the aggressor—she initiated, I was just stupid. We didn't even have conventional sex—no, that came out wrong, I'm not implying anything weird or kinky, I'm just saying we didn't have intercourse. Understand?"

"Not fully, Jim."

"She went down on me, okay?" Winterthorn sprang up, walked to the French doors, looked out at impatiens, begonias, ferns, a cute little pathway fashioned from round pond stones. "And then it was over and we never talked about it and it's not relevant because Elise wasn't significant to me and I'm sure the same went for her."

He faced us. "I was *nothing* to her. She made that clear."

"How'd she do that, Jim?"

"After she finished, she wiped her mouth and laughed and said, 'Don't make a big deal of that, Jimmy. I was just in a mood.' "

"That kind of attitude could make someone mad."

"The only one I was mad at was myself. I've always prided myself on being faithful and up until that point I had been. I was a total ass, no excuse. I still don't understand how it happened but I certainly didn't pursue her. Just the opposite, I wanted nothing to do with her."

"She took you by surprise, Jim."

"She sure as hell did but I was an ass, nonetheless. I know this sounds like something a woman would say but the entire episode made me feel dirty."

"Feeling dirty could make someone mad."

"I didn't *kill* her!" Winterthorn pounded a pane. Rocked on the balls of his feet. "Goddammit!"

"Why don't you sit back down, Jim?"

"I prefer to stand."

Milo said, "I'm going to give you a time span and I'd like you to tell me where you were during that period."

He outlined the parameters of the murder day.

Winterthorn said, "I was with—no, I wasn't with Emily, thank God. I was with my mother. She wasn't feeling well and my father was at a conference so I went and sat with her." Facing us. "There's no reason to drag Emily into this, right?"

"Hopefully not, Jim."

"*Please.* I had nothing to do with Elise's death."

"Even though she made you feel cheap."

"An isolated event," said Winterthorn. "I put it behind me."

"Something like that, a lot of guys would remember it fondly."

"I'm not a lot of guys."

"Guess not."

"That doesn't mean I'm a killer."

Milo said, "Let's go back to that event for a sec. You tell it as Elise coming on to you, she tells it as persistent sexual harassment."

"That's insane, I have no idea why she'd say that. Why me, of all people?"

"Who, then?"

Winterthorn looked to the side. "That's not what I meant."

"What did you mean, Jim?"

Winterthorn slumped. "This is crazy, totally crazy. Dr. Helfgott pulls me out of class and now I'm being interrogated like a criminal."

"Interviewed," said Milo.

"I feel interrogated. Worse—intimidated. Like Guantánamo."

"How did you and Elise get along after the 'event'?"

"I avoided her."

"She made you nervous."

"Maybe *that's* why she made those insane accusations. She felt rejected."

"She came on to you again and you turned her down?"

"No, no, I'd avoid eye contact, she never had the opportunity. Maybe it annoyed her, I don't know. But what was my choice?"

"Science teachers not hobnobbing with English teachers made it easier for you," said Milo. "But general job stuff must've thrown you together."

"What do you mean?"

"Gripe sessions in the faculty lounge."

Winterthorn's laughter was quick, too emphatic. Grateful for the opportunity to be other than scared. "There are no gripe sessions at Prep. They'd be considered unseemly."

Milo said, "That sounds like a word Dr. Helfgott would use."

"As a matter of fact, it's one of his favorite adjectives."

"Unseemly," said Milo. "Guess that could apply to murder."

"That Dr. H. would probably call abominable."

"Hmm . . . okay, Jim, I'll need your mother's phone number and address."

Winterthorn's eyes bugged. "You're kidding."

"She's your alibi, Jim."

"I need an *alibi*?"

"Jim, look at the facts objectively: A woman accuses you of sexual harassment and now she's dead."

"I'm the only person she accused?"

"Should there be others, Jim?"

Silence.

"If there's something you know," said Milo, "now's the time."

Winterthorn sat down, lowered his head. "I'm probably opening a can of worms."

"Sometimes that's what it takes to catch fish, Jim."

Seconds passed. A sparrow settled on a rock in the garden. A raven swooped down and scared the smaller bird away.

Winterthorn covered his mouth with one hand, moaned into

his palm softly. The hand lowered. "If you want to pursue that angle, I'd have a look at Enrico—Enrico Hauer. I'm sure he and Elise were seeing each other."

"Why?"

"They weren't exactly subtle, Lieutenant. Long looks, smiles, brushing against each other."

"Sounds like you were watching them, Jim."

"No, no, that's my point. It was hard to miss."

"What else can you tell me about Mr. Hauer?"

"He's from Argentina . . . he's . . . self-assured. Teaches urban studies and psychology."

"He and Elise had something going on."

"That was my impression."

"Problem is, Jim, that boils down to consensual hanky-panky, not harassment."

"The same applies to me! It was *totally* consensual—she *initiated* for God's sake—and it was only one time. Enrico, on the other hand . . ."

Winterthorn trailed off.

Milo said, "Okay, thanks for the help, Jim. Now, what's your mom's number?"

"What are you going to tell her?"

"That your whereabouts are part of a routine investigation."

"That's going to freak her out," said Winterthorn. "Could you say I'm not a suspect, you're checking out other people?"

"Hmm—if you've been totally truthful I guess I could do that."

"I have been, I swear. And you won't tell Emily, right?"

"Same answer, Jim."

"Thank you. I meant that." Winterthorn's eyes misted. Milo held out a tissue. Men usually refuse the offer.

Winterthorn didn't.

CHAPTER

12

Enrico Hauer smiled dreamily, as if aroused from a pleasant nap. "How bizarre."

Windsor Prep's head of social studies had arrived ten minutes late, giving Milo time to call James Winterthorn's mother and inquire about the science teacher's whereabouts. Martha Winterthorn, Esq., played lawyer for a while, finally filled in the time frame. Her account left an hour or so unaccounted for and mothers were dubious guarantors, but Milo hung up saying, "At this point, you see any reason to bust the poor bastard's life wide open?"

"Not yet."

Bell ring number two.

The man we found striding into the empty living room was thirty-five to forty, tall, muscular, broad-shouldered, and handsome in a mirror-junkie way: thick, black, pomaded hair worn shoulder-length, perfectly arched eyebrows, glossed and buffed fingernails. He wore a body-conscious chocolate turtleneck, black slacks, two-tone brown-and-black clogs. His gold watch was thin, his pinkie ring bulky. As we got closer, the aroma of a lemony cologne thickened.

He took in the house's interior. "Nice. When can we open escrow?" Mellow baritone, the barest hint of Latin accent.

Neither Milo nor I laughed.

Enrico Hauer said, "I'm joking because I'm upset and disoriented. Being called to face the police is Kafkaesque."

Milo said, "One of those days, huh?" and guided Hauer to the back of the house. Seated in the chair James Winterthorn had occupied, Hauer slipped his hand between buttock and metal. "Already warm. This is the hot seat?"

"It's good to have a sense of humor, Mr. Hauer."

"Rico. As a defense mechanism it's less damaging than others."

"What have you been told about this meeting?"

"Dr. Helfgott's secretary informed me Elise Freeman was dead and that the police wanted to talk to some of the faculty."

"How well did you know Elise?"

"Not well at all."

"It's been suggested that you and Elise Freeman had an affair."

"An affair? How silly."

"Never happened, huh?"

"By silly I meant that word. *Affair*. As if formal invitations were printed. We had sex." Hauer shook his head. "That's why I'm here? For having sex."

"For having sex with a dead woman."

Hauer laughed. "I am not a necrophiliac."

"Correction," said Milo. "A woman who ended up dead."

"Well, I'm sorry for that, but here are the facts: Elise and I had purely physical sex many times. Surely you guys don't see that as strange. A woman I can see objecting. The blending of emotion and physicality. But we are different, no?"

"You teach psychology, right?"

"I love it," said Rico Hauer. "One day I may pursue a Ph.D."

"What other subjects do you teach?"

"Social justice. That's a two-semester course spanning the nine-teenth and the twentieth centuries. As well as an honors seminar in urban studies and a super-honors mini-course in poverty and social adjustment."

"Super-honors?"

Hauer winked. "Kids who are really motivated get rewarded with extra homework and long papers."

Milo said, "Sounds like you've got a busy schedule."

"One who loves his work is never busy, only engaged."

"Ah . . . that apply to sex with Elise?"

"Oh, yes, Lieutenant. We were both definitely engaged—engrossed, really."

"How often did you and Elise get mutually engrossed?"

"As often as we could—no, forgive me, I'm being flippant again because this really has unnerved me."

"Being here."

"Being here to discuss Elise's death. Which I'm assuming was unpleasant and irregular, otherwise why would I be here, forgive the teleology—the circular logic."

Milo handed over his card.

Hauer said, "I hope she didn't suffer, Elise did not like to suffer."

"She told you that?"

"Oh, yes, explicitly. 'I'm not into pain, Rico.' "

"How did the topic of pain come up, Mr. Hauer?"

Hauer crossed long legs. White silk socks thin enough to suggest chestnut ankles contrasted with the black pants. "You're probably assuming paraphilia—pain in a sexual context. But not so, Lieutenant, the conversation was postcoital. Elise did what many women do in that situation. Began talking about herself." Conspiratorial grin.

Milo remained impassive. Hauer turned to me for empathy. I pretended to be a DMV clerk.

He said, "What I'm trying to get across is, Elise began talking about her childhood. A very unpleasant childhood, as it turned out."

"How so, Mr. Hauer?"

"A father who withheld love. In my view, it had turned Elise needy and vulnerable. That particular night, her point was that she'd escaped an unsatisfying family situation and had no desire to repeat it. Hence, 'I'm not into pain, Rico.' To my mind it sounded like anxious denial—trying to convince herself that she was strong. On the other hand, not repeating history would be a positive step, so I didn't debate her."

Hauer turned serious. "She yearned for gentleness. In fact, I'd say that was the unifying concept of her sexually. That's why I find it so unnerving that someone has harmed her. Was it violent?"

"We're keeping the details to ourselves for now."

"Yes," said Hauer. "That makes sense."

Milo said, "You always treated her gently."

"I'm a guy who loves to make women happy, Lieutenant. The pleasure of others increases my own."

"So if a woman wanted it rough, you'd oblige."

"Within bounds, but that wasn't Elise. Quite the opposite, she was more tickle than tussle."

Milo flipped pages in his pad. Hauer looked out to the garden, smiled serenely.

"You like working at Prep?"

"For the time being."

"Thinking of leaving?"

"Not imminently," said Hauer, "but I do like to keep life well seasoned. A few years ago I rode my motorcycle from San Diego into Central America. Shortly after that, I managed to enter Myanmar—Burma—on a cargo ship. That is a place Americans are advised against visiting. I managed quite nicely for two weeks. I've lived on the isle of Gibraltar, observing the monkeys. I've studied flamenco guitar in Andalusia—as a historian, not a musician."

"So one day you might just pick up and take another adventure."

"Life is adventure."

I said, "Where are you from?"

"A place where Italians speak Spanish and think they're Germans." Smile. "Argentina. But America suits me better. The land of endless opportunity."

"Like a Ph.D. in psychology."

"Or a position at a think tank, or ten more years teaching bright, nervous kids." A big hand waved. "Whatever life brings."

"What aspect of psychology would you study?"

"I would become a master psychotherapist."

"Isn't the Ph.D. a research degree?" I said. "Least that's what my cousin the psychologist says."

"I would research becoming a master psychotherapist. My secondary topic would be psychotherapeutic valences as they enhance affective gestalt."

Gibberish; I nodded as if it were profound.

Rico Hauer said, "Dreadful, dreadful, poor Elise." Touching his chest, he blinked. All the emotional depth of a sheet of vinyl.

Milo told him about the DVD.

Hauer didn't move a muscle. Seconds ticked. A full minute of mute immobility.

Milo said, "That's a serious charge, sir. No reaction?"

"What reaction would you like? Denial? Fine, I deny. Shock and surprise? Fine, I am appalled. If I believe you."

"You think we're lying?"

"I think," said Hauer, "that the police use deception because the courts have granted legitimacy to that tactic. In fact, I cover that issue in my urban studies class, pose it to my students as a serious moral dilemma."

"No dilemma here, Mr. Hauer. Elise really did make that claim, took the time to record it on a DVD."

"Poor Elise. To engage in such delusions. Then again, she had her own moral issues."

"Such as?"

"Lack of fidelity."

"To who?"

"Some poor devil who believed she had special feelings for him."

"A boyfriend?"

"He may have thought so." Hauer smiled. "Elise enjoyed playing with his head. Used me as a vehicle for her mean little games."

"How so, Mr. Hauer?"

"She liked to phone him while we were having sex." Hauer's eyes brightened. "There you go, perhaps he found out. Jealousy's an excellent motive."

"Does the poor devil have a name?"

"Sal. Elise enjoyed making small talk with him as she wiggled in interesting ways. Sometimes she'd cover the phone and moan. Sometimes she'd hold a photograph of herself and him while she and I tangoed. So to speak."

"What kind of photograph?"

"Nothing erotic," said Hauer. "The two of them at a casino, this Sal had won some money. A bald little man. I attribute her hostility to him as a yearning for mastery after a childhood filled with affective helplessness."

"She kept that picture in her living room," said Milo. "That mean you tangoed at her house?"

"Of course. Where else, Lieutenant?"

"Your place?"

Hauer grinned. "My wife would object."

Avoiding the bait, Milo took him over the same ground. Hauer grew bored. A guy hooked on novelty.

The request for an alibi elicited a yawn and the explanation that he'd been with his wife, a Spanish teacher at a girls' school in Hancock Park.

"Feel free to ask her, Lieutenant."

"You don't care."

"Claudia will pretend to be resentful but she has her own diversions."

"Open marriage?"

"There is no such thing," said Hauer. "Let's just say Claudia and I are more forgiving than most people. I would, of course, resent your telling her about Elise's accusation, as it is patently false and defamatory."

"Defamatory," said Milo. "That's kind of legalistic."

"I studied law in Buenos Aires, Lieutenant. Decided not to live my life as an attack dog." Smoothing his hair. "Doesn't it bother you, dealing with the worst in people?"

"I manage to cope, Mr. Hauer."

"Good for you. Now, what else can I help you with?"

Milo's wave was dismissive.

Hauer sat there.

Milo got up and rapped the back of Hauer's chair with a knuckle.

Hauer flinched.

"Out, Rico."

◆

We watched him speed off in a yellow Mazda Miata convertible. Ten minutes remained until Pat Skaggs's appointment. Milo lit a cigar and we idled on the sidewalk.

Three puffs and two smoke rings later, he said, "Elise was a busy girl."

I said, "Esteemed educators molding young minds."

"It's like Hauer and Winterthorn own a testosterone time share but Winterthorn never gets to use it. Wimp or stud, cast your ballot for prime suspect."

"I'll withhold judgment until Mr. Skaggs tells his story."

"Who knew the faculty lounge was such a hotbed of naughty? What do you think of Elise's accusations now?"

"Same answer."

"C'mon, stretch your theoretical wings."

"Both men 'fessed up to sex with her, but consent's a rapist's favorite excuse because it can neutralize DNA. It's possible as soon as Hauer and Winterthorn were summoned, they conspired to hedge with partial truth. But I really don't know."

He cursed. "In a normal situation, I'da popped in on them, there'd be no chance to collude. What about their personalities?"

"Winterthorn's an excitable boy. My guess is nothing much shocks Hauer."

"Unflappable sociopath?"

"He's got the pretentiousness."

"Mr. Amateur Psychologist."

"Mile wide, inch deep," I said. "One day he can get his own talk show. Or run for office."

He laughed. Smoked, pulled out his cell, and punched in Claudia Hauer's number. The resulting conversation was brief, pleasant, ambiguous.

"Mrs. Rico verifies *Señor* Smooth was with her all night, which is worth about as much as Mommy Winterthorn vouching for Junior trouble."

I said, "Whatever Hauer's character flaws, if what he told us about Elise's childhood is true, it is a nice fit with her binge-drinking and promiscuity. Also with choosing a guy like Sal Fidella, then degrading him. I'd be interested in talking to her relatives. Someone's going to have to deal with the body, eventually."

"In a *normal* situation," he said, "I'd have already put Sean or Moe on a back-trace for nearest kin." He flicked ashes. "Prank-calling the poor fool while she romped with El Gaucho was pretty damn cold."

"Interesting word choice, Big Guy."

He lowered the cigar. "Gonna show me some inkblots now?"

"Got 'em back at the office. I'm serious. You've got good instincts, maybe you just hit on something."

"Elise freezes Sal out emotionally so he gets back at her with dry ice?"

"She staged her games," I said, "he devised one of his own. He had a key to her house and his alibi's no better than Winterthorn's or Hauer's."

"And what looks like a whodunit is just another stupid domestic. Talk about multiple orgasms for His Splendiferousness. Yeah, Sal needs to be looked at harder but so do our esteemed educators. Neither of them wasted time casting suspicion on someone else. For Winterthorn it was Hauer, Hauer aimed us back at Sal."

"Get on the love train," I said. "Reminds me of something one of my professors said when I was considering a teaching career. 'Backbiting is the mother's milk of academia, son, because so little is at stake.' "

"I had a graduate advisor tell me basically the same thing," he said. "Dr. Carter, chairman of my master's committee. That was a coupla days before he put a move on me." He checked his Timex. "Be interesting to see who Mr. Skaggs dumps on."

Just as Milo stubbed out his cigar, a small white car approached from the north, belching exhaust. Slowing, it parked across the street. Nissan Sentra, dusty windows, multiple dings.

The woman who got out was young, tall, sturdily built, with long dark wavy hair, a full face, gold-rimmed specs. Her gray pantsuit fit loosely, as did the yellow blouse underneath. A big brown leather purse arced wildly as she jogged across the street.

"Police?"

"And you are . . ."

"Pat Skaggs. They say you want to talk to me about Elise."

CHAPTER

13

Patricia Ann Skaggs's robust frame and broad shoulders were belied by a beseeching, little-girl voice. Frequent tic-like eyeblinks turned gorgeous cornflower eyes into sputtering gas-flames.

Ten seconds with her in the back room and Enrico Hauer's insouciance had been neutralized.

Milo said, "So you know why you're here."

"Marlene—Dr. H.'s secretary—told me Elise died, the police were talking to her colleagues. Was she murdered?"

"It's possible."

"Oh, that's horrid!"

"You two were close?"

"I liked her," said Pat Skaggs. "We socialized at work, but I really can't say much about her personal life."

Blink. Blink.

Milo said, "Workplace friend."

"The first time I saw her, she having lunch by herself in a corner of the faculty lounge. She subbed, so no one knew who she was. I introduced myself. I figured it was difficult to get into our circle."

"Faculty at Prep's like a club."

"Oh, no, nothing like that," said Pat Skaggs. "It's just that the rest of us were accustomed to each other."

"Not much faculty turnover at Prep?"

"It's a great place to work." Raising her volume on that proclamation.

"How long have you been teaching there, Pat?"

"Five years, starting right after college."

"Which college?"

"Wellesley."

"That's a great place."

Impish smile. "Now you're going to say Hillary went there."

I said, "Madeleine Albright and Diane Sawyer went there."

She laughed. "They, as well."

Milo said, "What do you teach at Prep?"

"Advanced Placement and honors history, honors world civilizations seminar, bonus chautauqua on women's rights in the wake of the Industrial Revolution."

"Elise tutored history and English, so you had something in common. Ever send any students to her for tutoring?"

"A couple. They seemed satisfied."

"No complaints from pushy parents about someone getting an A-minus instead of an A?"

Pat Skaggs pushed hair off a moist forehead. "I'm sure you've heard stories but for the most part Prep's not like that."

"No grade pressure?"

"By the time kids get to AP and honors they've pretty much self-selected."

"Still," I said, "some of them require tutoring."

She licked her lips. "Some people are extremely perfectionis-
tic."

"Some people get upset when perfection's not attained."

"You're not really saying some student did this because they
weren't pleased with Elise's performance?"

Milo said, "At this point, we're open to any theory, Pat."

"Oh, wow," she said. "No, honestly, I don't see that." Small
hands quivered. "Honestly, I just don't see that."

"Where did Elise go to school, Pat?"

"U. of Maryland."

"She talk much about her college days?"

"Not really."

"Not really?"

"She did tell me she'd preferred to go to a small college."

"Like Wellesley."

Nod.

"Why didn't she?"

"Money."

"What'd she have to say about her family?"

"Nothing," said Skaggs.

"Nothing at all?"

"She avoided talking about her family, Lieutenant. As to why, I
can only conjecture that her memories weren't pleasant."

"Avoided, how?"

"I just got a general sense of . . . avoidance. Okay, here's an example: Once, before Thanksgiving, I was talking about how much
I looked forward to seeing my family. Elise said, 'Sounds nice,' and
there was a wistful tone in her voice. I mistook that for her missing
her own family, said something along those lines. Elise shook her
head, rather . . . vociferously. Then she smiled and changed the
subject but I felt I'd touched a nerve. On the other hand, maybe
I'm reading too much into it."

"What else did you and Elise talk about?"

"Work stuff, girl stuff. She hadn't dated in a long time, said she might be getting ready for that but wasn't sure."

"When did she tell you that?"

"I'd have to say a few months ago . . . three?"

Well past the time when she'd started seeing Sal Fidella.

Milo said, "Where'd you have those girl chats?"

Blink blink blink. "We went out a couple of times after work. Had a drink to unwind. Not at bars, at restaurants *with* bars. Because of me, I'm not into places where people just sit and get drunk. Even at Wellesley I wasn't much for the bar scene. Poor Elise, I can't believe anyone would do that to her. Did she suffer?"

"Sounds like you really liked her, as a person."

"I did."

He frowned. Shook his head. "That makes it a little tough, Pat."

"Makes what tough?"

"Having to tell you something that might conflict with your opinion of Elise."

"I'm not following." Moisture darkened the armpits of her jacket. Enough sweat to seep quickly through heavy twill.

Milo pulled his chair closer, leaned in close. Pat Skaggs's lower lip shook.

"Pat," he said, "the sad truth is you may have thought Elise was a nice person but the feeling wasn't mutual."

"I—what are you saying?"

He summed up the DVD.

Patricia Ann Skaggs screamed and ran from the room.

We caught up to her in the hallway near the vacant kitchen, where she'd slumped against a wall and was sobbing into both palms.

"I'm sorry, Pat." Milo placed a hand on her shoulder.

"It's not true! It's an ugly, ugly, ugly lie!"

We waited until tears gave way to snuffles.

"Let's sit back down and hear your side of it, Pat."

She pulled away. Red-faced, and some of the color had spread to the sclera of her eyes.

Red, white, and blue; the patriotism of fear.

"Let's sit down, Pat."

"There *is* no other side! If she said that—I can't believe she'd say that, why would she *say* that?"

"That's what we're trying to figure out, Pat."

"She lied about Jim Winterthorn and Rico Hauer, too?"

"Why would you ask that, Pat?"

"They're the only other faculty members summoned to talk to you."

"Who told you that?"

"Marlene."

"Pat, have you discussed anything related to this case with Winterthorn or Hauer—or anyone else?"

"Absolutely not," she said.

"I need you to be straight about that, Pat."

"I am being straight, I've had no time to talk to anyone."

"So you tried."

Silence.

"Pat?"

"After Marlene told me, I tried to call both of them but neither picked up their phones."

"When?"

"An hour ago. I assure you there was no attempt to dissemble. I was merely curious about why only the three of us."

"Was any other faculty member at Prep as friendly with Elise as you?"

"I really wasn't that friendly, myself."

"Same question, Pat."

She chewed her lip. Shook her head. "Truthfully, I never saw Elise with Jim or Rico."

"Do you know Jim and Rico pretty well?"

"Uh-uh, no way, I'm not getting into personalities. Not when you drag me here and make vicious accusations."

"The accusations are not ours, Pat. They're Elise's."

"How do I know that's true?"

"Why else would we be talking to you?"

"And Jim and Rico."

"Let's concentrate on you right now, Pat."

"There's nothing to concentrate on. I want to get out of here."

"That's your right," said Milo. "But it will result in a subpoena and further questioning at the police station."

Pat Skaggs gaped. "Why are you doing this to me?"

"A woman's dead and leaves behind a taped accusation. If we didn't follow through on something like that, would we be doing our job?"

No answer.

"What kind of grade would you give us for that type of sloppiness, Pat? D? F?"

Pat Skaggs ground her teeth. "She may have said it, but it *never* happened. Elise's death has nothing to do with me."

"That's why we need to sit back down and hear what you have to say."

"Oh, God," she said. "This is Kafkaesque."

Same adjective Hauer had used. If a tormented, tubercular Jew hadn't penned a handful of stories, what would academics do for emotional shorthand?

"I'm sure it feels that way, Pat. Let's head back and clear everything up."

"There's nothing to clear up," she said, but his gentle prod got her walking.

When she was back in the chair, I said, "So the sex was consensual?"

Milo's turn to blink.

Pat Skaggs didn't notice, her eyes were on me, wild and red-veined and bulging. Stricken as if I'd stripped her naked.

In a way, I had.

She let loose another flood of tears but made no attempt to bolt. Sat there snuffling and mumbling.

Milo said, "What's that, Pat?"

"It was only twice." She sat up. "Now you're going to say it's because of Wellesley, well, it's not, I'm tired of all those Harvard-boy jokes and I wasn't gay at Wellesley, I had a boyfriend, I was engaged to be married."

"Your sexuality doesn't matter to us, Pat, except as it relates to Elise Freeman."

"Twice," she said. "Two damn times. Okay? Satisfied? And you *cannot* tell my girlfriend, you simply *cannot*!"

The girlfriend was a harp teacher from Glendale named Michelle Washburn. She and Pat Skaggs had been living together for three months in an apartment not far from the Galleria.

The dual sexual encounters with Elise Freeman preceded that arrangement, though Skaggs and Washburn had been dating seriously. Skaggs's account evoked James Winterthorn's story: Following drinks and dinner, Elise Freeman had initiated contact. Substituting "soft kisses and affection" then a grope up Skaggs's skirt for the sudden fellatio she'd performed on Winterthorn. Both times, the women had ended up at Elise's house. Both times, Skaggs had left without spending the night, worried about giving herself away to Michelle Washburn.

"Brief encounter, then good night," said Milo.

"That makes it sound . . . I guess it was tawdry. I was an idiot, I still don't understand why I acceded. The first time could've been written off as Mojitos and bad judgment, the second? Moronic— and now I have to talk to you about it. Good Lord, this is humiliating."

"We hear all kinds of things, Pat. If it's not related to homicide, we couldn't care less."

"Well, *I* certainly didn't kill her. I never, never, never did anything remotely abusive or coercive with Elise. I just can't see why she'd *say* that." Tears. Abrupt panic. "You don't have to notify Prep about this, right?"

"Of course not."

"Please, I beg you. I love my job."

"Pat, if you've told us the complete truth, no one will know."

"I have, I swear. Please!"

"Okay, then. You can go."

"That's it?"

Milo smiled. "We could stretch this out a bit if you'd prefer."

Pat Skaggs inhaled, stood. Ran from the room looking smaller.

14

When we were alone, Milo paced the vacant house. I stayed in the back room, enjoying the view of the garden and wondering.

His footsteps lingered in the kitchen; the primeval urge. When he stomped back in, I said, "My bet's on Freeman making it up."

Milo said, "The teachers are horny but not monsters?"

"If they were drama coaches I might feel differently but all three seemed genuinely surprised about the accusation and it's hard to see the three of them cooperating on a campaign to torment poor Elise. Also, Elise made the DVD but never did anything with it. Maybe she contemplated an extortion scheme but changed her mind?"

"Seducing teachers for blackmail? Not exactly deep pockets."

"These are teachers who work for the richest school in the city," I said. "Talk about a massive workplace harassment suit. And something that waitress at the bar said makes me wonder if Fidella was involved. She pegged him as a get-rich-quick type."

He circled the room. Stopped. "Winterthorn and Skaggs I can see as vulnerable to extortion, but Rico Suavisimo doesn't care what wifey thinks. Why would Elise pick him as a stooge?"

"Maybe she didn't know about his wife's tolerance. She'd see a married man, one clearly giving off sexual vibes."

"Using the three of them to get to ultra-deep pockets . . . then why change her mind? Given what we're learning about her, I don't see a burst of moral growth."

"Could be she lost her nerve about doing battle with an institution like Prep. Especially after they gave her a permanent gig."

"Maybe the gig was payoff for not suing, Alex."

I thought about that. "Doubt it. She'd hold out for a lot more than a steady job. Another reason could be Rico. Unlike the other two, he describes a prolonged affair. Maybe Elise decided making love beat making war."

"She falls for *Señor* Stud, decides not to drag him into the muck?"

"And if things went bad, she always had the disc."

"Best-laid plans," he said. "So to speak."

"Which brings us back to Fidella," I said. "If he was involved in the scheme, he'd lose twice: another jackpot dashed and his girl-friend's making a fool of him with another man. I keep going back to his having a key to her house. What if he dropped in one night, found Elise and Hauer together but left without a scene?"

"He stews, builds up the rage, finally accepts the fact that Elise won't go forward with her threats."

"He also was aware of Elise's binge-drinking. Who better to lace her vodka with some kind of opiate? He waits until she's wasted and helpless, lowers her into the tub, packs her like crab legs at the fish market."

He grimaced. "And here I was thinking seafood for dinner. Wonder where that waitress hangs out when she's not drinking at Arnie Joseph's."

The octogenarian bartender held a glass to the light. "That's Doris, she does the three-to-eleven shift at Fat Boy."

"Where's Fat Boy?"

"Two blocks north. If you're thinking Doris had a thing with Sal, she didn't."

"Who did?" said Milo.

"Some blonde."

Milo showed him a snap of Elise Freeman.

"That's her."

"She in here a lot?"

"A few times. Grey Goose, up. Sometimes a twist, sometimes nothing."

"Not an ice freak," said Milo.

"Nope."

"Heavy drinker?"

"One drink, period. Thank God most ain't like her."

"What else do you know about her?"

"Nothing, I know drinks, not people." Studying Milo. "You're beer." To me: "Blended scotch, maybe a high-end single malt if you're feeling flush. Both of you drink wine when your wives want you to."

"Let's hear it for the wives," said Milo. "You're an oracle."

"Been doing this for fifty-three years, nothing changes."

"What does your crystal ball tell you about Sal?"

"Beer, same as you. Only difference is you I might let run a tab."

"Sal's not a good risk?"

"I'm a trusting sort," said the old man. "But jerk me around enough and it's cash on the barrel."

"Sal has trouble meeting his obligations?"

The bartender laid down his towel, folded it neatly. "What kind of dumb-ass empties a slot machine of ten grand and blows it the same day? When it comes to settling up, he's always got a sad story. So now it's cash on the barrel."

"Sal react okay to that?" said Milo.

"What do you mean?"

"He have a temper?"

"People don't do that."

"Do what?"

"Fuss when I read 'em the law." He reached behind the bar, hefted a Louisville Slugger. Black worn to gray, same for the tape around the handle.

Milo said, "It came to that with Sal?"

"Nah, but he knows it's here. Everyone does. Got robbed twenty-eight years ago, coupla cholos pistol-whipped me, my skull was like eggshell. I got smart."

"A bat's enough?"

The old man winked. Watery eyes dropped to a spot behind the bar. "Gotta be seeing as how normal people can't get carry permits for firearms, only rich dumb-asses who know the mayor."

"You got that right," said Milo. "Sal ever hit you up with easy-money schemes?"

"People don't do that with me."

"He ever hit up your patrons?"

"Probably."

"Probably?"

"People drink, their lips flap. Sal flaps a lot even before the first beer. But he never impresses anyone. I ignore all that noise and think about my grandchildren."

"Hear no evil?"

"Crap floats by me, why would I touch it?"

"Still," said Milo, "you smell it. What kinds of things is Sal into?"

"Mostly he bitches about how he used to have money. Stocks, bonds, real estate. Back when kids played instruments. You believe that, I'll sell you GM. Want anything, a soft drink? On the house."

"No, thanks. Tell us about the blonde."

"Not much to tell," said the barkeep. "Quiet, but not friendly quiet, more like nose in the air, she was too good for the place. She'd drink her one Goose, get all fidgety, make Sal leave. He followed her like a puppy dog."

Lifting the towel with deft fingers, he snapped it midair. "You want Doris, she's on shift right around now. Don't tell her I sent you."

"Doris likes her privacy?"

The old man returned the bat to its hiding place. "I don't give a rat's ass what she or anyone else likes. My age, I keep things simple."

Fat Boy was a holdout against franchise fever, a glass-fronted fifties cube with an upwardly thrusting roof that evoked manned space travel. Breakfast special banner taped to the glass, breakfast smells late in the afternoon. Blue Naugahyde booths, counter stools, and aqua carpeting had long conceded the war against dirt and wear.

The place was empty but for two bearded truckers inhaling bacon and eggs at the counter and a young Hispanic woman tending to them with good cheer and banter. Same unflattering pink uniform as Doris but she made it work.

"You guys can sit up here."

No sign of Doris. Then she emerged through rear doors, carrying a two-foot stack of yellow paper napkins.

Milo waved.

She ignored him and began filling dispensers. Her name tag said *Dorrie.*

"Afternoon, Dorrie."

"To you it's Doris," she said. "What now?"

"A few more questions about Sal."

"I already told you what I know." Moving on to the next booth, she spotted a crumb, flicked it away before dry-wiping the Formica, pressed the spring-latch of the dispenser, crammed in paper.

Letting go with an audible snap, she did the same at the neighboring booth.

"Soon as you're done, Doris."

"I'll be done in five hours."

"Doesn't look too crowded."

"Rub it in."

"How about we help you load the napkins, you spare us a few minutes."

"Soon you'll be wanting to split tips."

The truckers turned. Milo stared them down and they returned to their food.

Doris said, "How'd you find out I was here? Adolph told you, right?"

"Who's Adolph?"

"The mummy pours drinks at Arnie's."

"Just a few questions," said Milo.

"Damn Adolph—look, it's not like me and Sal are buddies."

"You mentioned get-rich-quick schemes. What kind?"

"That card you handed out said homicide, not con stuff. What, Sal killed his girlfriend over money?"

"What girlfriend is that?"

"Some blonde. Was it her?"

Milo produced Freeman's picture.

"That's the one," said Doris. "He really did her? Jesus, I never woulda thought."

"He's not a suspect at this time."

She snorted. "You're here for your health."

"A woman dies, we look at her boyfriend, Doris. If you've got information about their relationship, that would be helpful."

"He brought her to Arnie's, that's all."

"Often?"

"Sometimes. She never talked to no one, wasn't exactly fun in the drinking department."

"Timid drinker."

"One vodka she sometimes didn't even finish." She scowled. "Expensive stuff—Grey Goose. Making like she was superior."

"A snob," said Milo.

Doris put her napkins down. "The way she talked, overly pronouncing her words, you know? Like *I* went to college and *you* didn't. Like anyone gives a rat at a place like Arnie's."

"Why'd she hang with Sal?"

"How should I know? The other guy I saw her with was a lot cuter. Too young for her, but maybe she was one of those Goldilocks girls, know what I mean? One day it's too hot, the next too cold. No nose for just-right."

"Tell us about the other guy, Doris."

"He's the one killed her, not Sal?"

"We don't know who killed her, Doris. That's why we're here."

Doris's smile spread like a rash. Her teeth were randomly placed. "You didn't even know about the other guy, did you? Well, don't get me involved, I just saw him once."

"Where?"

"Walking down Van Nuys with her. They stop short of Arnie's, there's an alcove, this old office building. They duck in there, there's an overhang, soon they're in there doing kissy-face. She plants a big one on him, takes his face like this." Cupping her chin. "In goes the tongue. Blech. We're talking young enough to be her kid."

"May-December romance."

"You could say that. Or you could say they had the hots for each other, I ain't Dr. Ruth."

"You saw all this because—"

"I was walking behind them from my bus stop like I always do."

"What time of day?"

"Two, two thirty, I like to get to Arnie's, lubricate the throat before I arrive at this gourmet palace. Only reason I noticed her was I'd seen her with Sal. Also her getup. Tight red dress, talk about advertising the goods. I said to myself, *Hey, that's Goose gal but that cutie sure ain't Sal.*"

"What happened after they kissed?"

"She pats him on his cute little butt, he leaves, she goes to Arnie's. Soon after, Sal shows up, Blondie's smiling at him like it's true love. One drink and she's bugging him to leave, he doesn't even finish his beer, what a limp onion. So maybe he found out she was cheatin' and got mad, huh? That's what you're thinking, right?"

Calling out to the young waitress behind the counter. "Guess what, Rosie, I'm a big-time detective now."

Rosie said, "How much they payin' you, Dorrie?"

Milo said, "How young was this other guy?"

"A lot younger than her—what was she forty, forty-five?"

"Thirty-eight."

"I'da pegged her as older."

"What about him?"

"Twenties—twenty-two, twenty-three."

"Not younger?"

"That's not young enough?"

"Could he have been a high school student?"

"To me he looked twenties," she said, "but who knows? He dressed like one of those preppies. Nice buttondown shirt, khaki pants—but tennis shoes, kind of nerdy. Pen protector in the pocket—that I remember 'cause I thought it was real nerdy. But he didn't look like a nerd, too cute. More like a surfer—the peroxide hair." Grinning. "Real tight butt. I'd think he could do better than her but guys want one thing. Give it to 'em and they're burgers on the griddle."

"Hot?" said Milo.

"Hot and sizzly and bad for your heart."

"Let's talk about Sal's money schemes."

Doris said, "Who listened—okay, here's one I remember because it was so stupid. I'm enjoying my drink before work, Sal comes in, sits at the other end of the bar, pretends he's not gonna talk to me, has a beer and gives out this big sigh. All of a sudden, he's next to me. Pretends to make small talk, then: 'Would you believe this, Dorrie, I just got a huge commission check for some tubas'—he sells instruments, or so he claims, I never saw him do nothing but sit and drink. I say congratulations. He says, 'Problem is it won't clear for a week, I got a pile of bills, do me a little favor, I'll make it worth your while.' "

Milo said, "Lemme guess: You deposit the check in your account, he withdraws some of the money and pays you interest. If the check bounces, you're saddled with the charges."

"Guess *you're* a big-time detective, too."

"How much money we talking about, Doris?"

"Two thousand and some change, he said he'd give me a hundred for my trouble. Like I'd do it. Too good to be true always is."

"Why would he try to scam someone at a place he frequented?"

"Why don't you ask him?" she said. "Far as I know no one at Arnie's ever says yes to his b.s."

"He tries that kind of thing regularly?"

"He's always inching up to someone with that look, like he's carrying around the biggest secret in the world. Oh, yeah, I remember another one: He had truckloads of surplus trumpets and trombones coming in, just needed some money to ship them to Indiana or wherever it is they melt trombones down for brass. I pitch in, he'll split the profits with me. Another time he tried to sell everyone New Jersey lottery tickets at a discount. He's annoying but he gives up quick, not pushy and no one gets mad because he's pathetic. I got him pegged as a spineless worm, no guts no glory. That's why it surprises me you think he killed her."

"We don't, Doris—"

"Whatever. He's at his finest after a few," she said. "Six, seven beers and he's creative. You really think he killed her?"

We left Fat Boy, got back into the car.

"Clumsy con man," he said. "Yeah, I can see him getting tumescent over a big-money squeeze job on a place like Prep."

"And correspondingly mad when Elise pulled out of the scheme. Plus, the jealousy angle just got stronger."

"Our tutor and a young guy. She sure covered a lot of ground. Meaning there could be who-knows-how-many partners out there." Chuckling. "She might as well have tutored biology. You got where I was going with that age question."

"A preppie type," I said. "If Doris's age estimate is off Elise could've been sleeping with a student."

"Pens in the pocket—maybe a math brain but he needed help in English. Be nice to get hold of some Prep yearbooks, have Doris go through the boys."

"If Prep even has yearbooks."

"Why wouldn't they?"

"Mere paper and ink? I'm thinking sacred tablets."

15

Back at his closet-sized office, Milo belly-dived into the cyber-world. If Windsor Prep issued yearbooks they weren't cataloged online and none of the pay services promising to hunt down alumni had anything on the school.

No snarky critiques on the Internet, either, just paeans to the school's physical plant and academic standards.

I said, "Didn't know police protection could reach that far."

His smile devolved to an abdominal growl. "Time to subpoena Elise's phone records. Something traces back to a student, I'm bee-lining for the damn school." Rubbing his face. "That'll be so much fun I'll follow it up with do-it-yourself open-heart surgery using a rusty can opener."

I drove home, cleared paper, drank two black coffees, and began my own computer search, starting with MySpace and Facebook and using *windsor prep* as keywords.

No shortage of smiling, attractive kids attending the school, along with the usual friends lists, music choices, poetic excerpts ranging from lewd to sad, some home-drawn comic strips, the occasional photo of a cat or dog.

A handful of postings about Elise Freeman, but nothing more specific than *did u hear? ms. f. died. bizarre.*

No memorials or calls for tribute. Not a hint of rumor about sexual indiscretions.

Returning to the commercial alumni sites, I plugged Elise Freeman's name into the U. of Maryland database. No such person. Pairing her name with *maryland* pulled up a five-year-old search for graduates of Blessed Heart College on Garrison Boulevard in Baltimore, the school wanting to get in touch for a centennial celebration.

What else had she lied about?

I clicked the reunion link. Elise Freeman appeared in the *Where Are You?* column. So did Sandra Freeman Stuehr, graduation date two years later.

Four forty p.m. made it past working hours in Baltimore so I tried the city's white pages. Over five hundred Freemans.

But only one Stuehr, a business address: *Stuehr's Crab Cooker, E. Pratt Street.*

The woman who answered put me on hold. A minute or so later, she returned, talking over restaurant clatter. "When do you want your reservation?"

"I'd like to speak to Sandra."

"Who?"

"Sandra Stuehr."

Two beats. "Hold on."

The silence lasted nearly three minutes before a man got on. No more clatter, maybe a private office. "This is Frank, what now?" Clipped diction, vocal cords that sounded as if they'd been dragged a few miles on a gravel road.

"I'm looking for Sandra. You're Mr. Stuehr?"

"Yeah, right."

"Pardon?"

"Another lawyer heard from. Christ, stop bugging me."

I told him who I was, played up the LAPD connection more than reality justified.

"Yeah, right, more cock and bull. Look, pal, I can't stop you from calling but trust me, next time you won't get through, just like those other guys."

"This is a homicide investigation, Mr. Stuehr. The victim's Elise Freeman. If she's not related to Sandra—"

"Elise? Someone killed her? You're kidding."

"I'm not, Mr. Stuehr."

Silence. "I haven't seen Elise in a long time. Not since the wedding."

"Which was?"

"I married Sandy nine years ago. Wish I could forget the date. Sandy and Elise aren't close, Elise showed up, drank herself silly, left early."

"Sandra is her sister."

"One and only."

"Could I talk to Sandra?"

"Be my guest, pal. She's where you are—California. Or maybe it's Arizona by now, she likes warm weather, could be Florida for all I know. Or care. We've been divorced three years, she's still filing paper on me, she's money-mad—what's the diff. For all I know, this conversation really is cock and bull and you're one of her lawyers."

"Call the LAPD West L.A. station and ask for Lieutenant Sturgis." I gave him Milo's cell.

"You just told me another name."

"I'm Delaware. Lieutenant Sturgis is the chief investigator on the case. Talk to him directly."

"About what?"

"We're trying to track down Elise's family. There's a body that needs to be dealt with."

"Oh . . . well, that's not my problem."

"How about the last known address and number for Sandra?"

He rattled off the information as if he chanted it daily. Gutierrez Street, Santa Barbara. Three years of animosity but he kept his ex close at hand.

I said, "Thanks. Anything you want to tell me about Elise?"

"From what I hear, she's just like her sister."

"How so?"

"Hot-pants, thinks she's an intellectual, lies like a convict. My family's been running one of the best crab joints in Baltimore for sixty years. Listen to Sandy, it's a greasy spoon, I'm imposing by wanting her to occasionally help out."

"Hot-pants," I said.

Frank Stuehr said, "I'm not talking fashion, that's an old-fashioned expression for slut. Okay, you want to know something about Elise—and Sandy? Both of them got bothered by their old man. Know what I mean?"

"Molested."

"That's another word for it."

"Sandy talked about that?"

"Only once, when she was in one of her weepy moods, wanted me to put my arm around her or something. After that, nothing, like it never happened in the first place. Only other time I raised the topic was when Sandy and me tried mediation. She was making a play to steal a big chunk of the Cooker and that really pissed me off so I put forth the case she was morally turpitude. Spelled it out. She gets up, walks around the table, smacks me wham across the face. That ended mediation, she screwed herself, the judge didn't look kindly on her. You find her, *don't* give regards."

"What kind of guy was the father?"

"He died before I met Sandy, but I hear he was a run-around. That's what people said in the neighborhood. Outward, he was respectable, never met a Mass he didn't like. Principal of a school, top of that. I'd love to hear his confession. A virtuous father don't turn out two sluts."

"Sandy was promiscuous?"

"Sandy was a *slut*. Never stopped banging other guys the whole time we were married. Out at night all the time, I was a dumb-ass, believed those stories about Scrabble club, bridge, gardening."

"Same for Elise?"

"Elise once came on to me. Sandy was in the kitchen, Elise makes a grab for my you-know-what. I look at her like are you out of your mind, she pretends it never happened. They're both good at that. Pretending."

"What was their mother like?"

"Also dead by the time I met Sandy. Sandy never talked about her, like she didn't exist."

"At what school was the father principal?"

"Some black public school, I don't know."

"What was his name?"

"Cyrus Freeman," he said. "Ph.D., Sandy kept reminding me of that, how she'd lowered herself marrying a guy with only one year at Towson. Meanwhile, she's screwing half the population of Baltimore and spending my money like she's a member of Congress."

S. Freeman Stuehr was listed in the Santa Barbara book. Her voice-mail message was warm and friendly, offered in a voice as silky as her ex's was ragged.

"Hi there, whoever you are, this is Sandy. I'm sure I'd love to talk

to you but either I'm out or just catching a little California sunshine. So please leave a message."

Tempting offer, but I resisted.

One hit for *cyrus freeman:* a tiny squib in the Baltimore *Sun.*

Plans to name the auditorium at Chancellor Middle School in West Baltimore after its former principal had been deferred due to "institutional and budgetary concerns, including the expense of new signage."

I got on the phone. Milo picked up.

"Found you some next of kin, Big Guy." I filled in the details.

"Nothing like bitter exes for filling in blanks. Thanks for taking the time, Alex. Two lying sluts, huh? There's a clinical diagnosis for you."

"Sandy lives ninety miles away but hasn't contacted you, so most likely she doesn't know Elise has been murdered. That suggests the sisters weren't close. That could make her a less useful informant. On the other, she may be willing to give up some interesting details."

"I love Santa Barbara. Give me her number."

After he copied it down, I said, "Frank Stuehr's judgment is clouded by animosity but he's right about the link between a sexually abusive father and promiscuity." I told him about the change in Chancellor School's plans.

"The expense of signage," he said. "That's a new one. You're thinking something came out about ol' Cyrus's past. A middle school, oh, man."

"Inner-city kids would be easy victims. Especially back then. Elise told Fidella her father was rough on her but she never said it was sexual. Clouding the truth is a common defense mechanism and that could've led to a lifelong pattern. Case in point: lying about where she attended college. I checked out Blessed Heart and it's a small, well-thought-of Catholic woman's college with high standards, by no means inferior to U. Maryland. So it's not like she was padding her résumé."

"Lying for the hell of it?"

"That's possible," I said. "But I thought of something else: Turns out Blessed Heart's campus is two blocks from Chancellor Middle, so maybe she grew up in that neighborhood. That district is also close to the Pimlico racetrack. What if she developed an early affinity for gambling—and gamblers."

"Fidella," he said. "Yeah, blowing a jackpot in one day says he's probably got gaming issues. Maybe she did, too, and that's why one or both of them hatched up an extortion scheme. Then she changes her mind. My dear vic led a complicated life, talk about multitasking."

"Maybe just the opposite. She compartmentalized—divided her life into little boxes—trying to keep things simple."

"Esteemed teacher by day, wild girl by night. And somehow she ends up in the freezer compartment."

CHAPTER

16

Milo was at my house by nine the following morning. We took the Seville to Santa Barbara because "two hours on the road, pal, I like leather and functional A.C."

I said, "How'd the sister react to the news?"

"Gasped once, then she got calm pretty fast. Sexy voice. Like Elise's on the disc minus the depression."

As I drove up the Glen, he unwrapped the skirt-steak/baked-chicken/bacon/fried-potatoes-on-rye sandwich he'd constructed from leftovers scrounged in my fridge. Hydration came from slurps of Diet Dr Pepper in a half-liter bottle he'd brought with him.

By the time I reached Mulholland, he was phoning and eating, trying to find out why his priority request for Elise Freeman's phone records had received no response. Drones at her carrier kept transferring him, then cut him off. A second attempt produced "technical issues" as an excuse.

When he inquired about the subpoena of her financials at the

D.A.'s office, he was informed of "transfer delays." He tried Deputy D.A. John Nguyen, who put him on hold.

One minute later, Milo clicked off, scowling. "John can't cut through the fog, either."

"Everything gets shunted to the chief's office."

"Hardening of the procedural arteries." Clutching his chest in mock horror, he buried his face in animal protein. Gulping fast, without taking a breath. More distraction than gustatory pleasure.

I picked up the 405 North at Sepulveda, merged to the 134 West, coasted through the western reaches of the Valley as it turned into the 101. Speeding past brown-felt hills and plugs of the heroic trees that gave Thousand Oaks its cachet, I cut through the widening gullies and ambitious peaks of Camarillo. A few exits north and plein-air ceded to concrete: one beige mall after another.

A razor-straight shot through the agricultural bounty of Oxnard and Ventura took us past Carpinteria, where the Pacific became a western neighbor. Flat, blue, breaking frothily, the water soft-sold peace of mind. Sea lions bobbed, surfers took advantage of swells, tankers big enough to merit a zip code floated on the horizon. A few miles before Santa Barbara, the rich green buffer formed by the old-growth vegetation of Montecito cooled and sweetened the air. Global warming on your mind? Plant a tree.

Santa Barbara announced itself with a glorious lagoon that rimmed Cabrillo Boulevard's eastern edge. To the west, the ocean persisted. Tourists worked both sides of the sun-kissed thoroughfare on bikes and pedicabs. Sandra Freeman Stuehr lived a few miles past Stearn's Wharf, west of State, in a mint-green bungalow on a quiet, shady street. Three individual units on an eighth-acre lot. Hers faced the street.

Not that different in style from her sister's home, but none of the isolation.

She came to the door holding a coffee mug and flexing a bare foot. She wore a crisp, black linen mandarin-collar blouse, butter-yellow walking shorts, hoop earrings, half a dozen gold bangles. Her toenails were polished scarlet, her fingers glazed flesh pink. Honey-blond hair was clipped in a pageboy.

Thirty pounds heavier than Elise and two years younger, she had bone-china skin, clear blue eyes, and a way with makeup that widened the age gap; she could've passed for late twenties.

Milo made the introductions. Sandra Stuehr's handshake was topped by a quick little after-squeeze, the merest pressure of warm fingertip on knuckle. She beckoned us in, curling hair around an index finger, cocking a hip, and secreting Chanel No. 5. A perfect hourglass shape was enhanced by an even cushion of firm flesh. Back in Reubens's day, painters would've lined up for the privilege.

Milo said, "So sorry for your loss."

"Thank you. I'm ready to help you with whatever I can." Brief pout but no evidence of tear-tracks and her sapphire eyes sparkled. "Coffee? I'm having a refill."

"If it's no trouble."

"It's no trouble at all." Pivoting like a dancer, she crossed to a bright, open kitchen with a view of coral bougainvillea.

The aroma of French perfume permeated the little house's interior. We were miles from the beach but Sandra Stuehr's décor did its best to evoke sand and surf: overstuffed seating slip-covered in white canvas, pine tables waxed to a soft gleam, seashells and driftwood and bits of tumbled rock placed cleverly, so as not to crowd the limited space.

"Here you go."

The mug she handed me was pearl gray, embossed with a gold crucifix and a gilt legend.

Blessed Heart College. The First Hundred Years.

She settled on a love seat, folded her legs to one side. "How was the traffic from L.A.?"

"Easy," said Milo. "Great coffee, thanks."

"French press and I grind the beans myself." Soft, sad smile. "If you can't do something right, why do it at all?"

"We're trying to investigate your sister's murder the right way, Ms. Stuehr."

"Of course you are." Too-quick, too-wide smile; the tension of a first date.

I rotated the mug so Milo would notice. He pointed and said, "Blessed Heart is how we found you."

"Really."

"They put a call for alumni on the Internet."

"That silly reunion," said Sandra Stuehr.

"You didn't attend, huh?"

"Only sad people live in the past, Lieutenant. Blessed gave out my number?"

"No, that we got from your ex-husband."

"Good old Frank. I'm sure he had all sorts of wonderful things to say about me."

"We didn't get into personal details, Ms. Stuehr. Did Elise happen to attend the reunion?"

"I tend to doubt it."

"You don't know for sure?"

"If that's a subtle way to ask if Elise and I were close, the answer is far from it. Still, I'm devastated by what happened. Did she suffer?"

"No," said Milo. "How often did the two of you see each other?"

"Seldom verging on never," said Sandra Stuehr. "Even after I moved to California—two and a half years ago. Not for lack of trying on my part, one of the first things I did was drive down to L.A. to have lunch with Elise. It was pleasant but not intimate and afterward we both lied about staying in touch. Elise didn't even invite me to her home. I've never seen it."

I said, "So you've never been close."

"Elise always resented me and I got tired of trying to earn her approval. Despite that, I'm crushed by her death. Do you have any idea who could do such a terrible thing?"

Milo shook his head. "That's why we're here."

"Well, I wish I could tell you something profound, Lieutenant, but the harsh truth is, my sister and I have been virtual strangers since birth."

"Why'd she resent you?" I said.

Instead of answering, she said, "I always felt it, a wall—there might as well have been a physical barrier. When we were teenagers it blossomed to outright hostility and we ended up barely tolerating each other. Being the baby, I grew up thinking it was my fault, something I'd done to alienate her. Eventually, I came to realize it was because of what I *was*." Pause. "The favored child." Eyelash flutter, a flicker of frown. "Which, in our family, meant the *ignored* child."

I said, "Parental attention wasn't much of a prize."

She waved a hand. "Like I said, guys, reminiscence is for losers."

"Your parents—"

"We had one functional parent, Father. Mother was a non-entity, a shadow, just a total dishrag. She came from a poor family, never finished high school. That allowed Father to convince her he'd bestowed a great gift by deigning to wed her. I always suspected they married because he got her pregnant with Elise."

"His family was prominent?"

"Not in the sense of being rich, but they were highly educated. His father was a physics professor at Hopkins, his mother taught violin. I'm sure Mother was initially impressed." Dagger-point laugh. "She died when I was three and Elise was five and I'm not even sure the memories I have of her are accurate. All of them re-volve around drudgery—down on her knees scrubbing something, as if she was the maid. I suppose she was, we never had help."

I said, "After she died is when the problems began."

Her mouth hardened. "What are you getting at?"

"Paternal attention not being welcome."

Her mug faltered. She held it with both hands until it steadied, ran a finger under her bangs. "I've worked hard at resolving, so I can talk about it. But I don't see how it relates to what happened to Elise."

"Anything that helps us understand Elise is useful."

More hair-curling. She picked up a cowry shell, massaged it, laid it down. "He was a monster. He damaged Elise and that pre-vented the two of us from becoming real sisters. The pathetic thing is Elise and I had so much in common. We liked the same music, enjoyed the same subjects in school, both of us became teachers. Though I never need to work. We could've had a fantastic relation-ship if that bastard hadn't fucked things up."

Her mug went down hard on an end table. Coffee sloshed, wood thrummed. She stared at the stain. "He abused her but not me. I'm sure she blamed me. I refuse to feel guilty. Maybe if she'd talked about it, we could've worked it out, I don't know."

Milo said, "Physical abuse or—"

"Oh, it was sexual, all right," said Sandra Stuehr. "It was noth-ing *but* sexual, those good old, dependable late-night visits to Elise's bedroom. You could set your watch by it. Eleven twenty p.m. and his slippers were making those vile, scraping sounds on the carpet. Like a slithering snake, I still hear it from time to time."

"You shared a room?"

Rapid head shake. "Elise and I had adjacent bedrooms but I

could hear his footsteps, hear the bed bump—feel it, my head-board was right next to the wall. Then everything would grow quiet and I'd hear Elise whimpering. I could hear her. I was too scared to do anything but stay in my bed, what if he paid me a visit and started bumping my bed? But he never did. I was relieved. When I wasn't wondering if it was because Elise was the slim, pretty one and I was the chubby little Pillsbury dough-girl."

Her lips folded inward. She got up, took her mug to the kitchen, opened the refrigerator, popped a can of Fresca and sat back down.

"Sure be nice to put some vodka in this, but I don't drink any-more. Not that I had a problem, nothing like that, I was always moderate. But since I moved here, I decided to get healthy. Yoga, meditation, walking on the beach, I quit smoking. Put on fifteen pounds, but I can breathe again."

I said, "Your father was a middle school principal. Did you see any sign he abused his students?"

"I'm sure he did. All those little girls running around, easy for the taking? He ran Chancellor for nearly forty years, why miss out on a great opportunity? But what goes around comes around, as I'm sure you've found out."

"Something happened to him?"

"You don't know," she said. "Nine years ago, someone put a bullet in his head."

Milo said, "Who?"

"Unsolved," she said, grinning. "The cops said it was a street robbery, but I've always wondered if it was some father or brother getting even. Or even a girl who'd grown up and gotten in touch with her rage."

"Someone like your sister."

"Did Elise do it? Maybe. I have no knowledge of her being in Baltimore when it happened, but who knows?"

"Was he still working when it happened?"

"First year of retirement. They found his body on the sidewalk, two blocks from his house. His pants pockets were turned inside out, his wallet was gone, and he was lying facedown with a hole in the back of his head. There was certainly no shortage of muggings in the neighborhood, that part of West Baltimore had changed since he was a boy, he was the last white man standing. Not that it stopped him from taking his nightly walks. Denial, I guess. Or plain old arrogance."

"How did Elise react to his murder?"

"Neither of us talked about it and we had his body cremated. I'd like to think part of her was happy. If she allowed herself to get in touch with her feelings."

"Part of her?"

"There was probably sadness. Even I occasionally feel that, crazy as it is. He did make me breakfast every morning for fifteen years. Combed my hair until I was eleven. Everyone said he was a wonderful, nurturing man."

Milo said, "You and Elise never talked at all about his murder."

"Not a word. In his will, he asked to be buried next to Mother. I had one of Frank's busboys toss the ashes into the Chesapeake Bay. Out in back of the Cooker, where the garbage cans are. Can I warm up that coffee for you?"

As we drank, she excused herself, returned with a yellowed newspaper clipping in a plastic sleeve.

Former Principal Murdered.

Milo said, "Could we make a copy?"

"You think it's relevant to Elise's murder? I don't see how it could be."

"I'm sure you're right, Ms. Stuehr, but two murders in one family is worth looking at."

"The Freeman curse?" she said. "You know, last night, when

you called and told me what happened to Elise, I actually started thinking about that. Wondering if our family is doomed and I'm next. This morning, I woke up, decided that was stupid superstition, it was time to have a lovely day—you know, don't even bother copying, keep it. I don't know why I held on to it in the first place."

I said, "What you've told us about your father might help explain why Elise made some high-risk choices."

"Such as?"

"She binge-drank."

Sandra Stuehr's eyes got huge. "You're kidding. Are you sure?"

"We are."

"Wow," she said. "I've always thought of her as the moderate one. From the time she turned twenty-one all I got were pompous lectures about the need to control my drinking. We were both attending Blessed, she was a senior, I was a sophomore. Got into partying pretty hard."

"Did you see each other much in college?"

"Not even then. It's a small school but we managed to avoid each other. What did she drink when she binged?"

"Vodka."

"Interesting," said Sandra Stuehr. "Something else we had in common."

She drank her Fresca. "Not a coincidence, I suppose. Part of her sermon was, 'If you're going to be pigheaded and make a fool out of yourself, Sandy, at least drink vodka, it'll keep your breath fresh, no one will know you're a reprobate.' "

I said, "You avoided each other but she found time to lecture."

"Exactly. My best years were the two after she graduated, I could finally be myself. Did she do anything else high-risk?"

Milo said, "The coroner found opiates in her system."

"Like heroin?"

"Or something similar."

Sandra Stuehr placed the flat of a hand against her cheek, as if propping her head. "Unbelievable."

"People change," said Milo.

"There's change and there's charade," she said. "All this time I've seen her as the smart one. Are there any other crushing insights you want to give me about my sister?"

Milo said, "You lived near Pimlico. Any sign Elise played the ponies?"

"She *gambled*?" said Sandra Stuehr. "This is like meeting her for the first time. No, I never saw her wager on anything and I sure spent some time at Pimlico. She was the smart one, guys. Summa cum laude at Blessed, Hopkins offered her a scholarship to go to grad school in English. I, on the other hand, barely passed the teacher's licensing exam. Though that was 'cause I was distracted by my relationship with Frank. She went to the track?"

"No, but she did go to Reno and play blackjack."

"Must be genetic. *He* played the ponies. Nothing serious that I knew about, he'd take twenty, thirty dollars to the track, rationalize his losses as 'recreation.' Otherwise, he was a total cheapskate. How often did Elise go to Reno?"

Milo said, "We know about once. She went with her boyfriend, guy named Sal Fidella."

"Sounds like a Mafia type."

"He's an unemployed salesman. He and Elise won a five-thousand-dollar jackpot in Reno, lost it the same day."

"Like Father, like daughter," said Sandra Stuehr. Her mouth turned down. "Hope that doesn't end up applying to me. I can't see how it would."

I said, "What else can you tell us about Elise?"

"She enjoyed lying."

"Lying about what?"

"Anything, really. My theory is it began with him. When she was around twelve she began faking illness, probably to keep him out of her bed. She did it all kinds of ways—putting a finger down her throat and vomiting all over herself, soaking a thermometer in hot water, rubbing her skin with one of those sandpaper dish-sponges to bring up a rash, complaining of horrible cramps. She also lied about things that seemed pointless. Not eating the lunch he fixed but telling him it was delicious. Or just the opposite, finishing every bite but coming home and telling him she'd lost her lunch, was starved. I guess she was trying to feel in control. She'd pull sneaky pranks on him. Hiding his slippers, putting his reading glasses where he'd have trouble finding them. Once, I looked out my bedroom window in the middle of the night and saw her letting air out of one of his tires."

"How old was she?"

"A teenager . . . maybe fifteen."

"Did you let her know you'd seen her?"

"No way, I wanted her to like me."

"Did she lie to anyone but your father?"

"Sure," she said. "She cheated in school, stole old tests and sold them. I found out because a boy who'd bought one bragged about it to his friend. That night, I searched Elise's drawers, found a wadded-up bunch of money. I didn't count it but it looked like a lot. She never got caught, at graduation she won honors and commendations for character."

"Did your father ever figure out she was pranking him?"

"Not a chance. In his eyes, Elise could do no wrong. She was the clear favorite."

I said, "Too bad for her."

Sandra Stuehr turned to me. Her eyes were wet. "Good, bad, right, wrong. Sometimes it all gets scrambled. You're sure she didn't suffer?"

◆

Further questioning produced nothing and we were preparing to go when a soft knock sounded on the front door.

Sandra Stuehr said, "It's open, honey, come on in."

The man who entered was midtwenties, good-looking, Asian, with expensively spiked hair. He wore a white silk Nat Nast bowling shirt with blue vertical stripes, cobalt linen slacks, brown hand-stitched deck shoes, and a rose-gold Rolex.

She got up, took his hand, kissed his lips lightly. "Perfect timing, we're finishing up."

Milo introduced himself.

"Will Kham."

Sandra Stuehr said, "Will Kham, M.D. Chief resident in rheumatology at Cottage Hospital."

Kham toed the floor. "It's okay, Sandy—"

"Will's been on call for three days, finally has a day off. I'm sure you guys won't mind if we get going."

Milo said, "Thanks for your time, Ms. Stuehr. If you think of anything else, please let us know."

"Of course," she said. To Kham: "They don't think she suffered, baby."

Kham said, "That's good."

As we closed the door, she was saying, "I'm thinking San Ysidro Inn, baby, that new chef they've got is fantastic."

17

Milo scanned the clippings on Cyrus Freeman's murder before slipping them back into the sleeve. "Nothing more than Sandy just told us." Flipped the sleeve onto the backseat and checked his Timex. "Four hours of freeway for the Sister Who Knows Nothing."

"And yet she told us so much," I said.

"Elise might've killed Daddy? Maybe so, Alex, but I'm not curious enough to find out."

"I meant Elise developing her lying skills early, as a survival strategy. Faking illness to avoid getting raped was as good a ploy as any, but there's always collateral damage. That's consistent with chronic depression, drinking, using sex as a means of control, and hooking up with a hustler like Fidella. Same for concocting an extortion scheme involving her sexuality. But what really interests me is her selling tests back in middle school. That kind of thing would come in handy at a place like Prep."

Traffic slowed along the beach. We caught the long stoplight at State. More tourists, easels full of sidewalk art, a few homeless guys lounging on the grass, playing critic.

He said, "She peddles exams, then tries to beef up the take with a little extortion?"

"Picking the wrong sucker could be hazardous to your health."

"Wonderful. Even if I put the rape aside, I can't avoid the damn school."

He closed his eyes, rested his head against the seat. "Best way to find out if she was raking in a lot of extra dough are those god-damn financials."

Another set of calls made him smile. "On their way and her phone records are on my desk. What do you think about Elise two-timing Sal with a young guy, and Sandra leaving her husband for a young guy? Some sort of symbolic distancing themselves from their *old* man?"

"Could be," I said. "Or they just prefer younger men."

"For that I need a pal with a Ph.D.?"

We were back at his office by three thirty p.m.

To the left of his computer sat a loose stack of paper. He began pawing, crumpling and tossing departmental memos, sheet after sheet of the city and county junk mail taxpayers pay for but never read.

Toward the bottom, eighteen months of Elise Freeman's bank records at Wachovia and her phone history for sixty days.

The financials elicited an immediate "Whoa." Ninety thousand and some change in a passbook account, most of it accounted for by sixteen five-thousand-dollar deposits posted irregularly over the last three years.

"It ain't buried treasure but it's a lot for a teacher making thirty a year," he said. "Wonder what five grand buys you at Prep."

Turning to the phone records, he used two felt-tipped markers to highlight. Yellow, pink, pink, pink, yellow. The end result was a cheery zebra: thirty-two yellow stripes for Sal Fidella's 818 number, seventeen pinks for someone in 626. The rest was uninteresting.

"Pasadena," he said. Phoning the number, he listened, wide-eyed, hung up. "Caltech, some chemical engineering lab. Everyone's out at this time—probably blowing something up—but leave your name blah blah blah."

"Far be it from me to stereotype," I said, "but Elise's young guy wore a pocket protector."

"Mr. Not-quite-a-nerd." He found the Caltech website, zeroed on chemical engineering. The only bios were of faculty members but a few more clicks brought up an account of a research presentation two months before. A quintet of doctoral students summarizing their research projects. No pictures.

Ellen Choi, Vladimir Bobrosky, Tremaine Franck, Mitchell Yamaguchi, Arlen Arabian.

He said, "Long years of detective training tells me it's unlikely Ms. Choi has undergone a sex-change operation, same for Mr. Yamaguchi undergoing surgery to look Caucasian. So let's pare down and see what MySpace has to offer."

Within seconds he'd pulled up a trio of pages. "Guess even brainiacs crave their fifteen nanoseconds of fame."

Arlen Arabian was mid- to late thirties, with Brillo hair and a rabbinic beard already graying. Skin-headed Vladimir Bobrosky was built like the super-heavyweight power lifter his page claimed him to be.

Tremaine L. Franck was young, slim, pleasant-looking in a doe-eyed, anemic way. Long, lank brown hair swept diagonally over a broad, unblemished brow.

"So he peroxided to blend in with the dudes at County Line."

He Googled Franck, found the young man's name in a Windsor Prep newsletter dated the previous year, and pumped his fist.

> After completing Harvard, summa, in three years, Trey's been accepted at Caltech for Ph.D. studies in chem-eng and looking forward to getting back to sunny Southern California. But he admits he will miss the bonhomie of Cabot House, as well as selected undergraduate courses, particularly those of Professor Feldheim, who was a shining beacon of erudition, coherence, and tolerance despite Trey's attempts to convince him of the benefits of application as opposed to pure cogitation.

"Couldn't agree more," said Milo. "Pure cogitation gives me gas."

He switched to the LAPD data bank, plugged in his departmental password, got to work on Trey Franck's stats.

No criminal record, a few parkers, one speeding ticket two years ago. Twenty-two years old, five eleven, one fifty-two, blond, blue.

"First he darkens, then he lightens," said Milo. "Embrace change."

"Look at his address," I said.

South side of Brentwood, an apartment number.

"Not the high-priced spread," he said, "but close enough to Prep. Maybe Franck was one of their deserving scholarship students. Elise started four years ago when he was a senior. Maybe she liked 'em *real* young and tutoring turned to something else."

"He doesn't sound like the type who'd need tutoring."

"Not in math or science, Alex. But Elise coached English. I need to meet this genius and screw due process."

He used his personal cell to contact a source at the phone company, and copied down the landline matching Franck's address.

Ten rings, no answer, no machine.

Milo said, "What the hell, Brentwood's close. What's your gas situation?"

"Half a tank," I said. "No problem if we don't cogitate too much."

The building was a space-clogging twenty-unit heap two blocks south of Wilshire, faced with poorly tended balconies and satellite dishes perched on railings.

Security door. No answer to the bell-push for *Franck, J.*

We were about to leave when a woman with short gray hair and sturdy limbs stepped out with a black brindle French bulldog.

Dead ringer for Blanche's feisty predecessor, Spike, and a smile hijacked my mouth. The woman noticed, smiled back. Serenely, as if used to the attention. So was the dog. He planted his legs, faced forward, stacked like a champ.

Milo said, "Brings back memories, huh?"

The woman said, "Pardon?"

"My friend here had one of those, same color."

"They're the best, aren't they?"

"Quasi-human," I said. "How long have you had him?"

"Three years, he just finished filling out."

"I'm guessing twenty-six pounds?"

"On the nose. May I ask how long yours lived?"

"He was a rescue, so I don't know for sure. Best guess is twelve, thirteen years."

"Thirteen would be great. I hear some are making it longer."

"What's his name?"

"Herbie."

"Hey, Herbie." I bent, rubbed the broad, knobby head. Herbie panted, gathered his dignity, and continued to pose.

Milo said, "Do you happen to know a young man who lives in this building? Trey Franck?"

The woman's eyes grew wary. Milo showed her his I.D.

"Police? Trey's such a nice boy."

"He hasn't done anything wrong, ma'am. We're looking for information."

"Trey was a witness to something?"

"It's possible."

"Wow," she said. "Well, he doesn't live here anymore. Has been at Harvard for years, may still be, for all I know."

"Who lives here?"

"His parents. June's a nurse and Joseph's some kind of scientist. A little distant, but overall nice. They both work long hours."

Herbie blew out air. His flews vibrated. He tugged on the leash.

The woman said, "The boss needs his walk, bye."

Herbie led her toward Wilshire, jaunty walk suggesting life really was wonderful.

Milo said, "Rush-hour drive to Pasadena, there's a concept. Let's hedge with a stopoff at the office, then another in the Valley. No sense pursuing a nice boy unless he's the one Doris saw."

He inserted Trey Franck's face into a six-pack photo lineup composed of similar young white men, then I hazarded Beverly Glen toward Van Nuys.

Brutal congestion at Sunset continued as far as I could see. As I neared the road leading up to my house, Milo said, "Go home, I'll pick up my wheels, continue solo."

"Not necessary."

"Feeling benevolent?"

"Feeling curious." I called Robin, told her not to keep dinner waiting, I might be at Caltech for a while.

"You've already got a bunch of degrees," she said.

"I was thinking chemical engineering."

"And here I thought our chemistry was great."

"Wait up and I'll engineer something."

"Long as it's structural, babe, not civil."

I drove up to Fat Boy just after six. Half the counter stools were occupied, same for the booths. The same scalding-oil smell.

Doris was tending to a party of cheerful Hispanic kids, unloading a tray full of fried food. "Uh-uh, too busy, can't break my rhythm."

We stood to the side. She finished and walked past us and we tagged along.

"Enough, I told you everything I know."

"Two seconds to look at a picture and we're out of your way."

"It goes to three seconds, you're tipping me."

Milo showed her the six-pack. A blunt-nailed finger jabbed Trey Franck's face. "That's him, satisfied?"

"Extremely. I'm even willing to tip." He reached into his pocket.

"Don't insult me," said Doris. Then she laughed, punched his shoulder lightly. "I'm giving you attitude 'cause that's what I do, boys. What, the kid's a dangerous criminal?"

"Not so far."

"But maybe."

"Not even maybe, Doris."

"Tease," she said. "You ever solve this thing, come back and I'll trade you the gory details for lunch." Another punch. "But you still have to tip."

18

Milo worked the phone as I picked up the freeway.

Well past working hours at Caltech but he tried the chemical engineering department again. Same recording.

"They're definitely blowing something up."

DMV gave up an address for Tremaine L. Franck two blocks from campus. Forty-five minutes later we were pulling up to a six-unit dingbat, enhanced by two flowering magnolia trees but otherwise sad. A tilting bicycle rack stood near the entrance. A single chain coiled around the slats but no bikes in sight.

Inside, the place smelled like a dorm with two-wheelers crowding a dim hallway. Green walls were chipped and cracked, ravaged carpeting was worn down to the padding in spots, hip-hop blared through plywood doors. One section of the hallway had been glued with hundreds of pennies. Crude black-marker lettering above the array: *Penny Paved Is Penny Ioned.*

No music leaked from Trey Franck's unit. No answer to Milo's knock. He slipped his card between the jamb and the door, with a message to call asap.

"Let's grab a bite in Olde Towne, try him again. I know a fish-and-chips place, got the whole English pub thing going on. Ever throw darts?"

Five minutes later, as I neared Colorado Boulevard, his cell beeped a Bach fugue.

"Mr. Franck, thanks for calling back. Listen, I was wondering if we could talk about Elise Freeman . . . you haven't heard? Sorry to be the one to tell you but she's passed . . . no, not naturally . . . we're not certain yet . . . that would be good, Mr. Franck . . . Trey it is . . . no, it won't take long at all, Trey.

"Pull a U-ey, Dr. D. Haddock will have to wait. He was in the apartment next door, we just missed him. Sounds like a nice kid, appropriately freaked about Elise. On the other hand, he snuck around with her while she was supposedly going with Fidella and he changes his hair like I change shirts. So maybe he got involved in more than May-December hoohah."

"Multifaceted," I said. "That could help get you into Harvard."

"You bet. Look at His Flawlessness."

As we returned to Trey Franck's building, the fugue repeated. "Sturgis . . . Dr. Jernigan, what's up? No, I haven't . . . probably . . . yeah, it does, what can I say, you play the cards you're dealt . . . that's pretty quick, not that I'm complaining . . . okay . . . makes sense . . . no, I haven't, thanks for letting me know . . . yes, I will keep it close to the vest."

He hung up, bounced his lower teeth against his uppers. "The unnamed opiate has been identified as oxycodone, possibly administered as a liquid because there was no pill residue in Elise's stomach, but Jernigan won't swear to that. Not enough dope for an O.D. but the interaction with all the booze in Elise's system would significantly kick up the risk for heart stoppage."

"Someone gave her a chaser," I said. "Liquid form would make it easier to doctor the alcohol."

"Jernigan was double-checking to see if there were Oxy bottles at the scene or in the trash. When I told her no, she said that clinched it, she's calling it a homicide."

"What are you keeping close to the vest?"

"The fact that she called me. The labs came in yesterday with instructions from Above not to disseminate without official permission. Jernigan was surprised when I didn't do a follow-up call, so she went out on a limb."

"Nothing like a pal at the coroner."

"Too bad I need one."

Trey Franck slumped on the Murphy bed of his shabby single room. Near his left hand was a contact-lens case and a bottle of eyedrops. The orbs to which he'd just applied the drops were big and round, gray-blue flecked with gold, shiny with moisture.

Hanging on a grimy wall opposite the bed was the room's sole nod to decoration: a black poster curling at the corners, bearing a single line of white script limned in electric blue.

DIGITAL CLOUD BOSTON

Milo pointed. "That a band?"

"Art exhibit," said Trey. "Allison Birnbaum, a friend from college."

"Harvard?"

"Indeed, that's a college." Franck shook his head. "I can't believe this."

"How'd you know Elise?"

"I did some work for her. This is utterly horrifying."

"When's the last time you and she had contact?"

"We spoke on the phone around . . . two weeks ago."

Confirmed by the records.

"Social call?"

"She called me to catch up." Franck's speech had an odd delay to it, lips forming words milliseconds before any sound emerged.

"About?"

"Work." Franck knuckled an eye, touched a chin dotted with sparse blond stubble. He had on a baggy blue Yale T-shirt, gray sweatpants, rubber thongs. His hair was longer than his DMV shot, a good two inches below his shoulders and tinted coppery brown with white-blond tips. Smooth, hairless arms hung like vines from narrow sloping shoulders. Nails bitten to the quick. A bright green beanbag chair and a splintering dresser comprised the décor. Atop the dresser, a hot plate shared space with food spatter, used and unused cans of Pepsi, a bag of cheese curls, books, spiral notepads. One corner was filled with a jumble of dirty clothing. A laptop and a printer sat on the floor.

Milo had considered the beanbag, eyed an ambiguous stain, and opted to remain on his feet. "What kind of work did you do for Elise?"

"I took tutoring jobs when she was full up."

"Did she pay you or just recommend your services?"

"Elise handled the business aspect. For every hour I worked, I earned half."

"So she had plenty of business, gave you the overflow."

"Her business is seasonal," said Franck. "But, yes."

"Did Elise ever tutor you? Back in your high school days?"

Franck blinked. "No." Reproachfully, as if the question was absurd.

"Perfect SATs all on your own?"

Shrug. "It's just a test."

"What subjects do you specialize in, Trey?"

"Anything that's required."

"Math-science as well as English?"

"Yes."

"Elise only tutored English and history."

"She could do basic math but she preferred not to go beyond that."

"So for algebra, calculus, APs, and such, you're the man."

"Was," said Franck. "I don't do it anymore."

"Too busy?"

"I've got a research assistantship that pays for room, board, and tuition." Taking in the room. "It's not luxe but I'm fine."

"This building a dorm?"

"Not officially," said Franck. "It's owned by an alumnus and he gives a substantial break on the rent. What exactly happened to Elise?"

"All we can say at this point is that she's deceased, Trey. Tell us how you met her."

"That's relevant because . . ."

"It's relevant because I asked."

Franck stared up at him. "Sorry, I'm still trying to integrate."

"You were close to Elise."

"She helped me by sharing her business—"

"When did that start?"

"I was a senior at Prep, she knew I needed the money."

"And you were smart."

Shrug. "She thought so."

"No problems tutoring your peers?"

"I had something they needed. For the most part, they were smart kids."

"Why would smart kids need tutoring?"

Franck's smile said we couldn't hope to understand.

Milo said, "Smart but not super-smart?"

"At a place like Prep, boosting a 740 SAT to 780 is profound."

"How much do smart kids pay for something like that, Trey?"

"Their parents pay a hundred an hour with a one-thousand-dollar retainer up front. My cut was fifty percent."

"How many clients a week did Elise send you?"

"At the peak I was putting in fifteen hours a week. I still can't believe she's gone." Franck's eyes drifted to the ceiling. Gray stains marred the plaster, as if a greasy-haired giant had butted his head.

"Seven fifty a week," said Milo.

"Well earned, Lieutenant."

"You don't have time for it anymore."

"I need to concentrate on my research," said Franck, slapping hair from his brow.

"What are you researching?"

"Catalysis and response engineering."

"Oh, yeah," said Milo. "Saw a *TV Guide* special on that."

Franck didn't react.

Milo edged an inch closer. "You're into color, huh?"

"Pardon?"

"Your hair, you dye it."

Franck licked his lips. "You take your fun where you find it."

"What's the next step, a catalysis tattoo?"

Reluctant smile. "I don't think so, Lieutenant."

"Were you Elise's only employee?"

"I was."

"When you went off to Harvard, she didn't hire anyone else?"

"No. When I was back for summers, I resumed. It beat flipping burgers."

"Guy with your talents," said Milo, "I don't see you in fast food."

"Guess what, Lieutenant, that's exactly what I did for two high school summers. McDonald's, Burger King. Then I promoted myself to busboy at Shecky's Deli. You want corned beef sliced thin, I'm your man."

"No summer fellowships available for smart kids?"

"There's no shortage of *un*paid internships," said Franck. "And the best summer programs, like Oxbridge, you pay for. My father teaches math and my mother's a nurse. Ergo a funny hat and playing solo deep-fryer."

"So it was a match made in heaven," said Milo. "You and Elise."

"It worked out for both of us."

"How come you're wearing a Yale T-shirt?"

Franck blinked. "Why wouldn't I?"

"Why advertise the opposition?"

The young man's smile was wide and toothy. "It's an Ivy thing. Flaunting your own school is pretentious."

"So when some jerk cuts me off in traffic and he's got a YooHoo University decal on the rear window of his Mercedes he probably didn't go to YooHoo?"

"If he's a jerk, he probably did," said Franck. "Can I assume you have no idea who killed Elise?"

"I never said she was killed, Trey."

"You're homicide detectives."

"Sometimes we investigate suicides."

"You think *that's* what it was?"

"You see that as possible, Trey?"

"What do you mean?"

"Any signs of depression on Elise's part?"

"No."

"Just like that," said Milo, snapping his fingers. "No hemming and hawing."

"I never saw any depression. Not in the clinical sense."

"Meaning?"

"She had her moods," said Franck. "Like anyone. Mostly when I saw her, she was in fine spirits." He picked at a cuticle. "I probably shouldn't get into this, but I feel duty-bound. Not that I think it's necessarily relevant. But . . ."

Pick pick.

"There's a kid named Martin Mendoza. He's a senior at Prep and Elise tutored him. But he didn't come to her in the usual way, Prep assigned him to Elise."

"And?"

"And there were problems."

"What kinds of problems?"

"Anger management," said Franck. "He didn't want to be there—at Prep, or working with Elise—and he let her know. He came in as a junior, recruited to pitch for the baseball team, he'd been a star in public school. Early in the season, he got injured, couldn't play anymore, but Prep had already contracted with him for the full two years."

"Contracted?" said Milo. "Sounds like the major leagues."

"In a sense it is, Lieutenant. When a prize athlete from the inner city fits a niche at Prep, Prep draws up a written agreement. If it works out, everyone gets their money's worth. If it doesn't and the student has significant academic issues to begin with—which is fairly typical—the problem generally fixes itself. In a Darwinian sense."

"The student drops out because he can't handle the workload."

"It's a high-pressure environment to begin with," said Franck. "Unless you're academically oriented, you're likely to be miserable."

"Blow your knee, back to Urban Sprawl High."

"Well put, Lieutenant."

"Martin Mendoza didn't oblige?"

"From what Elise told me, transferring to Prep wasn't his choice, it was his parents'. His father works as a waiter at a country club, that's where he met an alum who hooked him up. But overcoming historical deficits is tough."

"What's a historical deficit, Trey?"

"Public school," said Franck. "Martin had some monumental catching up, Prep hired Elise to help him."

"Nice of them, even though he wasn't pitching anymore."

"Guess so."

"You don't think it was altruism."

"I think by seventeen a kid should have some control over his life and when you neglect that, you're playing with fire. Martin got pretty aggressive with Elise. It upset her."

"Physically aggressive?"

"Verbally, but it bothered her enough to tell me about it."

"Did she ask you to protect her from Mendoza?"

"Nothing like that, she just wanted to talk about it. Normally, I wouldn't be thinking about it. But now that she's . . . I have to tell you, I'm not comfortable talking out of school."

"So to speak," said Milo.

Silence.

"So Elise was scared of Mendoza."

"More like . . . I guess she was, Lieutenant. She tried to do her job but he kept missing appointments and messing up her schedule, never followed through on homework assignments, went out of his way to be uncooperative. Elise finally told him he was wasting her time and Prep's money and not doing himself a favor. He got in her face, started screaming. Elise said she backed away, was ready to call 911. But he just cursed and ran out and she never saw him again."

"When did this happen?"

"A month or so ago. When's the funeral?"

"At this point, that's unclear." Milo produced his pad, flipped it open, scanned. "Arnie Joseph's."

"Pardon?"

"It's a bar on Van Nuys Boulevard. Elise used to drink there occasionally but you know that."

"I don't drink." Franck's finger worked a cuticle. A seam of blood appeared and he stanched it with a thumb.

Another look at the greasy ceiling.

"You're saying you've never been to Arnie Joseph's."

Franck licked his lips. "I haven't."

"But you have been near Arnie Joseph's, that's how we found you, Trey. You walked Elise over there, then the two of you shared a bye-bye kiss. Hot and heavy was the way it was described to us."

Trey Franck blurted, "Oh, God." Plopping back on his bed, he lay on his back, closed his eyes, breathed fast.

"Anything else you want to tell us, Trey?"

Franck mumbled something.

"I didn't catch that, Trey."

"We did it."

"Did what?"

Franck propped up on his elbows, stared past us. "We made love. Not regularly, once in a while. Nothing emotional, for fun."

"Fun," said Milo.

"Stress relief." Franck swiveled and met our eyes. Held the gaze defiantly. "Dealing with idiots, hour after interminable hour. It helped us forget."

19

Trey Franck sat up and spread his shoulders.

Admitting his affair with Elise Freeman had enlarged him.

Milo said, "When did you and Elise begin your stress-reduction program?"

"Don't worry, I was over eighteen."

"I'm not worried, son, I'm looking for details."

"I still don't see why *anything* I've done is relevant."

Milo squatted and put his big face close to Franck's. Franck edged back.

"When we investigate a nasty death, Trey, we begin by looking at people close to the deceased, because statistically, most nasty deaths are perpetrated by someone the victim knows. When we ran Elise's phone records, you popped up as a frequent contact. One thing in your favor is that you didn't lie about not speaking to her in two weeks. The record backs that up. But that doesn't mean we're not interested in learning more about you."

"Statistics," said Franck, "are group measurements intended for samples, not individuals. They possess absolutely no validity when applied to individuals."

"Thanks for the math lesson, son, but right now you're what we call a person of interest and if you want to stop being a person of interest, you'll just answer the questions."

"I just don't see why my sex life is—"

"Here's a theoretical situation, Trey: What if you and Elise had a hot-and-heavy romance going and she broke it off? Jealousy and resentment are great motives."

"It may be theoretical but it's definitely not empirical," said Franck. "Elise and I got together occasionally for recreational sex and no one broke anything off. If you're looking at jealousy, pay attention to a loser who had a serious thing for her named Sal Fidella. Since you've got phone records, I'm sure you've seen his number."

"You know Mr. Fidella."

"No. I know *of* him. Elise said she'd dated him on and off, he was getting annoying."

"Annoying in what way?"

"Wanting to keep getting with her but she was over it. She thought he was a loser, always talking to her about get-rich-quick schemes."

"Such as?"

"She didn't elaborate and I didn't ask. It wasn't anything we dwelled upon."

"Did Elise ever say Fidella had actually gone through with any of his schemes?"

Franck smirked. "So you already suspect him."

"Don't second-guess us, son."

"She never got specific beyond saying he was all heat, no light."

"She ever say he was violent?"

"Unfortunately, she never mentioned that."

"Unfortunately?"

"You'd concentrate on him and I wouldn't have to talk about my sex life."

"You've seen a photo of Elise and Fidella in her living room?"

"Okay. So?"

"That didn't make you think?"

"About what?"

"She's over him but hangs on to his picture?"

Franck's knees pressed together. "I suppose that was incongruous. But so what? I wasn't romantically attached to Elise."

"Obviously," said Milo. "She kept no picture of you."

Silence.

"Unless she did and you removed it after she died."

"No way, I haven't been to her house in months! You keep coming back to total irrelevancies—"

Milo said, "Of course, there could be another reason—another theoretical. Elise had students coming in and out. Parents, too, sometimes. Flaunting a nonromantic, recreational relationship with a former student wouldn't do much for business."

"I was *never* her student."

"You were eighteen when you met her."

"That made me legal."

"We're not talking legal, Trey, we're talking appropriate."

Silence.

Milo said, "How soon after you started working for Elise did it get personal?"

"I don't recall."

"Guy like you with memory problems?"

"My memory's fine," said Franck. "I never made note of the

precise date because I never thought I'd have to explain myself to—"

"Was it soon after, or did it take a while to develop?"

Franck shook his head. "This is humiliating."

"So was Elise's death."

The young man lowered his head.

"How soon, Trey?"

"Not weeks. Months." Franck looked up. "You want the voyeuristic details? Fine. One night I went over to Elise's house to collect my money. She was wearing a tank top and shorts. White top, blue shorts. All the other times I'd seen her, she'd dressed in dresses to the knee or slacks, her hair tied back, no makeup. That night, her hair was loose, she wore makeup. She had on perfume. She told me I was doing a great job, invited me to sit down, have a drink—not alcohol, I don't drink alcohol, never have, she meant a soft drink, that's what she was having. We sat down together on the couch, talked." His eyes moved to one side, drifted back, cloudy with reminiscence. "It just happened."

"And kept happening," said Milo. "We're talking four years."

"On and off. Have you heard the expression *booty-call*?"

Milo smiled. "Yes, son. Who booty-called who?"

"She always called me. The last one was two weeks ago—the phone call you saw, but that time I didn't go over."

"Why not?"

"Other obligations." Franck scratched a corner of his mouth. "I'd grown ambivalent about the relationship. For one thing I came to learn that Elise has a drinking problem. Nothing chronic, but she binges. My mother has a problem in that area and I've seen how it's affected her. Secondly, I prefer to date women my own age. I'm not claiming to be some kind of big-time player, but right now there's someone I'm involved with. She knows nothing about Elise and I'd like to keep it that way. I'm deeply sorry Elise is dead, I couldn't feel worse, she did a lot for me. But I'm really nervous about my personal life going public. That would be hell."

"No reason for your girlfriend to know, unless she's your alibi."

Franck's eyes widened. "I need an alibi?"

"Let me give you some—I guess you'd call them parameters—for the period of Elise's death."

As Milo outlined the time frame, Franck's shoulders loosened almost immediately. His grin was Christmas-morning bright, a kid in a room full of presents.

"During that entire time, I wasn't even in L.A., I was in Palo Alto for a series of research meetings with Professor Milbank—Professor Seth Milbank. He's conducting research at Stanford that might conceivably relate to mine. Professor Moon—my advisor, Professor Norman Moon—thought it would be a good idea for the three of us to sit down face-to-face and discuss possibilities. Professor Moon has travel money on his grant so we flew up. Feel free to check my plane tickets and my hotel reservation. I'd show you restaurant receipts—we ate out every meal—but Professor Moon paid for everything with his business card."

Milo said, "Tickets and hotel sound like a good start, Trey."

The young man slid off the sofa bed, retrieved his laptop from the floor, held the computer like a glockenspiel, and typed while standing.

Seconds later he showed us an online travel site screen.

Four-day stay at the Palo Alto Sojourner Inn, incoming and outgoing flights on Southwest.

"Satisfied?" said Franck.

"Four days," said Milo. "That's a lot of meetings."

"We made a side trip to Berkeley to confer with Professor Rosen."

Milo phoned the hotel, spoke with the desk, hung up. "Looks like you're cleared, Trey. Unless you've figured out how to be in two places simultaneously."

"Not yet, but maybe one of these days," said Franck.

"You're working on that?"

"Wait long enough, Lieutenant, and everything happens."

We left the shabby building, nearly collided with a helmeted student speeding up the footpath on a skateboard.

"Hey, watch it!"

Milo said, "Put more time into your physics homework."

"Huh?"

"Plotting trajectories, pal. Yours sucked."

The kid stared, waited until Milo's back was turned before flipping us off. Back in the car, I said, "Fish-and-chips?"

"Something's off with Franck but I can't pinpoint it."

"There's a minuscule speech delay," I said. "Like a machine processing."

"That's it. Reminds me of a witness on the stand who's been coached. A four-year affair leaves plenty of room for rage. Too bad he's alibied tight."

"You're not buying the booty-call defense?"

"That's what it was to Elise. But young guy, experienced older woman? I'll bet Franck was a virgin when she seduced him and he grew a lot more emotionally involved than he's letting on."

The door to Franck's building opened. Franck stepped out and walked straight toward us.

"This should be interesting," said Milo, starting to roll down the window.

But Franck, staring down as he hurried, never saw us. Cutting across the lawn, he continued south.

We waited a few minutes before following him.

Two blocks south, he entered another apartment building. A whole different world from Franck's dump; this one was thirties Spanish architecture, immaculate upkeep, thoughtful landscaping.

The right side of the building was a wide veranda arranged with wrought-iron furniture. Real estate ads would call the place charming and, for once, they wouldn't be lying.

We didn't sit long before Franck was out again, arm in arm with a petite dark-haired girl in jeans and a Brown sweatshirt.

Milo said, "Obviously, she went to Columbia."

Franck and the girl faced, pecked lips. Strolling to the veranda, they pushed a love seat toward the shadows, settled, held hands, kissed some more. The girl's head rested on Franck's shoulder.

Milo said, "Now I feel like a voyeur. And now it is fish-and-chips."

The pub was gone, replaced by half a storefront peddling vintage jeans, another serving fast-food Thai.

"Time to be geographically eclectic," he said. "What can I get you?"

"I'm fine."

"Don't think your discretion will shame me into fasting."

I idled by the curb as he loped into the Thai place. Something he told the counter girl made her smile. He got back in the car with bags full of takeout.

"Double order of *pad* to go, just in case you change your mind. Extra spice, extra shrimp, extra everything she could think of."

I cruised west on the 210 as he wielded a plastic fork and gobbled.

When he stopped to breathe, I said, "The daisy chain continues."

He wiped his mouth. "Meaning?"

"Another helpful witness. Winterthorn punted you to Hauer, Hauer to Fidella, now Franck gives you a twofer: Fidella and Martin Mendoza."

He flicked the prong of the fork. "Let's hear it for upright citizens doing their duty. Maybe two votes for Sal should put him square on my radar. If he did find out Elise was cutting him off sexually and financially, we're talking big-time hurt feelings. Which puts me right back where I started: the so-called boyfriend."

He poked noodles, wrapped up the bulk of the Thai food and bagged it.

"Not good?" I said.

"Good enough."

He appeared to doze off, but a few miles later, without opening his eyes, he said, "As far as young Master Mendoza with the temper, he's Latino, meaning he might know Spanish. Meaning he'd find it easy enough to pay Mr. Anteater for buying ice. On the other hand, murder's a pretty strong reaction to being tutored against your will and according to Franck, Mendoza had stopped showing up at Elise's place."

I said, "For tutoring."

His lids rose. "She was doing him, too?"

"Another younger man."

"Oh, boy . . . but with a young offender, something sexual gone bad, I'd expect disorganization, overkill. This was just the opposite, Alex. Antiseptic, staged. It doesn't feel right."

"It doesn't, unless Martin's one of those long-simmering types."

He called in an AutoTrack on Martin Mendoza. Plenty of registered drivers with that name but none in the age range. Same for a criminal record.

"Kid doesn't even have a license. Must love watching rich kids zoom into the student parking lot. Okay, gotta find him."

I said, "His father works at one of the country clubs. That narrows it down a bit."

"Hell with that." He bared teeth. "It's back-to-school for Uncle Milo."

20

The Hotel Bel-Air sits on twelve of the most expensive acres on the planet, sharing precious dirt with eight-figure estates. No sidewalks in Old Bel Air discourages pedestrian riffraff. So do high walls and gates, closed-circuit cameras, guard dogs, and rent-a-cops.

Try building a hotel in Old Bel Air today and the *Not-in-my-backyard* roar will set off sonic booms. But when the foreign potentate who purchased the property several years ago proposed to convert the hotel to his private Xanadu, the avalanche of neighborly rage caused him to fly back home and become an absentee innkeeper.

Time can rot but it can also lay on patina, and people learn to love what they're used to. That, it occurred to me, might explain the pride north-of-Sunset Brentwood takes in hosting Windsor Preparatory Academy's sixteen-acre campus. A core belief in the value of education isn't the reason; the merest suggestion of constructing a public school in the district can bring down a city councilman.

Prep occupies a remote pocket of Brentwood, at the end of a northern cul-de-sac. No signage advertises its presence. A thousand feet of two-way, cobbled drive heralded by fifteen-foot gateposts winds its way toward a guardhouse equipped with a yardarm. Beyond the barrier, a generous roundabout leads to baroque iron gates offering a glimpse of the rarefied world beyond.

Sixteen acres is ample space, per the school's website, for a dozen buildings *fashioned in classic Monterey Colonial style,* an Olympic pool, an indoor gym complete with yoga room and full-court basketball, a regulation football field, ditto baseball diamond. The nine-hole golf course is a recent addition in response to *student interest.* Even with all that, *when season and air quality permit, expansive lawns and drought-tolerant plantings provide the opportunity for outdoor seminars, or simply for gaining an appreciation of environmental integrity during moments of contemplation.*

The Prep day begins at eight thirty a.m. By eight, Milo and I were watching the motor traffic that streamed in and out of the entry road. Long queue but well mannered, no one fussing. The slow pace gave us plenty of time to scan vehicles for the face that matched Martin Mendoza's MySpace page.

It also allowed drivers and passengers to study us, but Milo didn't seem to care.

Mendoza's social networking seemed halfhearted: some underplayed baseball triumph, no list of friends, not a word on the career-killing injury. The few photos provided depicted a tall, husky, dark-eyed, crew-cut boy with muscular shoulders, thick eyebrows, and full, downturned lips. Even while posing with a middle school MVP trophy Martin Mendoza came across grim.

Milo read the printout for the third time, pocketed it just as a flame-red Infiniti slid past the gateposts. A silver Lincoln Navigator took its place. Teenage girl in the passenger seat. She rolled down her window, smiled saucily.

Milo smiled back.

The woman at the wheel said, "Close it, Lisa." Fed the Navigator gas and lurched out of view.

I said, "Let me guess: After sleeping on it, you decided on a new phase in the investigation. To hell with the chief."

He worked his tongue inside his cheek. "Me an insurgent? Perish."

The next car was a white Jaguar. Hispanic kid in the passenger seat, but not Mendoza. Diplomatic plates. Uniformed driver.

Nearly all the older students drove themselves. The younger kids were chauffeured by attractive, sharp-jawed women and preoccupied men gabbing illegally on cell phones. Being driven appeared to turn them sullen.

One of the most morose riders looked closer to senior than freshman, a skinny, red-haired boy pressed to the passenger door of a bronze Lexus LX. Resting his chin on a bony fist and staring into nothingness.

Bubble-coiffed strawberry blonde at the wheel.

Noticing us shook the boy out of his torpor. He studied us. Kept staring until the Lexus rolled out of sight.

I said, "Carrot Top seemed to know you."

"Don't know him, but I do know his mommy."

"Mrs. Chief and the vaunted Charlie."

He sighed.

I said, "He looked a little down."

"Would you want Him for your dad?"

"Touché."

"Maybe he'll be happier when he's in New Haven warbling the Whiffenpoof Song."

"How do you know about stuff like that?"

"Been reading up on the Ivy League. A little cultural anthro-
pology never hurt."

"What'd you learn?"

"That I'd never have gotten in."

A navy Bentley Continental rolled up. Pretty black girl staring
straight ahead and chewing gum energetically, gigantic dad at the
wheel wearing a white tracksuit. Several seasons since he'd performed buzzer-beaters for the Lakers.

"Whole different world here," said Milo, rubbing his face.
"C'mon, Marty, show yourself."

By eighty forty-two, the last car had passed through, with no
sign of Martin Mendoza.

Milo said, "Onward," and we continued on foot. The cobble-
stone was smooth under my shoes, as if someone had hand-
polished every inch. Monumental Chinese elms flanked the drive,
creating a shady allée. As we got closer, smidges of youthful vocal-
ization filtered from behind the school's façade, but the rustle of
leaves in the breeze was louder.

Rounding a curve exposed the guardhouse. Two people walked
toward us.

Woman in a black pantsuit speeding several steps in front of a
large man in a khaki uniform.

Headmaster Mary Jane Rollins said, "Oh, it's you," in a flat
voice. "I've just fielded a storm of complaints."

The guard remained behind her, hands folded on his buckle.
Midsixties, beefy and ruddy, with piercing blue cop eyes that tran-
scended retirement. Flashlight and walkie-talkie on his belt, no
gun. A brass name tag read *Walkowicz*. Rollins's back to him gave
him the courage to wink at us.

Milo said, "Complaints about what, Doctor?"

"Two men lurking at the entrance," said Rollins. "Needless to
say, parents were alarmed."

"Never been called a lurker, Doctor."

"I fail to find humor in the situation, Lieutenant."

"Sorry about the inconvenience, Doctor. Luckily for everyone concerned, we're here to protect and serve."

Walkowicz grinned.

Mary Jane Rollins said, "Given the tense world we live in—now exacerbated by Ms. Freeman's death—upsetting our students is the last thing we needed this morning. They've barely achieved closure."

"About Ms. Freeman's death?"

"We've held two Town Halls as well as a voluntary grief counseling seminar for anyone interested. It's been an emotional experience."

I said, "How was the turnout for the seminar?"

"What difference does that make?"

"Just wondering about student interest."

"Why? So you can interrogate them? Turnout was fine, our people are doing well. All things considered. Or they were until two men were spotted—"

"Lurking implies underhanded," said Milo. "We stood right out in the open and to my eye none of the kids seemed bothered."

Mary Jane Rollins fingered eyeglasses hanging from a chain. "With all due respect to the acuity of your eye, Lieutenant, you created stress and bother. Now, if there's nothing more—"

"You're not curious why we're here, Dr. Rollins?"

"I've too many things on my plate for idle curiosity."

Walkowicz rolled his eyes. Rollins sensed something and pivoted toward him. By the time their gazes met, the guard had returned to stoic immobility. But when Rollins faced us again, his mouth flirted with mirth.

Milo said, "We need to talk to one of your students. The intention was to find him before he entered the school grounds. To *minimize* disruption."

"A student? Who?"

"Martin Mendoza."

Silence.

"He is a student here, Doctor?"

"Why do you want to talk to him?"

"We didn't see him enter. Did he arrive extra-early?"

Rollins's eyes moved past us. Engine noise huffed from the mouth of the drive. Seconds later, a gray Crown Victoria rolled into view, picked up speed, came to an abrupt, tire-squeaking stop. Captain Stanley Creighton got out. Brown suit in place of the cream getup he'd worn at the crime scene.

"Morning, Dr. Rollins, I'll take it from here."

"Thank you, Captain."

She turned to leave. Walkowicz remained in place. Staring at Creighton, a bushy gray eyebrow arced.

Rollins said, "Return to your post, Herb."

"Yes, ma'am." To Creighton: "Captain, ay? Congrats."

Creighton squinted. Nodded. "Herb."

Rollins said, "You know each other?"

Walkowicz said, "Sure, we go back. Right, Stan?"

Before Creighton could answer, Rollins got between them. "How wonderful for you, Officer Walkowicz. Now let's put aside auld lang syne and get back to our respective jobs."

"Yes, ma'am." Saluting conspicuously, Walkowicz followed Rollins as she race-walked up the drive, veered to his booth, and closed the door hard. Putting a little hip-roll into his stride, the cop-waddle that came from a Sam Browne laden with gear.

Milo said, "Old officers don't die, they just sit on their asses and pretend to be useful."

Stan Creighton said, "He was one of my training officers at Central. Then he transferred to Glendale PD and we lost—" His eyes hardened. "What the hell were you thinking, coming up here with no authorization?"

"Working on my improv skills, Stan."

"Cut the shit, man, this is a major problem. What possessed you?"

"A problem for who?"

"Don't play with me," said Creighton. "What was going through your head?"

"I need to talk to a student, I figure school's the logical place to find a student."

"What student?"

"Kid named Martin Mendoza." Milo offered a sketchy summary.

Creighton said, "Kid's got a temper so he's a suspect?"

"I'm open to suggestions, Stan."

"Whatever. The point is even with a student the school's *not* the logical place because the rules were made clear to you. Kids have homes, start there. Now get the hell out of here."

"And here I was thinking a stroll on campus would be educational for all concerned."

"You really have a death wish, don't you?"

Milo smiled. "I'm assuming you're talking metaphor, Stan."

Creighton's pupils were pinpoints. His right eye ticced. "Go. *Now.*"

The elms rustled. From the distance, a girl's laughter sweetened the air.

"You're defying a direct order?"

"Just looking for a shovel so I can dig that grave."

Creighton's nostrils flared.

Milo's jaw worked.

I thought of a trip Robin and I had taken to Wyoming. Herds of bison, face-offs between pairs of massive bulls until someone limped away.

Creighton said, "Don't make me ask you again."

Milo said, "Can I check first to see if I've got rope in my car?"

"Rope? For—"

"So you can tie one of my legs back so I can't walk without falling on my ass, then you can bind both of my arms to my side and oh yeah, maybe I've got some rags in the trunk so you can gag me if God forbid I should talk to a goddamn witness without seeking permission, then you can use some other rags for the blindfold so I walk into fucking walls. After that's done, Stanley, you can tell me how to do the job."

Creighton's neck veins bulged. His fists were the size of cabbage heads.

Rapid pulse in the veins. Audible breathing.

Suddenly he laughed, forced himself into a relaxed posture. "Oh, man, you are really fucking *up* the job."

"I can only fuck up the job if I've *got* a job."

"What's that supposed to mean?"

"What do you think it means, Stan?"

Creighton snickered. "Right, like you'd quit."

"Like I *do,* Stan," said Milo, tossing his badge to the ground. "Life's too short, send my regards to the Emperor. If the brain-dead battalion surrounding him grants you access."

Turning heel, he marched away. I followed, catching my breath.

Creighton said, "Yeah, right."

Neither of us spoke until he drove away. Keeping a light touch on the gas. Humming a weird minor-key tune—maybe some old Druid chant buried in his Celtic consciousness.

"Did I mean it? Hell, yes. Or no. Or maybe. Goddammit. Will I regret it? Probably. Okay, let's find Martin Mendoza."

"Off the job but on the job," I said.

"As an independent citizen."

"How're you going to approach him?"

"With my usual tact and sensitivity."

"I meant under what authority?"

"Hmm," he said. "How about power to the people?"

21

L.A. County hosts scores of golf courses but exclusive enclaves for the big-rich number less than a dozen.

Milo began with the Westside, used his suddenly defunct rank to get through to human resource directors. Success on the third try: Emilio Mendoza was a waiter at Mountain Crest Country Club.

I'd been there a few years ago, as the lunch guest of a psychiatric entrepreneur wooing me to direct a nonprofit home for wayward children. Amiable meal, but the devil had messed up the details and I'd declined, despite a great steak. Soon after, the home closed down in a corruption scandal.

The club occupied lovely, rolling bluffs where Pacific Palisades abuts Malibu. By the sixth hole, ocean views distract. Stout fees and extensive vetting limit the membership to people of a certain type. That day at lunch the only dark faces had been those of the staff; I wondered if Emilio Mendoza had been the one to place a platter-sized rib eye before me as if it were a sacrament.

The HR woman on the phone said, "He's at work, I'll have him call you."

Milo said, "It would be better if I talk to him now, ma'am."

"May I ask what this is concerning?"

"A family matter," said Milo.

"Emilio's family?"

"Yes, ma'am."

"The police—oh, dear. You're not saying something terrible has happened?"

"Terrible things happen all the time, but Mr. Mendoza's family is fine."

"Then why—"

"If you'd prefer, I can drop by, talk to him in person. Maybe shoot a few holes."

"Hold on, I'll try to find him."

A few minutes later, a soft, lightly accented male voice said, "This is Emilio."

Milo misrepresented himself again as still active, but made no mention of homicide. "Sorry for bothering you, Mr. Mendoza, but I need to talk to Martin."

"Martin?" *Marteen,* emphasis on the second syllable. "Why, sir?"

"It's concerning his tutor, Elise Freeman."

"Her," said Mendoza. "She's no longer his tutor."

"She's no longer anyone's tutor, sir. She's deceased."

"You're kidding—my God, that's terrible. The police? She was hurt by someone? Why do you need to talk to Martin?"

"We're talking to all her former students, Mr. Mendoza. Trying to learn everything we can about her."

Long silence. "That's the only reason?"

"What do you mean, sir?"

"You don't suspect Martin of something?"

"No, sir, we'd just like to talk to him. You can be there, or his mother can, I'm happy to come to your home, keep everything low-key."

"Martin didn't spend much time with her, sir. He took a few lessons, that's all."

"I know, sir, but we've got a list to go through. Routine, nothing to be worried about. Is Martin ill today?"

"Ill?"

"He wasn't at school."

"You went to the school?" Mendoza's voice cracked on the last word.

"We did."

"They told you he was ill?"

"No," said Milo. "Just that he wasn't there. Is he home?"

Silence.

"Sir?"

"No," said Emilio Mendoza. "He is not at home."

"Where is he, then?"

Silence.

"Mr. Mendoza."

"I don't know."

"Martin ran away?"

"His mother and I came home from work, he was gone. He left his cell phone. He didn't take anything that we can see. My wife is sick, she is throwing up."

"How long ago did he leave?"

"Three days ago," said Mendoza.

Shortly after the murder.

Milo said, "When you last saw him he was at home?"

"In bed, he said he was sick. We thought he looked okay, was just sick of school. We were tired of arguing, so we let him stay home."

"Sick of school in general, or Prep in particular?"

"He didn't like that place." Emilio Mendoza's voice faltered. "Three days. My wife is having a real hard time."

"Have you called the police?"

"I was going to. Today. I kept hoping he'd come home. When you called I thought maybe you found him. Somewhere."

Milo said, "Kids drop out for a few days all the time, I see it all the time."

"Martin has left before," said Mendoza. "Twice, he took the bus to his sister in Texas. This time, she says he's not there."

"You think she'd cover for Martin?"

"They're close, but no, after Gisella heard how upset her mother was, she wouldn't do that."

"Let's get together, Mr. Mendoza, I'm sure we can sort things out."

"What could you do?"

"Tell me about Martin, maybe I can help find him. If a missing persons report is the way to go, I'll see that yours gets full attention."

"You want to talk about Ms. Freeman," said Mendoza. "You don't suspect Martin of anything?"

Milo nodded and mouthed *Now I do.* "Not at all, sir."

"I don't know," said Mendoza.

"Brief chat, sir."

"I'm working all day and then maybe I do a double shift if they need me."

"Whenever you're free," said Milo.

"I don't know," Mendoza repeated. "Okay, enough of Anna throwing up, one way or the other we need to—in an hour, okay?"

"Perfect. Where, sir?"

"Not at the club, they won't let you in. Meet me on Pacific

Coast Highway, around half a mile north of the club. Malibu Mike's, you're hungry, they're okay."

"See you there, sir. Thanks."

"I don't know what I'll even say to you."

Malibu Mike's was a flimsy white-frame lean-to set on a patch of land-side asphalt. A grinning, overly fanged shark cutout teetered atop the fraying roof. Picnic tables canted on the uneven pavement, some shaded by wind-scarred umbrellas. Behind the property, a hill of iceplant-encrusted soil formed a bright green curtain.

The chalkboard menu listed burgers, hot dogs, fish tacos, and something called a Captain's Burrito. Milo said, "I'm under-ranked."

You're no rank at all.

I said, "Order half and call it a Lieutenant."

"Let's eat something, I need to fuel up for serious lying."

A young chubby brunette girl worked the counter, a young, floppy-haired Asian boy, the grill. The ocean across the highway couldn't compete with blaring hip-hop from a speaker placed perilously close to the burners. Some millionaire gangsta bragging about having no conscience.

"Help you guys?"

I ordered a chili dog.

Milo said, "Two half-pound cheeseburgers, anything extra you want to put on is fine with me."

The girl said, "All we got extra is onion and pickles—I guess we could throw on chili, too, but I'll have to charge you."

"Go for it. How's that Captain's Burrito?"

The girl grimaced. "Guys order it but I don't like it. It's messy, you end up with most of it on the paper, then it sticks to the paper 'cause a the cheese, then it hardens you can't peel it off without peeling off the paper. Then afterward, your hands smell of sauce, cheese, it's gross."

"Captains can be like that."

"Huh?"

"All show, no substance."

No comprehension in young, brown eyes.

Milo said, "But the burger's okay?"

"I like it."

Milo finished his first half-pounder, unwrapped the second but didn't touch it. The ocean was calm. He wasn't.

"Kid runs away, right. Maybe Franck did me a favor."

He studied the water, got up. "I will not be influenced by the opinions of others, gonna try the damn burrito. Get it to go, Rick's on call, I can eat with my hands, no one's gonna squawk. Should reheat okay, don't you think?"

He returned with a greasy cardboard box that he placed in the trunk of the unmarked. The car's built as tight as a drunk's resolve, so the ride home would be fragrant. Just as he returned to the table, a white Hyundai drove into the lot and a smallish man got out. Round face, thinning dark hair combed straight back, pale complexion, crisp features.

"Lieutenant?"

Milo waved.

Emilio Mendoza seemed disappointed. He'd arrived ten minutes early, maybe wanting to rehearse his own script. But we'd beat him by fifteen.

He wore a white drip-dry shirt, pleated black pants, tiny black bow tie. No sign of the red waist-length jacket I remembered from my lunch.

Milo said, "Thanks for coming, sir. We'll wait while you order."

"I'm not eating," said Emilio Mendoza. "Even if I wanted to spend the money, my stomach's jumping all over the place." Patting the offending area. "I can't stay long, there's a big dinner crowd, a couple rookies need educating."

Milo said, "Speaking of education, how did Martin come to Prep?"

"You mean how could a waiter from Uruguay afford to send his kid to a place like that? I can't, they gave him a scholarship."

"Baseball."

Mendoza's eyes narrowed. "You've already talked to the school?"

"I looked up Martin's MySpace. Only thing on there was baseball."

Mendoza looked at him, doubtful.

"That's why they call us detectives, Mr. Mendoza. So how'd Martin end up at Prep, rather than at another school?"

"You're talking to students? You don't think Martin did something?"

"Are you worried Martin did something?"

"Of course not." Emilio Mendoza's eyes watered. "Maybe I'll get a coffee."

After he sat down with a cardboard cup, Milo said, "Does Martin have a special friend? Someone he'd go to when he's upset?"

"Only his sister."

"Where in Texas is she?"

"San Antonio, she's a nurse at Bexar Hospital. Martin called her the day he left—after his mother and I went to work. Just to say hi, that bothered Gisella, it wasn't like Martin."

"Your son's not talkative?"

"He's a quiet boy."

"What was his mood with Gisella?"

"She said he sounded distracted. She couldn't say by what."

"Is Gisella Martin's only sibling?"

"Yes, it's only the two of them." As if he regretted that. "Gisella's seven years older but they're close."

Milo let him sip coffee, used the time to finish his second burger. "I'd still like to hear how you connected to Prep."

"Oh, that," said Mendoza. "A good man—a regular at the club, his kids and grandkids went to Prep, I was talking to him about Martin, how Martin was a smart boy, I wasn't happy with his education. We live in El Monte, Martin was happy with the public school but no way. Sure he liked it, everything was too easy for him, he didn't have to work. You go to college like that, you can't compete with kids who went to tough schools. The member, he's a rich man but a good man, treats everyone like a person—he said maybe there's a solution, Emilio. I say, what, sir? He just smiles. Next time he comes in, orders his tri-tip and his martini, gives me a brochure from Windsor Prep."

Mendoza's laugh was more nose than mouth. "That is what I gave Mr. Kenten. A big laugh. Then I apologized for being rude, a fool. He says don't worry, Emilio, I know I caught you by surprise. If it's money you're worried about, maybe we can find a solution for that, too."

Mendoza placed the coffee on the table. "I felt even more the fool. Then he says, didn't you once say your boy was an excellent pitcher?"

Mendoza shrugged. "I don't remember saying it, we don't get personal with the members, but the nice ones . . . he always comes in by himself, I figure it's good for him someone pays attention. I say, sure, Martin's a great pitcher. Strong, like his mother's side." Pinching his own thin biceps. "His mother's father was a blacksmith, muscles out to here, his uncle Tito, his mother's brother, played basketball for Miramar—that's a big team in Uruguay—before he got hurt."

Frowning. "Martin also got hurt, maybe that's from her side, too."

"What was Martin's injury?"

Mendoza touched his left shoulder. "Rotator cuff, it can heal if he rests. Maybe surgery, maybe no. Either way, no baseball for a long time."

Mendoza slapped the table. "Perfect opportunity, like from God. They need a star pitcher, Martin needs a good education. At South El Monte, there was talk some professional scouts came to see him. But no one said anything to me so I think it was just talk."

"When did Martin transfer to Prep?"

"Last year, second half of eleventh grade."

"Middle of the year."

"I was worried about them being snobs but let me tell you, they rolled out the carpet. Big deal, he wasn't impressed."

"Martin didn't like the attention?"

"Martin didn't like *anything.* The kids, the teachers, the buildings, even the trees. Too many trees, Papi, they put dust in my hair. I say are you crazy, man? It's beautiful, a Garden of Eden, you want South El Monte after seeing this? He says yeah, that's what I want. I say you're out of your mind, boy. He turns his back on me, says I like what I like and it's my life."

Head shake. "Stubborn, like his mother. Maybe it helps with baseball. Saturdays he went to the U-pitch. Throwing all day. One time he came home with the arm all black under the skin, he threw so much the muscles were bleeding under the skin. It looked like a disease, his mother screamed, I called his coach—this was middle school, he was twelve, thirteen, say talk to Martin, no more bleeding. He tells me Martin's gifted, maybe he overdoes a little but that's better than being lazy. Stupid man, I hang up, talk to Martin myself. Martin says Sandy Koufax used to pitch with black arms. I say who's Sandy Koufax? Martin laughs and walks away. Later, I look up Sandy Koufax, he's the greatest pitcher ever lived, fine, good for him, I still don't like my son with a black arm."

Another look at his watch. "I go to Martin's games, he says don't embarrass me by screaming and going crazy like the other fathers, just sit there. That's all I can tell you, I need to get back to work."

I said, "How did Martin adjust to the tougher curriculum at Prep?"

"Did he feel stupid?" said Mendoza. "Oh, yeah, and he let me know all the time I made him feel stupid by moving him."

"Did his grades suffer?"

"Sure, this was a real school. No more easy A's, now it's B's if he's lucky. I tell him a B from Prep is worth more than a public school A. He walks away."

Mendoza threw up his hands.

"That's when Elise Freeman stepped into the picture."

"She was their idea—the school's. What happened was Martin wrote a composition—a term paper, it was no good, sloppy, he can do better, I've seen him do better. Maybe he did it on purpose, you know?"

"To prove a point," I said.

"Exactly. Making himself look stupid so the school say bye-bye. I tell him instead of making a scheme, study hard, you're a smart boy, now with no baseball, you got extra time. He hands the paper in anyway. Got a D."

As if announcing a terminal diagnosis. "Never, ever before did he get a D, not him or his sister, never did I see a D anywhere in my house. I was ready to . . . I got angry, okay, I admit it. There was loud yelling. That's the first time Martin took the bus to his sister."

"How long did he stay away?"

"Just the weekend. Gisella convinced him to go home, she bought him an airline ticket. I paid her back every penny."

"What about the second time?" I said.

"A few weeks later." Blinking.

"What was that about?"

Sigh. "Her. Ms. Freeman. The school arranged a tutor for him, all paid. To Martin that was saying, You're stupid. Stubborn, like I said. Maybe for baseball it's okay but not for life."

Anger had winched his voice higher. No more fatherly protectiveness. He leaned closer. "Everyone helping him, he's spitting in everyone's face—not really spitting, you know what I mean."

Milo said, "Attitude."

"Oh, boy, he's got attitude." Mendoza swigged coffee, narrowly missed sloshing liquid onto his white shirt. He inspected the placket. Flicked off a speck of dust. "Lucky, I only got one more clean in my locker." Another glance at his watch. "I got to go, they need me."

I said, "How long did Martin stay in Texas the second time?"

"Same thing, three days, that time Gisella put him on the bus 'cause I told her no more airplane."

"There's no chance he returned to Gisella's?"

"Gisella never lies."

Milo said, "Could we have her phone number, please?"

"You don't believe me."

"Of course we do, sir. But just in case Martin shows up sometime in the future."

"You think he could?" said Mendoza.

"Kids do all sorts of things."

"That would be good. His mother could stop throwing up."

Milo copied as he recited.

I said, "You're sure Martin doesn't have any friends he could find refuge with?"

"That's part of the problem, he didn't like the kids there. Too rich, too snobby, too white—even the Latino kids and the black kids were white according to him. I say you're the one being a snob. Judge people by what they do not by who their parents are. He laughs, like you'd understand. I say you're a star athlete, good-looking guy, you're smart, what's not to like? He gets *really* mad with the attitude, starts screaming."

"About what?"

"About everything nice I said. I'm a star athlete? He shakes his bad shoulder. This is an athlete? He pinches his cheek, stretches the skin out. This is good-looking? Martin's dark, not like me, his mother's side, sometimes her brother—the basketball player—gets taken for a Brazilian. I say calm down. He keeps going. You think this is good-looking at a place like that? I'm a fucking outcast. Excuse the language, that's how he said it."

"He was pretty upset."

"He's waving his arms, gonna hurt that rotator cuff. He walks out but this time he comes back. With the D term paper. Rips it up, starts eating it." Still incredulous. "Chewing the paper, swallowing, I'm screaming now, what are you doing, fool, you'll get sick. He says since you stuck me in that place, I been eating shit, what's a little paper for dessert? Then he leaves the house, I don't see him until I get home from work the next day."

"Where'd he go?"

"He never says where he goes."

"He didn't want to be tutored but he showed up."

"He's a good boy," said Emilio Mendoza.

"How did he like it?"

"He says it's a waste of time and money, she doesn't care about him, all she wants is the money, all she does is sit there while he reads and writes, then she gives him extra homework that no way he's going to do." Mendoza's eyes shot to the sky.

I said, "Anything else about her bother him?"

"Not really." He gripped his cup with both hands, dented the cardboard.

"What is it, Mr. Mendoza?"

"Look," he said, "Martin can think things that are wrong. Like one time, he knew one of Gisella's friends was interested in him. But she wasn't. Gisella told him, they had a fight."

"Martin thought something about Ms. Freeman that you don't think was true."

"He said she touched him too much. Nothing sexy, his arm, his hand. I say what's the big deal, she's friendly. He says, what the hell, Papi, does touching have to do with English? I say you're making a big deal, she's there to help you."

I said, "Ms. Freeman tutored English and history. What about Martin's science and math grades?"

"In science—biology—he's better, got the B's. He hates writing, said Ms. Freeman figured that out and that's why she gave him extra writing. I say she's trying to fix what you need to be fixed."

"Then he walked out."

"You got it," said Mendoza. "He's a good boy, please don't think he did anything. The whole thing with her—Ms. Freeman—it's no big deal, he went three times, maybe four. Martin's a good boy, he has a lot of pressure, maybe I did the wrong thing by putting him in Prep, my wife says I did."

Split second of reflection. "But no, I don't think so, you need a challenge, without a challenge, you dress up in a bow tie and serve rich people who look at you like you're a piece of furniture. Now I have to go, please don't say a little more, Emilio. I have to go."

22

Mendoza's white Hyundai rolled down to PCH.

Milo said, "He started off protective but ended up giving up info. Way I see it, one of two things happened: Elise came on to Martin and it creeped him out. She got pissed at being rejected, he got pissed that she was pissed, it escalated and Martin bore a grudge. Or he succumbed to her charms but she made him feel inadequate. Or played around with him and rejected him later."

"There's a third possibility: He had nothing to do with killing her."

"He rabbited, Alex. That's his pattern, when the tension piles up, he leaves."

"Like you said, a teen with a short fuse still doesn't sync with the planning that went into the murder and nothing Martin's father told us depicts Martin as a good planner. Just the opposite, he's impulsive."

"True, but I've got to listen to my victim, even a lying victim like Elise. Martin scared her, enough for her to tell Trey Franck about it. Time to find this kid."

He found Gisella Mendoza's number in his pad.

"Ms. Mendoza? This is Lieutenant Sturgis from the Los Angeles Police Department. Your parents are worried about your brother, Martin, and I'm checking his whereabouts . . . yes, your father told me he wasn't but I was wondering if Martin's shown up since then . . . yes, of course you'd call your parents and that's still the first thing you should do. But if you don't mind, please let me know, too, because once I close the file on Martin I can pay attention to other missing kids . . . yes, unfortunately, we've got lots . . . I'm sure you are . . . yes, I know it's anxiety-provoking, though your dad does say Martin has left before and he always comes back quickly . . . yes, that was good of you, your parents really appreciated your convincing Martin to return. Let me ask you something, Gisella. The second time Martin showed up, your dad said he had issues with a teacher . . . right, a tutor. Did Martin mention anything about what bothered him about this tutor? . . . because maybe the same thing happened and it'll help us find him . . . that's it? Okay, thanks for your time—oh, yeah, could I have your address for the file?"

He clicked off. "Nice girl. I'm gonna ask San Antonio PD to do a drive-by at her place."

"What did Martin tell her about Elise?"

"He felt she didn't care about him. That could mean she blew him off sexually. Wonder if he's fluent in Spanish—shoulda asked his dad about that."

"Dr. Rollins might know," I said.

"Like she'd tell me."

I pulled out my phone, called Prep, asked for Rollins, got put on hold.

He said, "You're kidding."

"Nothing ventured."

Four minutes later, I had the answer, provided by a borderline-hostile headmaster eager to get me off the line. When I thanked her, she said, "Please note: Once again, I've been fully cooperative. Repay the kindness by respecting Prep's privacy?"

Milo said, "You gotta give me some charm lessons. So does he *habla Español?*"

"Well enough to pass out of the foreign-language requirement."

"Excellent, who better to pick some Spanish day laborer to do the heavy lifting. Hell, for all we know Mr. Anteater was directly involved with the killing."

"Mr. Anteater bought dry ice in Van Nuys. Martin's got no driver's license but he somehow managed to get from El Monte to the heart of the Valley, then over to Elise's place in Studio City?"

"Big deal, he borrowed wheels or stole 'em—or got someone to drive him. He calls himself an outcast but that doesn't mean he couldn't find another outcast. Can't you see a couple of bitter adolescents hatching a weird ice scheme?"

His cell rang. "Für Elise" again. I said, "Got the joke," but he was concentrating, didn't hear.

"Afternoon, sir . . . no, I suppose not, sir . . . in all fairness, sir, it wasn't a deliberate provoca . . . yes, sir. But still . . . yes, sir. I just felt . . . Stan Creighton came on a bit heavy . . . yes, sir . . . can I say one thing? Strictly speaking, if I'm off the job, I'm not actually obligated to . . . yes, sir . . . yes, sir . . . yes, sir, right now, sir."

Snapping the phone shut, he rubbed his face.

I said, "Out of retirement?"

"Apparently I never was in retirement. Apparently decisions about my career aren't mine to make. Apparently doing the job properly 'has nothing to do with your fucking ego or your histrionic, grandstanding bullshit, Sturgis.' I'm due at his office, A-sap. This time, you're explicitly *dis*invited."

"Aw shucks."

"His exact wording was 'Don't even think about shlepping along your Ph.D. nursemaid. This shit you wipe on your own. And be thankful your fucking badge doesn't end up in a bodily orifice.' "

"Maybe you can bring a peace offering," I said.

"Like?"

"Special-order a double-sized burrito. Tell him it's the Chief."

"Oh, man," he said. "There'll be enough gas without that."

I next heard from him at eight p.m.

Standing at my door holding a bouquet of flowers.

"For Robin," he said. "Because I'm invading her privacy."

He walked past me, stopped to pet Blanche, griping, as always, about a taller dog not killing his back. Blanche licked his hand and pressed her head against his shin. He muttered, "Yeah, you're cute . . . where's Robin?"

"Out for dinner with an old friend from San Luis."

He handed me the flowers. "Put 'em in water, they'll keep."

"How'd it go downtown?"

He strode to the kitchen, searched the fridge, pulled nothing out.

"I arrive expecting to be disemboweled with garden shears, he's all mellow, smoking a cigar, tie loosened, 'Come right in, Sturgis.' It's like nothing ever happened, he just wants a progress report. It was only after I finished that he reverted to type. 'I said progress, Sturgis, not a fucking exposition of the obvious. Why the hell haven't you followed up on the Italian boyfriend, seeing as he's a con and a loser? Work this one logically.' Which translates to forget about the school."

"He'd rather have you on supervised duty than freelancing. What does he think about Martin Mendoza?"

"Not impressed. Same for Trey Franck. 'It's always loved ones and lowlifes, Sturgis. The Italian guy is both.' "

He opened the fridge again, retrieved a loaf of bread, and snarfed a slice dry. Blanche looked up with customary fascination.

"So guess where I'm headed now? Reason I stopped here, first, is I'm not sure how to approach Fidella. He's cooperated so far, what's my reason for recontacting him without getting him antsy and pulling back into his shell?"

I said, "If he's a con man he'll be naturally suspicious, so I'm not sure you can avoid getting him wary. You could try telling him you've found some kids at the school who had conflict with Elise, figured if she confided in anyone it would be him."

"Which leads to an interesting point: Elise told Trey Franck about Martin but if she mentioned it to Fidella, he didn't pass that along. So either she felt closer to Franck or Fidella's keeping his cards under the table. If it's the latter, Fidella may be considering another extortion scheme."

"All the more reason to tantalize him with a possible link to the school. You're confirming his initial theory and making him feel like part of your team, as opposed to a suspect. He lets his guard down, you might learn something interesting."

"And Santa's on call twelve months a year." Yanking the fridge open for the third time, he scored a second slice of bread, deliberated, added a third. Pulled out a jar of boysenberry jam topped by a gingham-wrapped lid.

"Looks homemade. You guys going slow-food?"

"Robin's friend brought it."

Slathering both slices, he chewed noisily. "I'd love to see Fidella's spontaneous reaction to the mention of Franck's name. He gives off a serious tell, I've got a clear pathway to your basic crime of passion. But I can't risk showing my cards. Not that the odds like Uncle Milo. Unlike Sal, I never scored a jackpot."

"If you had, you might've held on to the dough."

"Well, look at that." He pinged the vase of flowers with a fingernail. "For the price of some stems and petals, I get therapy."

CHAPTER

23

The sky above Sal Fidella's block was moonlit, particle-clogged, heavy with mist. Houses and shrubs and trees appeared partially erased.

No Corvette in the driveway, dim yellow porch light over the door but no illumination from within.

Milo got out and rang the bell anyway, was greeted by the expected silence. Someone called "'Scuse me?" from across the street.

A man gestured from the lawn of a neatly kept ranch house.

Big man in T-shirt and shorts. Big shaggy dog on a leash sitting obediently at his side.

The dog studied our approach, dark, bear-like, unmoving but for intelligent eyes that cut through the haze.

The man was in his early thirties, bullnecked and crew-cut with a fuzzy chin-beard and the top-heavy physique of a silverback gorilla. "You're cops, right? I came out with Rufus and seen you." He hooked a thumb at Fidella's house. "What'd he do?"

Milo said, "What makes you think he did anything?"

"He didn't?"

"What's on your mind, sir?"

The man shifted his weight. The dog didn't budge. "Tell the truth, Officer, none of us likes him living so close."

"None of us being . . ."

"Me, my wife, also the Barretts—two houses down, they also got kids."

"You're worried about your kids?"

"Not yet," said the man. "So far, he just bothered the wives."

"Bothered them how?"

"Trying to sell 'em stuff they didn't want. With my wife it was a guitar for my oldest. But Sean don't play the guitar, Sean's into sports, she told him that. He kept pushin', telling Dara kids who played instruments were smarter than kids who didn't play instruments, he had some good cheap guitars, Sean could pick his color. Dara said thanks but no thanks. He follows her all the way up to our door, finally she has to say, really, I'm not interested, and he's still talking. Dara told me about it later, I said let me go over there, she said if he does it again, no sense making a scene. Later we were having a barbecue with Doug and Karen—the Barretts—and Dara found out he'd pulled the same stunt with Karen."

"Trying to sell her a guitar."

"Drums, their oldest plays the drums, you can hear it a mile away when he practices. One day *he* catches Karen as she's driving up, tells her doesn't sound like Ryan's drum kit's any good. She says it's fine. He says it's really not, he can get her a better one, cheap. Karen says no thanks, we're fine, he gets pushy the same way he did with Dara. Karen's tougher than Dara, she yells at him to back off."

"Did he?"

"Yeah. But he had a foot in her door, that's weird, no?"

"Anything else about him we should know, Mr. . . ."

"Roland Staubach," said the man. "I go by Rolly. This is a nice family block, he lives by himself, never goes to work. So tell me, how'd he get that Corvette? And that ginormous flat-screen?"

"You've been inside his house?"

"Me? Why should I?"

"You saw his flat-screen."

"It's right in front and sometimes he opens those sheets he uses for curtains. I'll be walking Rufus and he's right there for the whole world to see. Sitting on the couch in his underwear drinking and watching his flat-screen. When I saw you drive up in that unmarked, I said finally, someone I can talk to."

"You know about unmarkeds," said Milo.

"I used to drive for one of the tow-yard services used by your department. Van Bruggen's, over in Silverlake? Once in a while I hooked up an unmarked. So what'd he do?"

"Nothing," said Milo.

"Nothing? You knocked on his door."

"He's a potential witness, Mr. Staubach."

"To what?"

"Nothing that concerns the neighborhood. Is there anything else you want to tell me about him?"

"He gives me a bad feeling," said Staubach. "Anytime he gets in that Corvette, guns the engine like he does, Rufus is at the front window, all tense." Rubbing the dog's neck. "Also, he never goes to a regular job, this is a working block. I drive for UPS, work weekends at Mack's Aquarium in Tarzana. Dara's a teacher's aide at the kids' school, for tuition. Doug and Karen are both at Con Edison. The Millers down the block are respiratory therapists, everyone's working like crazy except him."

"How long has he lived here?" said Milo.

"He was already here when we moved in, that's a year and a half ago."

"Thanks, Mr. Staubach. We'll be back to talk to him."

"You could talk to him now, Officer."

"He's home?"

"I saw him pulling that Corvette into the driveway around four thirty, never saw him leave. Gunning it, like he always does, Rufus was up at the window, all tense. Then an hour ago the Corvette starts up again only this time no gunning and Rufus is relaxed so I go check it out. Some other guy's driving it away. Some kid."

"How old of a kid?" said Milo.

"Didn't get a long look at him but I could see him through the open window and it sure wasn't Fidella."

"We talking teenager?"

"Could be. I really didn't see that good."

"Caucasian?"

"Not black, that's for sure," said Staubach.

"Hair color?"

"Couldn't tell you."

"Could he have been Hispanic?"

"All I can say is light enough so he wasn't black. Or maybe he was black but a light black. I figured maybe he's Fidella's kid, a divorce situation, Fidella never sees him, that would fit. With his character, you know?"

"You figured Fidella loaned him his car."

"I guess . . . you're thinking the car got stolen?"

"Was the kid inside Fidella's house?"

"That I can't tell you. You're thinking this kid hot-wired it or something?"

"You're sure Fidella wasn't in the passenger seat?"

"I guess he could've been. All I saw was someone at the wheel."

Milo looked up and down the block. "There was enough light?"

Staubach pointed. "He passed right under that street lamp, Officer. I wouldn't tell you something I saw when I didn't."

"What was the kid wearing?"

"All I saw was his head," said Staubach. "That's my point, I'm not gonna make stuff up."

"Have there been any other car thefts in the neighborhood?"

"You know, last year, Mr. Feldman—he's an old man, his wife just died, that blue house with all the flowers. Last year, someone drove off in Mr. Feldman's Cadillac, middle of the night, rolled it right out of his driveway. It got found in East L.A., tires gone, the moonroof cut out. That's why you asked about Hispanic? Some kind of East L.A. gangbangers? Yeah, sure, he could've been."

"You saw this kid drive off an hour ago."

"What time is it now?"

"Nine fifteen."

"Then it's an hour and a quarter. So what's next, Officer?"

"I'll give Mr. Fidella another try."

"Great idea."

Milo said, "Looks like Rufus is itching for his walk."

"Already walked him," said Staubach.

"Then I guess he deserves a nice rest."

"Wha—oh, sure, I'll stay out of your way. But keep in touch, okay? We're a block likes to know what's going on."

Another try at Fidella's front door brought the same result.

He peered across the street at Staubach's house. Neatly pleated drapes ruffled as someone moved.

I said, "Your year for helpful citizens."

"Must be El Niño."

We continued up Fidella's cracked driveway. The yard was an

unlit patch of dirt or grass—too dark to tell which. High hedges loomed on three sides. The rear door was wood set with a glass panel. The single garage was bolted shut.

No illumination. Milo pulled out his little fiber-optic flashlight, held it high, the way cops are trained to do, aimed at a rusty light fixture over the rear door. "Empty socket, lots of rust. Sal's behind in his maintenance." A rap on the panel was followed by silence. He cast a cool white beam over the property.

Mostly dirt, some weeds, a single struggling orange tree. The hedge was ficus, worn bare in spots by disease and backed by cement block.

A second go-round, closer to the rear of the property, picked up something lying near the hedge.

What looked to be a roll of carpeting. Closer inspection showed it to be a cloth tube, fattened by substantial content.

Giant sausage.

Person-sized sausage.

Milo held me back instinctively, inched forward, scanned. Stopped.

Clamping the flashlight in one armpit, he gloved up. Lit up the dirt separating him from the package. Bent at the knees.

"Footprints . . . looks like some sort of sneaker."

Shifting to the left, he skirted the prints, checked the ground for other signs of disruption, inched his way toward the roll of cloth. Stooping, he held the flashlight in his teeth, peeled back a corner of sheeting.

"Bald head," he announced. "Cracked like an egg, lots of blood."

He got up, walked backward. "Can't move anything until the C.I. gets here but anyone taking bets this ain't Sal?"

I said, "No good odds on that one."

◆

Three hours later, Fidella's body had been taken to the crypt. Blood spatter freckled the kitchen of the house, including some fairly heavy ceiling castoff. A pool cue coated with skin and brain matter stood propped in a corner, bloody sneaker prints trailed through the hallway near the linen closet. Under strong light, red specks darkening the dirt outside grew visible.

Despite all the blood, no sign of a struggle. Milo's working hypothesis was a blunt-force blitz near the kitchen sink, followed by wrapping of the body in a blanket and three fitted sheets taken from the linen closet and a dump in a corner of the yard. No argument from the C.I. or anyone else.

Techs dusted and processed. Van Nuys uniforms guarded the yellow tape out front. A gray-haired, stoop-shouldered Van Nuys detective named Wally Fishell showed up after the body was gone, looking sleepy and put-upon. After getting the facts from Milo, he said, "I'm happy to work with you, Lieutenant, but if you see this as fruit from the tree you planted, that's fine with me."

"Meaning farewell and good luck."

"If that's your preference," said Fishell.

"Because you're a pal."

Fishell looked as if he'd been slapped. "I'm not dumping, I don't want to get in your way is all."

"No prob."

"Look, whatever you want, Lieutenant. I been working like a dog, supposedly I'm off. The plan was to spend time with my granddaughter. She lives in San Mateo, I don't get to see her often enough."

"Go home, then."

"Naw, it's okay, I'm here already."

"Forget it," said Milo. "This is definitely gonna hook into mine."

"You have an idea who killed him?"

"Probably the same person who killed my vic."

Fishell waited.

Milo said, "That's as far as it's gotten. Go home and enjoy the granddaughter. How old is she?"

"Five."

"Great age."

"You bet. We were watching *Dora the Explorer*," said Fishell. "That's a cartoon show—you got kids?"

"Nope."

"Oh," said Fishell. "Well, thanks, I get back now I can finish *Dora*."

We waited around longer, in case the crime scene crew came up with anything dramatic.

No signs of forced entry. Fidella's slippers and three empty beer bottles with Fidella's prints were found in the living room.

No prints on the pool cue, probably wiped clean. Same for a bloodstained leather case. Screening the house for physical evidence would stretch until morning. No sign of any computers, but clear space on a bedroom desk and an old laser printer in the closet suggested a linkup had once existed.

Fidella's cell phone lay on the bed. Milo checked recent calls. Nothing since morning. He returned the phone to a tech admiring the murder weapon.

"Look at this, Lieutenant. Ivory handle, probably genuine. And this is *real* cute." Eyeing a middle section of rosewood imprinted with silver hearts, clubs, spades, and diamonds.

"This cost some serious bucks, Lieutenant. No table in the house so he probably took it with him to bars, pool halls, whatever."

"Or the killer brought the cue with him."

"And risk damaging something so cool?" said the tech.

"Depends on the payoff."

"For what?"

"Bashing in Mr. Fidella's skull."

"Oh. I guess, maybe."

We left the scene.

Roland Staubach observed, accompanied by Rufus and a fair-haired woman also in shorts and a tee. Neighbors drifted out of their homes and stayed to watch.

Milo waved.

Staubach returned the gesture woodenly before looking away.

Milo drove on. "All of a sudden it's a block doesn't want to know too much."

Midway up Beverly Glen, he said, "Martin Mendoza's looking better and better. Bashing Fidella's skull then stealing the car is exactly the kind of poor-impulse crap a kid like him would do."

"What's the motive?" I said.

He had no answer for that and ignorance didn't sit well with him. Hunching over the wheel, he switched on the police radio, pretended to be interested in misdemeanors and traffic violations. By the time he dropped me at my house we hadn't spoken for ten minutes.

"Night," I said.

"Guess who I'm calling soon as you're out of the car?" Cursing under his breath. "Don't suppose he'll take the news well, seeing as he just lost his favorite suspect and this puts it right back at the school . . . why *would* Martin go after Fidella?"

"Don't know."

"Hey," he said, "that's my mantra. Be sure to tell Robin where the *flores* came from, I forgot a card."

He drove off as I climbed the stairs to my front door. Moments after I was inside, settled next to Robin, a familiar knock sounded at the front door.

Milo stood there, looking like a shy kid at the prom.

Robin stood on tiptoes and bussed his cheek. "Thanks for the bouquet, darling. What have you brought me now?"

"I *should* bring you something. Same reason, abuse of privacy."

"C'mon in, darling."

"Love to, but I've been summoned by the boss. As in now. Unfortunately, so has Alex. If you can spare him, I'll send you three dozen roses tomorrow."

"He's worth more than vegetative matter, but sure."

I said, "I'm re-invited?"

"Better. You're the guest of honor."

The freeway at one a.m. was slick black tape.

I said, "Chief's in his office this late?"

"He's home."

"You do house calls?"

"Now I do."

I said, "Anyone in the office notices a meeting at this hour, it arouses suspicion and documents his meddling. Meaning where he lives, no one'll notice. Last time, he met us in Calabasas. My guess is he's got one of those secluded West Valley spreads."

"Now you know why he likes you, Sherlock."

The chief's spread in Agoura backed up against horse farms, undeveloped pasture, the umber mass of the Santa Monica Mountains.

Getting close took us half an hour beyond the freeway, past the point where streets were identified by signs. Early on we'd sped past desperately cute strip malls, a Porsche dealership, a gas station charging ten percent more than in the city. Now we hurtled through dark, unfocused space.

Milo had trouble navigating the increasingly complex web of trails barely wide enough for a vehicle. Several wrong turns into frustration, he flipped on the dome light, read his own hand-scrawled directions while coasting. By the time we arrived at a small wooden sign he was sweating and cursing. Burned into rough plank:

SERENITY RANCH

I said, "Bit of a commute to Windsor Prep. Nothing like parental dedication."

"Nothing like mommy dedication."

We passed through an open swing gate—just a steel frame and a single diagonal cross-beam—and the Crown Vic labored up an asphalt ribbon worn to raw earth in spots, lumped unpleasantly in others. The car's overtaxed suspension whined at every concussion.

The gate wasn't much of a barrier. I said, "A lesser man might be concerned about intruders."

"Apex predators don't fret about that kind of thing."

A half-acre motor court spread tight as a fitted sheet fronted a wide, shallow-roofed, one-story house. Parking for scores of cars but no vehicles in sight. Maybe the family wheels were buttoned up in the quadruple garage.

The court was unadorned concrete. Other than a couple of huge oaks listing dangerously, no greenery graced the house. The rear was clear, flat acreage, lots of it. The trees were probably the last surviving remnants of an ancient grove decimated for Top Cop's lair. Too many wet years and they might topple vengefully.

The chief was waiting for us, rocking in a chair set at the front edge of the court, tastefully lit by a low-watt pole fixture resembling a gas lamp. The tip of his cigar created tiny orange curlicues. Wisps of smoke were ingested by the darkness.

Milo cruised to a halt, opened his window. "Sir."

"Over there." A stiff thumb jabbed to the left. Embers tumbled to the concrete, sparked, died.

We parked, got out. No other seating meant we stood like supplicants. The chief's white hair gave off metallic glints when the cigar tip favored it with transitory light. Otherwise, he was a charcoal sketch.

"Two murders, Dr. Delaware," he said, softly. "My diagnosis is 'big fucking mess.' What's yours?"

"I'll go with that."

"Inconsiderate bastard, the Italian guy. I liked him better as an offender." He clicked his tongue. "So we're looking at the Mexican kid for the Italian."

That made it sound like an international conspiracy. I suppressed the urge to say, *With an American pool cue.*

Milo said, "Like I said, a young man was spotted leaving the—"

"Exactly, you've said, let's move on. In terms of Freeman, we've pretty much eliminated those teachers?"

Milo said, "There's no evidence against them, but—"

"So we move on."

Long silence, then the sound of a slow, sucking inhalation. The cigar tip expanded, a miniature orange planet. Smoke-rings floated upward like tiny UFOs. "Not that you've got anywhere to move, Sturgis."

I said, "Hard to go anywhere when you're stuck in Park."

The orange disk bounced. "Meaning, Doctor?"

"Meaning this hasn't been a conventional investigation."

Throat clear. "You're a social observer, Doctor?"

"A casual observer. More isn't required."

"Maybe we'd all be better off, Doctor, if we stuck to our areas of expertise. Yours being psychopathology. In terms of that, does the Mexican kid sound potentially violent to you?"

"He sounds frustrated," I said. "His family's from Uruguay."

"Wherever he's from, he sounds like a fucking ingrate. *Señor* Daddy tell you which alumnus got his *niño* into Prep?"

"A man named Kenten."

"Edwin Kenten?" he said. "Another fucking layer of complication."

"Who is he?"

"A builder of cities, Doctor." Laughing bitterly. "A Titan among mere mortals. His game is partnering with municipalities, then evoking eminent domain to bulldoze private property. In place of which he nails up low-budget housing and big-box stores financed by taxpayer money. All in the name of the greater good."

His laugh was low, hoarse, ominous. "Ed Kenten served on the committee that recommended hiring me. We had an interview during which he led me to believe he supported me. When the time came to vote, he supported someone else because their dark skin mattered more to him than the ability to get the fucking job done." Another threatening snicker. "Yeah, can see him putting the Mexican kid in an awkward situation just so he could feel noble. Kid freaks out, gets violent, does Freeman, but that's not enough to quell his rage, so he bashes the Italian's brains."

He clucked. "Eddie's going to have to find himself another barrio darling. Meanwhile, he's playing his eighteen holes at Mountain Crest and getting chauffeured to Paradise Cove. Hell, the kid's daddy's probably still serving Ed his shrimp cocktail."

The cigar tip danced merrily.

I said, "Why does Kenten complicate matters?"

"Once the kid gets busted, Eddie being his mentor will come to light and first thing he'll assume is I'm out to make him look bad. So you be damn sure, Sturgis, that you've got rock-solid evidence before you stir up the cesspool."

A light went on in the big, low house. The chief shot a quick look back, faced us again.

"Okay, here's the deal, Sturgis: Concentrate on finding the Corvette. It shows up with the Mexican kid's prints in it, or if you get any kind of physical evidence from the house pointing to the kid, we'll be forced to deal with the consequences. You find squat in the car and the house, you leave the kid alone."

"And?" said Milo.

"And take a breather. Regroup. Put everything on ice until you've got evidence. Pun intended. And don't worry about getting bored. I just sat through a PowerPoint dog-and-pony from my math techies and they say West L.A.'s due for a fresh homicide in thirty to fifty days, most likely a gang shooting. Once in a while, even you can catch something easy."

Milo said, "Mendoza's never been in the system, AFIS won't have his prints."

"A nice, law-abiding *niño,*" said the chief. "How uplifting. Maybe Eddie Kenten sensed that. On the other hand, maybe the kid's kind of cute."

The orange disk dipped. "Catch my meaning, Sturgis?"

"Kenten's gay?"

Laughter. "A married grandpa? Tsk-tsk, I don't rumor-mong. On the other hand, you tell me Mendoza's a strapping, muscular stud, I'm not going to gasp in shock."

"Sir, in terms of Martin Mendoza's prints not being in the—"

"No sense what-iffing, you don't even have the car. Find it, have the techies do their thing, who knows, you might luck out and get prints from someone who is in the system. I just saw the GTA stats for Van Nuys. Shameful, it's something we definitely need to work on. So the Italian could've gotten brained by a jack-happy Eastside punk just like the neighbor assumed and we can all go home, have a beer, fuck whoever it is we customarily fuck."

"That doesn't close Freeman, sir."

"Some of life's mysteries, Sturgis, are destined to remain enigmatic."

Milo didn't respond.

I said, "Convenient. Except for the moral dilemma."

The chief's head shot forward. Cigar sparks flew like miniature fireworks. "Whose dilemma might that be, Doctor."

"Charlie's."

His next words came out tight, as if extruded from a clogged machine. "You don't know Charlie."

"I know kids and from what you said last time, Charlie sounds like a thoughtful kid. The murder of a teacher would get any student curious. A serious young man with a moral compass and a direct link to law enforcement might take that curiosity to another level. It wouldn't surprise me if this is the first time he's expressed any interest in your work."

The cigar tip dipped suddenly.

I said, "If Elise Freeman's murder languishes in bureaucratic purgatory, Charlie will want to know why. You'll give him an explanation and he might even pretend to accept it. Alternatively, he'll be assertive and push you and you'll embroider. Either way, he's smart, nothing short of the truth is going to satisfy his curiosity. The kind of curiosity that could linger well past graduation from Yale."

"Yale," he said. "Boolah Boolah."

"Fight songs endure," I said. "Surrender songs don't."

The orange dot bobbled. Shaky hand. He tried to steady it. Failed. Dropping the cigar, he stomped hard. Embers scattered, glinted, vanished.

He sat there, bracing his hands on his knees. Shot upright like a switchblade flicking open. Turning his back on us, he trudged across the cement court, grew small. Entered his house and closed the door silently.

Lights off.

I said, "Sorry, Big Guy."

"For what?"

"Messing you up with the boss."

"Screw that," he said. "Quitting and getting roped back in gave me a whole new perspective." Staring at the house. "Never seen him retreat like that."

"He could be too mad to speak."

"Who cares? You got to him, Alex. Trust me, he's in there right now, brooding about Junior. And being a rank opportunist, I'm grabbing the white card."

"What white card?"

"Carte blanche, *mon frère*. Until he specifies otherwise, I'm gonna do whatever the hell I please on Freeman and Fidella."

"He already specified the plan," I said. "Half-assed search for Mendoza, Freeman goes cold."

"That was before you tweaked his psyche and he didn't fight back. Silence is acquiescence, *amigo*. The lion wimps out, the wildebeests proceed to the drinking hole."

Carte blanche at two a.m. meant putting a BOLO out on Sal Fidella's Corvette as we sped east on the 101.

Milo said, "I get non-AFIS prints that aren't Fidella's, all the more reason to hunt for Marty Mendoza *seriously*. As in talking to every damn student and teacher at Prep who knew him, maybe flying out personally to San Antonio where I will enjoy tamales and carne asada and drive by his sister's apartment at frequent intervals, myself."

"I am detective, hear me roar."

"Beasts of burden make noise, too."

Nine hours later, he called me. "Top of the morning." Lightness in his voice.

"You found the car?"

"Nope, but I made a new friend."

◆

I met him at noon at the Culver City jail on Duquesne, where a guard named Shirronne Bostic led us to a locked holding room.

Tapping a foot, she shuffled through a key ring.

Milo said, "When did he come in?"

"Last night around ten. Picked up in a hooker sting, pretended *no hablo inglés* then changed his tune when he got hauled in instead of just a ticket like the last time. Your card was in his pocket along with some bullshit I.D. You were his one call."

"Flattered."

"He for real, Lieutenant?"

"Depends on what he has to say."

"Guess he is real," said Bostic. "You're here."

Inside the holding cell, a middle-aged balding man with a droopy mustache sat on a metal bench, dusky skin jaundiced by cruel light. White stubble dotted his face, his eyes were defeated.

Jumpy eyes and unstable hands, same as when he'd been part of the day-laborer crowd waiting for pickup work near the ice joint. The one who'd claimed a fake address in Beverly Hills.

Officer Bostic said, "He claims to be Hector Ruiz but he also claims to live near movie stars."

"That's my name," said the man.

Milo said, "I'll take it from here, thanks," and Bostic left. "Mr. Ruiz, how're things in B.H.?"

Hector Ruiz said, "The guy in anteater shirt," in barely accented English.

"What about him?"

"I know him." Ruiz rotated his wrists, tugged the side of his mouth into a grotesque demi-smile.

Milo said, "I'm waiting."

"I need to get out."

"Next time you get arrested, make sure it's in L.A. and it'll be a snap."

"Please," said Ruiz.

"Tell me about Anteater."

"Please," Ruiz repeated. "My wife coming from Juarez. She can't know."

"You got arrested for the same thing two weeks ago, Hector."

"That was a ticket," said Ruiz. "This time they take me in."

"That's called being a repeat offender."

"*Please.* I got no bail money, they gonna keep me here, she coming two days."

"Tough lady?"

Ruiz pressed a palm against a temple. "Oh, man."

"I'm LAPD, Hector. Most I can do is talk to Culver City Vice."

"Why just talk? Do," said Ruiz. "You say you *gran patrón.*"

"In L.A."

"They lie to me, she was a cop." Ruiz outlined female curves. "They give her the hot pants and the boots, she say I blow you for thirty."

"The boots'll do it every time," said Milo.

"She say she blow me before I say nothing."

"Clear case of entrapment, Hector."

"I need out tomorrow."

"Mrs. Ruiz isn't arriving for two days."

"I need clean the house."

"Hiding the evidence, huh?"

"I need *out.*"

"What's Anteater's name and where can I find him?"

"Get me out I tell you," said Ruiz.

Milo leaned in close. "It doesn't work that way, Hector. And just giving me information won't be enough until I make sure it's worth more than your I.D. card."

Ruiz looked away. "What you want with him?"

"Not your business, Hector, but if you want the wife to be happy, I need him in custody."

No answer.

"*Comprende,* Hector?"

"I know English."

"And a good English it is." Milo shot a cuff, checked his Timex.

Hector Ruiz said, "You promise to help me?"

"Once I've got Mr. Shirt in custody."

"Okay, okay, okay, he live in my apartment."

"You're roommates?"

"No, no, same building. He number five, the bottom. I number seven, the top."

Milo suppressed a smile. "Beverly Hills?"

"No, no, here," said Ruiz. "Culver City. Venice Boulevard, near the freeway."

Out came the pad. "Address."

Ruiz tugged his mouth. Complied.

"Now I need a name, Hector."

"Gilberto," said Ruiz. "Gilberto Chavez, he say he a painter, in Juarez he never paint, just drywall and no good at drywall."

"One of those darn painter wannabes," said Milo.

"Don't say I the one tell you."

"What else do you know about Mr. Chavez?"

"He smoke a lot." Miming a two-fingered cigarette grasp, Ruiz brought his hand to his mouth, scrunched his eyes, hollowed his cheeks, gave a goofy look.

"*Marihuana que fumar,*" said Milo.

"All the time," said Ruiz. "That's what they pay him with."

"Who?"

"Kids."

"What kids?"

"They pay him with weed to buy dry ice. He say lucky day."

"Tell me about these kids, Hector."

"That's all he say. Kids."

"How many?"

Ruiz shook his head. "That's all he say."

Milo waited.

Ruiz said, "You got to get me out before Lupe come."

"If you've done your best, Hector, I'll do mine. Tell me about the kids."

"That's what he say." Crossing himself. "Kids, that's all."

Milo headed for the door.

Hector Ruiz said, *"Please."*

A call to a Vice D named Gerald Santostefano revealed that Ruiz was scheduled for release in three hours due to overcrowding at the jail.

"Why'd you take him in to begin with?"

"He's a chronic, Lieutenant."

"Likes the ladies, huh?"

"Likes 'em in boots, real pest," said Santostefano. "You know what it's like, we can't get 'em unless we nab 'em in the act. We put one of our cuter rookies in a pair of knee-high white plastics with stacked heels, he was toast."

"There's an idea for *Project Runway.*"

Santostefano cracked up.

Milo said, "Any way you can keep him in for a while?"

"What's a while?"

"Until I call you and let you know his info's good."

"Well," said Santostefano, "I got no personal problem with that but it's a jail issue. Who's on shift there?"

"Officer Bostic."

"Shirronne's okay, I can maybe get her to lose paper for another few hours. Beyond that, I can't promise."

Milo thanked him.

"Hey," said Santostefano. "Who knows, maybe one day I'll need you."

"Not for fashion advice."

The building besmirched a corner lot on the south side of Venice just west of Sepulveda. Two gloomy stories of cracked, gray stucco were rust-striped like a tabby cat. Waist-high chain link boxed in a yard coated with powdery brown dust. Cans and bottles and trash bags had been kicked into a corner. Errant flecks of garbage dotted the dirt near the doorway.

During the quarter hour we watched the premises, two Hispanic males left and three others entered, the third swaggering arm in arm with a chubby, heavily made-up woman wearing a floral micro-dress.

Gilberto Chavez, aspiring housepainter, didn't show up in DMV, AutoTrack, or any other database, making the surveillance guesswork.

Milo watched another man enter. "Could be any one of them." A few more minutes passed, then: "Might as well."

Unit Five was at the rear of the ground floor. A bumper sticker issued by a Spanish A.M. station was glued diagonally across the door.

Milo put one hand near his Glock and knocked three times.

The door opened and the sweet, vegetative aroma of marijuana blew out.

The man who blinked at us in surprise was small—five four, tops, with thick black hair that shrouded his forehead and grazed the top of bushy eyebrows. The eyes below were brown meatballs floating in hot-pink soup. His mouth hung open, showcasing half the teeth he'd grown by six.

He was dressed for stoner comfort in loose, grubby pale blue sweatpant shorts and a T-shirt. The tee was white, three sizes too big, emblazoned with the UC Irvine logo in gold lettering and an anteater of matching hue. The animal was caricatured in profile, extravagantly snouted, hipster-slouching in a way that evoked Robert Crumb.

Milo said, "Gilberto Chavez?"

The man blinked. "Ah . . . no."

"On the contrary, ah yes."

Chavez tried to close the door. Milo had him spun around, cuffed, patted, and trundling toward the curb before Chavez got out another denial. One of the sweatpant pockets gave up Mexican I.D., a tin of organic rolling papers, and a Baggie of clean-looking marijuana.

"No Gilberto," he insisted.

"That Juarez driver's license sure looks like you."

"No Gilberto."

"Gimme a break," said Milo.

"Okay."

Milo stared down at his diminutive quarry. "Okay, what?"

"I Gilberto."

"So glad we've reached a consensus."

"No my weed."

We waited until traffic thinned to cross Venice, put Chavez in the car. The dope reek embedded in his clothes saturated the interior and Milo cranked open a window. "Tell me about dry ice, Gilberto."

"Huh?"

"Kids paying you to buy dry ice."

"Huh?"

"Last week, in the Valley. Some kids gave you marijuana after you bought them dry ice."

Blank stare from Chavez.

"Hielo seco," said Milo. *"Muy frio.* Some kids asked you to—"

"Oh," said Chavez, grinning broadly.

"Something's funny, Gilberto?"

Chavez turned serious. "This no about weed?"

"It's about dry ice."

"What the problem?"

"No problem, just tell me about the kids."

"Girls."

"The kids were girls?"

"Oh, yeh, nice," said Chavez. "Very nice."

"How many?"

"Two."

"How old?"

"I dunno."

"Guess."

"Huh?"

"How old?"

"Eighteen?"

"Why'd they want dry ice?"

"I dunno."

"How much weed they give you?"

Silence.

Milo dug up a business card and flashed it in front of Chavez's bloodshot orbs. "See what it says here? Homicide. I don't care about dope."

Chavez's blank look said he wasn't processing. Illiteracy or too much THC.

"Homicide, Gilberto. Know what that is?"

"Someone get kill?"

"Yes, Gilberto."

"So?"

"So the ice you bought was involved in someone being killed."

Chavez's mouth dropped open. Anxiety burned through some of his high and his eyes sharpened. "Oh, no. No no, no, no, no!"

"Yes, yes, yes. Tell me about the two girls."

"I dint do nothin'."

"Then you have nothing to worry about."

"I dint do nothin'."

"Okay. Now tell me about the girls."

"I dint do *nothin'*."

We drove Chavez to West L.A. station where a claustrophobic solo cell was available because no psychotics were in residence in the holding jail. Milo's repeated attempts to open Chavez up failed. He seemed to drop in and out of lucidity.

We left him curled on the floor, snoring, and climbed to Milo's office on the second floor. He shuffled through messages, tossed everything.

"There's enough product in that bag to keep him here on a possession with intent. Maybe jail food'll convince him to look at pictures of those girls."

"You think they're in a mug book?"

"I think they're in another book. Let's get outta here."

This time we drove straight up to the Windsor Prep guardhouse. Herb Walkowicz emerged, khakis pressed, an old-fashioned visor cap jaunty on his head. "Hey, guys, gonna get me in trouble again?"

"We'll do our best," said Milo. "Dr. Rollins in?"

"Since eight a.m." Eye roll. "Unless she climbed over a back fence or something without snagging her designer pantsuit. She in trouble?"

"I just need to talk to her."

Walkowicz looked disappointed. "I'd like to see that one in an interview room without her damn BlackBerry."

"Not a pleasant gal, Herb?"

"You could say that." Wink wink. "You could also say she's a tight-assed, snobby bitch. But you never heard that from me."

"What about her boss?"

"Dr. Helfgott? He's okay, not around much. Day to day, Rollins runs the place."

"Know any of the teachers?"

"Know 'em by sight, that's all," said Walkowicz. "Everyone goes in and out, I'm in my cage watching. The invisible man. Take my advice: Don't retire, just die on the job."

"I'm working on that, Herb."

Walkowicz laughed. "So you want to go in? I got a key to that big front gate. Only problem is, I have to let the office know before I let anyone through and when Rollins finds out it's you she's for sure gonna make a stink. Last time she told me not to let you get within twenty feet."

"Call her and tell her we're being obnoxious, then put me on the line."

"Yeah," said the guard. "That would be better."

Ten minutes later, Mary Jane Rollins emerged swinging a royal-blue book bag marked with the school's crest. She wore a charcoal pinstriped pantsuit, red flats, a withering frown.

"Here." Thrusting the bag. "I'm sure you could've gotten one on eBay."

"Nothing like straight from the source," said Milo. "How much is it gonna cost me?"

"Oh, please. What I don't see is why you need it to identify Martin. You already know what he looks like."

"It's called careful documentation, Doctor."

"Of what?"

"Everything associated with a case."

"So Martin is . . . we still haven't seen him. Not for days."

Matter-of-fact, not the least bit upset.

I said, "What's he like, Dr. Rollins?"

"In what sense?"

"What kind of kid is he, personality-wise?"

"I have no idea."

"While he was here you didn't have much contact with him?"

"Nothing out of the ordinary."

"No special attention," I said, "despite his circumstances."

"We were acutely aware of his circumstances. That's why we paid to hire a tutor for him. Obviously *that* didn't work out."

Irritation, not a trace of horror.

"So he got no other help besides tutoring?"

"Such as?"

"Counseling, maybe from someone on the faculty who knew him well."

"Sir," she said, "we have two hundred and ninety-three students preselected for intelligence, character, and the ability to reason independently. That means minimal need for babysitting."

"Other than academic tutoring."

"That is a matter among students, their families, and their tutors. Our paying was an additional courtesy we extended Martin. Obviously, it didn't work out as we'd hoped. Now, in the future, if you people believe there's something you absolutely *must* have immediately, use the phone." Crooked smile. "During these days of fiscal austerity, I'd think city agencies would prefer to save on gasoline."

Milo said, "We like the personal touch."

"Good day, gentlemen."

"Thanks for your cooperation, Doctor."

"I'm not cooperating," said Rollins. "I'm acquiescing."

When she was back behind the gates, Herb Walkowicz whistled softly through his teeth. "Welcome to my world."

"Working with Stan Creighton was better, Herb?"

"Let me tell you something about Stan. He used to be a good guy before he got involved."

"Involved with what?"

"Suits and weenies and other assorted bullshit artists," said Walkowicz. His mouth tightened. "Kinda people send their kids to a place like this."

As we headed to the car, Milo reached into the blue bag and drew out last year's Windsor Prep yearbook.

Three-hundred-plus gilt-edged pages bound in royal-blue calf-skin. Each student's headshot in full, high-def color.

I said, "Nice production values."

"Only the best for show-pooches." He inspected a few photos. "Some of them even look happy."

Gilberto Chavez remained curled on the floor of his cell.

"He been that way all this time?" Milo asked the uniform on duty.

"For the most part. He peed once, we made him clean it up. Hey, Dr. Delaware, how come the deceptive ones always sleep like babies?"

I said, "Minimal or no conscience."

Milo said, "Pop the lock on Rip Van Winkle."

The uniform opened the cell, made sure the door clanged loud.

Chavez stirred but but didn't awaken. When Milo called out his name, he opened his eyes briefly before clamping them shut.

Milo toed his shoulder. "Sit up. *Now.*"

Chavez groaned, struggled to his elbows, finally complied with theatrical sluggishness. Milo took him by the shoulder, propped him up, slid him to the edge of the bench. Flipping the yearbook to the freshman page, he placed it on Chavez's lap.

"Start looking."

"Uh-uh."

"Uh-uh, what?"

"I dint do nothin'."

"I know you didn't. But those two girls you got weed from were involved in something bad so unless you want to take all the heat and go up for murder, you'll show me who they are."

"I dint—"

"Show me who they are, Gilberto, and we're finished. Don't cooperate and you're never getting out of here."

"I dint—"

"Shut the fuck up," said Milo, softly. "Now start looking."

Seventy minutes later, Chavez had been through every photo three times.

Same baleful head shake after each pass.

He tried to return the book to Milo.

"Again, Gilberto."

"I don lie," Chavez whined. "No in here."

"You ever wear glasses, Gilberto?"

"No way."

"Try again. And take your time."

Fourth pass, same result.

Chavez looked ready to cry. "I wanna go home but they no in here."

"Let's talk about them, Gilberto. What makes you think they were eighteen?"

"I dunno—they wasn't fifteen."

"How do you know?"

"In a car."

"What car?"

"Black Honda." Retrieving memories that had eluded him.

"Anything different about the Honda?"

"No."

Milo flipped to the front of the senior class. "These are eighteen-year-olds. Take another look."

"Mister, they no *in* here. These *white* girls."

"The girls who wanted ice weren't white."

"One white, yes. Other Mexicana."

"She speak Spanish to you?"

"English. But Mexicana."

"A white girl and a Latina," said Milo.

"Yeh."

"First time I asked what they looked like you said you couldn't remember."

"I couldn't."

"Now you remember one was white and one was Latina."

Chavez touched the side of his head, gave a dreamy smile. "I wake up, you know?"

Milo took the yearbook from him, held it at his side, like a bludgeon poised to bash. "Get more awake right now, Gilberto, and tell me exactly what they looked like."

"Nice."

"Pretty?"

"Yeh."

"Who was driving?"

"The Mexicana."

"You're walking, they pull up?"

"Yeh."

"Then what?"

"The white one she 'Hey, can you help us?' "

"Pretty girl."

Chavez grinned and outlined the jut of enormous breasts.

"Big girl."

"Big titties," said Chavez. "I say 'What?' She get out." Shaping bulbous hips. "Nice."

"What about the Mexicana?"

"*Flaca* but nice face."

"Skinny," said Milo. "So she got out of the car, too."

"Yeh. Laughing."

"Something funny was going on."

"I figure a joke."

"What were their names?"

"No say names."

"They didn't talk to each other and use names?"

"Never," said Chavez with surprising clarity. "First they say money for you help, then the Mexicana come out of the car with you know."

"I know what?"

"You kn—okay, okay, a bag. Say 'This better than money.' I say for what do, they say 'Go buy something.' Lots of laugh."

"They were having a good time."

"I think a party, ice is a party, no? I dint do *nothin'* bad."

"What were they wearing?"

"The white one, black on top, tight jeans." Shaping lush hips again, he blew out air. "Long hair." Reaching behind, he touched a spot below his waist.

"What color?"

"Black."

"What about the Mexicana?"

"Also black, but the blond here." Fingering the fringes of his own dense coiffure.

"Streaked," said Milo.

"Yeh."

"The Mexicana also had long hair?"

"Yeh. Red top—the tank. Tight jeans." Whistling apprecia-tively. "Sandals, also heels. White, yeh, white."

"You're doing good, Gilberto. What else?"

"I bring the ice to the Honda, they gimme the bag."

"Same bag I found in your pocket?"

"Yeh."

"Who else was in the Honda?"

"Nobody."

"You're sure?"

"I put the ice in the backseat, nobody else."

"Where'd they wait while you bought the ice?"

"A block, I had to carry."

"That didn't make you curious?"

"Whuh?"

"Them paying you to buy something they could buy them-selves. Waiting a block away."

"No," said Chavez.

"No, what?"

"Two weeks I got no work. I don wonder about nothin'."

We left the station and walked up Butler Avenue.

Milo said, "Girls and not Prep students. Lord, hand me the Prozac."

I said, "Teenage girls like to please teenage boys."

"Getting ice for a young stud. One of them being Latin could mean she knows Martin from his former life in El Monte." Smiling. "God forbid I should racially profile."

He called the lab about Fidella. Listened, turned serious. Hung up. "One palm print showed up on a gutter that runs down a corner of the garage. The sneaker impressions are probably Nikes, a common model, but too shallow to have evidentiary value. All the blood's Sal's and wherever there was no blood, the house was clean—definitely a wipe-down, same as with Elise. That and the computer theft tells me we're dealing with the same guy. In terms of the palm print, the garage is near where the body got dumped so maybe a glove slipped while it got dragged past. Nothing shows up on AFIS but palms haven't been cataloged long enough to make that meaningful. I get a suspect, it's sufficient for a match."

He phoned Martin Mendoza's house, got the boy's mother, listened for a long time with what sounded like sympathy.

But when he hung up, he said, "She said all the right things, but her tone wasn't right, Alex. Too . . . composed. Like she was reading a script. This after her husband said she'd been throwing up nonstop."

I said, "Not enough anxiety because she knows he's safe."

"Safe," he said, "is a relative concept."

Hitching his trousers, he growled. "Time to hunt."

San Antonio PD agreed to two daily drive-bys of Gisella
Mendoza's apartment for the next three days.

The shift supervisor said, "You got a serious fugitive, call the
marshals."

Milo phoned Gisella again, reached her at work at Bexar Hospital.

"Too damn polite and she worked hard at telling me nothing.
Time to get some pix of the South El Monte student body, maybe
Gilberto can pick out our enterprising twosome."

No yearbooks available on a site that trafficked in academic
nostalgia but the high school's website linked to its store where
Eagle Pride DVDs sold for ten dollars.

Milo tried to placed a rush order, was told by an administrative
assistant named Jane Virgilio that he had to purchase online and
shipping would take at least ten working days.

"Even for the police?"

"Why would the police want our DVD?"

"It's related to a former student, ma'am. Martin Mendoza."

"Martin? Why in the world?"

"You know him?"

"He was one of our stars, everyone said he'd go to the major leagues, then that prep school stole him away. He's in trouble?"

"He's gone missing so knowing who his friends are might help locate him. Any idea who he hung out with?"

"Missing?" said Virgilio. "For how long?"

"Several days," said Milo.

"His parents must be frantic."

"They are, Ms. Virgilio. Who were his closest friends?"

"I can't really pinpoint any."

"No one?"

"Actually, Martin was kind of a loner."

"Team player but *not* a team player?"

"I—oh, I see what you mean. Guess that's true. Martin practiced pitching all the time, maybe he didn't have time to socialize."

"Any girlfriend?"

"I have no idea. The family didn't say?"

"They're not aware of any special girl in his life, ma'am."

"Then I guess there isn't one. I knew Martin more by reputation than personally."

"Athletic star."

"All he had to do was throw that ball straight and fast and the game was ours. When you say missing, do you mean he might be hurt?"

"Sure hope not, ma'am," said Milo. "Tell you what, I'll come by and pick up that DVD right now."

"Um, okay, I think we have some in stock—if you're moving this fast, it sure doesn't sound good. Those poor parents. Mrs. Mendoza volunteered for every bake sale and Cinco de Mayo celebration and Mr. Mendoza didn't mind serving food to hundreds of people. I should call them."

"Not a good time, ma'am. They're sequestered."

"Oh."

"Anything else you can tell me about Martin?"

"Hmm," she said. "Terrific kid, that's all."

We were just out the door when the phone rang.

Sierra Madre PD: Sal Fidella's Corvette had been found early this morning, abandoned and partially burned in a ravine along the northern edge of that pretty city.

Milo checked a map. "Ten miles north of El Monte. Forget Texas, the kid's sticking close to home."

The high school was on the way, so we stopped there first. Clean and well maintained, but your basic institutional architecture and no evidence of a golf course. Jane Virgilio wasn't in but her assistant handed us the disc.

Another check of the Thomas Guide: The Mendoza residence was five blocks away and we headed there. I thought of Martin getting up early for the commute to Brentwood, rewarded for the trek with frustration.

Emilio and Anna Mendoza's residence was small, white, nondescript. Drapes blocked every spotless window. No answer to Milo's ring.

A vest-pocket backyard shaded by an umbrella-like agonis tree was overstuffed with bromeliads, ferns, palms, coleus. A bulk-rate sack of plant food was propped against a trellis wall and the grass had been watered to emerald. A knock on the rear door evoked the same silence.

Milo put his ear to the panel. "Can't hear anything but they could be holed up."

He phoned the house, got no answer.

I said, "Maybe they've all packed up to Texas."

"After the car was dumped? Family that flees together? Yeah, why not?"

That theory was shattered when a call to Mountain Crest Country Club revealed that Emilio Mendoza was on shift.

"May I speak with him please?"

"I'll see." Moments later: "Sorry, he's tied up."

Click.

A quick ride through Pasadena took us into the northeast corner of Sierra Madre. Houses were long gone and brown hills rolled lazily.

No police presence announced itself in advance of the dump spot. We drove right to the rim of a shallow depression, far short of being a ravine. A female uniform stood next to a black-and-white, talking on a cell phone. Forty, dark hair drawn into a ponytail, smile on her face as she chatted.

She waved languidly.

No tape cordon, no evidence markers, nothing to say this was a crime scene. Nothing to guard, the Corvette was gone.

The site was a forty-foot beige soup bowl, sides eroded and bearded by serpentine roots and the stumps of long-dead trees. At the bottom, nothing but flat dry space. Scorch marks scarred the first few feet of drop along the southern wall. The Corvette hadn't rolled to the bottom.

A large clump of petrified root boll beneath the burned area seemed a likely culprit. White flecks said someone had tried to cast prints.

The cop pocketed her phone. Two stripes on her sleeve. *E. Pappas.* "L.A.? All yours, I was just on my way out."

Milo handed her a card. "No debate on my place or yours?"

"My chief isn't much for jurisdictional quibbles, Lieutenant. Car got towed to your auto lab."

"Good riddance, huh?"

"You bet," she said, without a trace of regret. "We're a force of twenty-one people, I'm the only corporal, and in six years I can remember exactly one homicide and that was an open-shut domestic. Arson's another story, we get the usual pyros during dry season, our FD has its hands full. Thank God this one didn't spread. It won't even appear on our stats."

"Did you see the initial scene?"

"First to arrive."

"Who called it in?"

"Elementary school chaperone—a parent with some little kids on a field trip. I'm no arson detective but it looked like an amateur job. Gasoline got poured on the passenger seat but the windows were left closed so the fire got starved out quickly. Your offender wasn't any wizard at hiding evidence, either. Tried to roll the darn thing down to the bottom but it got caught on that chunk of root. Even if it had made it to the bottom, it still would've been in plain view. You want to conceal something, I'll show you gullies ten minutes from here so overgrown you could hide stuff forever."

"Anything on the casts?"

"Nope, sorry. After the car had been moved we saw what looked like shoe prints, but they turned out to be twig marks. Maybe you'll pull up some latents from the vehicle. Only thing left behind was a hat and I made sure it got bagged and tagged for you."

"Thanks. What kind of hat?"

"It was partially burned but I'd say a baseball-type. The little color left was blue."

"Where was it left?"

"We found it on the passenger seat, where the accelerant was squirted. That tells you how dinky the fire was, couldn't even finish off a cloth cap."

"This spot isn't particularly hard to get to," said Milo. "People come here a lot?"

"Would you?" said Pappas. "We've got gorgeous areas all over the place, my opinion, this is one of the uglier ones. Only reason that field trip was here was the teacher wanted to scare the kiddies about erosion."

As Corporal Pappas drove off, we inspected the scene, achieved no insights. A call to the auto lab supervisor verified the arrival of the Corvette.

The trunk and glove compartment had been emptied but the VIN number traced to a vehicle registered to Salvatore Fidella. Moderate fire damage to the interior left plenty of vinyl and metal to process for prints, fluids, and fibers. Same for the remnants of a partially burned blue cap already processed and found devoid of prints or DNA. A handful of scorched fibers with metallic content suggested brass or gold thread, maybe an insignia.

Milo reached Detective I Sean Binchy at the station, directed Binchy to run an image search on *south el monte baseball team.*

"When do you need it, Loot?"

"Now."

"Sure . . . here we go, they're called the Eagles . . . here's a group picture, game they won from Temple City, they're all smiling."

"What color are their caps, Sean?"

"Navy blue."

"Any insignia?"

"Looks like a snake—no, it's an *S,* probably for 'South.' "

"Gold?"

"Right on, Loot. Anything else you need?"

"Pray for world peace, Sean."

"I already do that every morning, sir."

◆

We drove back to L.A., stopping at a place on Colorado for take-out coffee that we drank while in motion. Just west was Pasadena and that got me thinking. But I didn't have enough for sparkling conversation.

Milo said, "The kid pays girls to buy ice so he can ice Freeman in a dramatic way, then mops up Fidella for good measure, only question is why. With Elise's proclivities and Fidella being a lowlife, maybe sex and education got jumbled up together in a particularly nasty way."

I said, "Martin was careful enough to set Elise's murder up with surgical precision and to wipe Fidella's house clean amid a horrendous scene but left his hat in the car—and the car out in the open?"

"Teenagers, Alex. You're the one always saying they're unpredictable. Or maybe he's reached that point: big drop in adrenaline, tired of running, and ready to get caught. We can discuss this till forever but right now he's a good lead. The car gives up the same prints as Fidella's garage, I'm going public."

I said, "Prep school makes noble attempt at diversity but best intentions fail, the manor-born sail into their dream schools, Martin Mendoza ends up in jail. The chief—and Darwin—will be pleased."

"Yeah, it stinks, but that doesn't make it untrue." He finished his coffee, chewed on a cold cigar, drove faster. A few freeway exits later, he said, "Life ain't a surprise party. We both know that."

No message from Darwin on his desk but the chief had left an unfamiliar number.

One ring then a familiar voice on conference. "Talk, Sturgis."

Milo filled him in.

"Fool leaves his hat in the car. He's that strong for the Italian, we'll get him for Freeman."

"It's looking that way, sir."

"Find those girls."

"I've got a DVD of the South El Monte student body, about to show it to Chavez."

"Should've done that before calling me."

"Sorry, sir."

"You get verification on those little bitches, we're pressing full-court."

Loading the *Eagle Pride* DVD into his computer, he brought up pages of fresh faces, printed every one, and X'd out the boys with a sharpie. "Make Gilberto's job easier."

Back at the holding cell, Chavez was wide awake, jumpy, complaining about the food.

The guard said, "No more dope in his system, he's getting grumpy." He unlocked the door.

Milo said, "More pictures, Gilberto."

"You kidding." Chavez reached behind, scratched his back. Clawed hard. "I think you got bugs in here."

"No, we're clean, Gilberto. Start looking."

Chavez flipped pages too quickly.

"Take your time."

"I see, I know."

Upon turning the final page: "Oh, shit."

"You found them?"

"*No*, that's the *shit*," said Chavez. "They no *here*, now you gonna *keep* me!"

"Go through them again, Gilberto."

"*They no here!*" Chavez shouted. Small, rough, workingman's hands curled. "I want out!"

"Easy, Gilberto."

"You lock me *up*, I do what you *say* and you still lock me *up*."

"That weed locked you up."

"That no mine."

Milo flashed him a pitying look.

"Weed," said Chavez, "is jus a ticket."

"Not that much weed, Gilberto."

Tears filmed Chavez's eyes.

Milo said, "Do your best for me and I'll help you."

"Fine, fine, fine! You want me look say *yes,* I say *yes.*" Jabbing the first page. "*This* one. This one. And *this* one, I give you three, okay? You want four, five? Okay, this one and—"

"Settle down, Gilberto."

"*Madre de Dios*—they no *here!*"

"Go through it one more time," said Milo. But his heart wasn't in it.

27

Milo slouched back to his office. Tried the lab again for prints in the Corvette.

The car had been wiped clean.

He knuckled both eyes. "Yeah, yeah, he's that careful but leaves the damn hat out in plain view. Maybe it fell off his damn head when he lit the damn fire and he got scared and ran. Figured the damn blaze would get rid of damn everything."

I said nothing.

"Don't use that attitude with me, sonny." He called San Antonio PD about the first drive-by of Gisella Mendoza's place.

Been and gone, no sign of unusual activity.

"When in doubt, gluttony."

At Café Moghul the bespectacled woman heaped his plate with every item on the buffet, added lobster just out of the tandoori.

"At least somebody loves me," he muttered, tucking a napkin under his chins.

The woman beamed.

As he finished his third bowl of rice pudding, Sean Binchy entered the restaurant. "Wouldn't bug you but some guy called twice in the last half hour, Loot, says it's about Martin Mendoza. I tried your cell but it was off."

Milo fumbled in his pocket, flipped the phone open. "Switched off by accident." Glancing at me. "Unless Freud was right and there are no accidents."

I said, "Freud was wrong about lots of things but this one I'll leave up to you."

"Huh." He turned to Binchy. "What'd this guy have to say about Mendoza?"

"No details, just that he wants to talk to you."

"How did he know to ask for me?"

"Beats me, Loot." Binchy pulled out his pad. "Name's Edwin Kenten, here's the number."

"Kenten phoned personally?"

"Yup. Why wouldn't he?"

"What I've been told, he's a guy gets people to do things for him."

Edwin Kenten put the lie to that by answering his own phone. His voice was nasal, thin, softened by a musical accent—wetlands Florida, southern Georgia.

"Lieutenant Sturgis, thanks for calling back promptly."

"No problem, Mr. Kenten. Who referred you to me?"

"Marty Mendoza's family gave me your name and it's Marty I'd like to talk to you about. I know you're extremely busy, sir, but if there's some way we could meet, I'd be grateful. We could have tea in my office. I'm in Westwood, Wilshire near Broxton."

"What's a good time, Mr. Kenten?"

"At your convenience, Lieutenant."

"I can be there in twenty."

"I'll leave your name with my parking man."

A gracious fourteen-story office building clad in limestone and brick and crowned by hand-carved moldings took up the southwest corner of Wilshire and Glendon.

Butting up against all that architecture was Edwin Kenten's fifteen-story headquarters, an assertively ugly off-white rectangle striped with garish blue glass.

"The gift," said Milo, "and the box it came in."

KNT Enterprises took up the top floor of the shipping carton, accessible by a key-operated elevator marked *Private.* The parking lot attendant was built like a bouncer, with a wide smile as deep as a decal. Phoning for authorization, he produced the key, turned twice. "Mr. K.'s ready for you. Have a nice day."

We stepped into a windowless, off-white waiting room carpeted in shag the color of a puppy's accident. An unmarked door at the rear was painted matte gray. The amenities consisted of four folding chairs haphazardly positioned, a coffee table hosting a jar of crumbling biscotti, a few plastic bottles of generic water, and two leaning-tower heaps of old magazines.

The man waiting for us was sixty-five to seventy, pudgy and bald on top with gray curls tufting above leprechaun ears. A powder-blue silk shantung shirt billowed over pink linen pants and white patent loafers. The shirt matched the man's curious eyes. The trousers color-coordinated with a diamond pinkie ring. The face of his wristwatch was larger than some cell phones.

He inspected both of us, guessed correctly. "Lieutenant? Eddie Kenten."

"Good to meet you, sir. This is Alex Delaware."

"Pleasure. You boys come in."

Kenten's sunburned face was a near-perfect sphere. Same for his torso and abdominal region, as if a trio of apples had been stacked carelessly. When he turned toward the door, each segment rolled with eerie independence. He appeared on the brink of falling apart and I felt myself tensing up to prevent disaster.

We followed him past a maze of plain-wrap cubicles. Twenty or so people worked quietly at phones and computers. Kenten waved to a few, smiled at everyone. Continuing toward the requisite corner office, he exuded gingery aftershave that hit us in gusts.

His personal space was predictably vast with blue-glass walls, but northern and western vistas were blocked by taller structures. To the east, the tops of Wilshire Corridor condos were barely visible. Only the southern view was free and clear: miles of houses and low-profile shopping sinking into the flight paths over Inglewood. Everything clouded by a milk-chocolate puff of smog.

A cheap-looking desk was heaped with papers where it wasn't crowded with framed snapshots. Some of the pictures were positioned for visitor viewing: a younger, thinner, crew-cut Kenten in formal army dress marrying a bony woman nearly a head taller, a slew of kids and grandkids in various stages of development.

A circular folding banquet table and plastic chairs served as the conference area. A plug-in kettle, tea bags strewn loosely, and more crumbling biscotti were the refreshments du jour.

Kenten said, "Can I pour for you fellows?"

"No, thanks, sir."

"You don't mind if I indulge, do you?" Ripping open a packet of Earl Grey, Kenten poured, steeped, pawed a biscotti, chewed noisily, unmindful of crumbs on his shirtfront.

Blowing into the teacup, he pursed his lips. "Nice and hot . . . thank you for coming."

"What can we do for you, Mr. Kenten?"

"Everyone calls me Eddie. I'll come right to the point: The Mendozas are worried you're looking into Marty as having something to do with the death of Ms. Elise Freeman. I'm here to tell you Marty had nothing to do with it."

"You know that because—"

"Because I know Marty, Lieutenant. I'm the one who brought him to Prep." Kenten put down his tea. "I thought I'd done him a favor."

"You feel differently now?"

"With the police chasing after him?" Challenging words, but twinkly eyes and grandfatherly cheer.

"We're not chasing him, Mr. Kenten. We'd like to talk to him."

"Why?"

"We can't get into that right now."

"Kind of a catch-22?" said Kenten.

"No, sir. Just the early stages of an investigation."

"A murder investigation." Head shake. "Never thought I'd be talking to the police about murder. Especially in regard to Marty. Trust me, Lieutenant, he had absolutely nothing to do with Ms. Freeman's death."

"He's told you that?"

Kenten put down his teacup. "No. I'm being logical."

"How well did you know Ms. Freeman?"

"I knew of her," said Kenten. "By reputation."

"What reputation was that, sir?"

"Sexually inappropriate."

"Marty told you that?"

Kenten lifted the cup. "She tutored many students, not just Marty."

"You heard it from another kid at Prep?"

"At this point," said Kenten, "I'd prefer not to get into *those* details. Suffice it to say they don't impact your investigation."

"I should be the judge of that, Mr. Kenten."

"Lieutenant, I didn't need to call you in the first place, so please don't punish civic responsibility. Let's just say that Ms. Freeman had acquired what you people would call a jacket—that is the correct term?"

Milo said, "A jacket is a criminal history, backed up by an official record."

"Well, then, let's say Ms. Freeman had acquired a . . . sweater. Something jacket-like—a cardigan."

Kenten chuckled. Encountered two stoic faces.

"Please forgive me, I'm not making light of her death. Terrible, terrible thing, no one should die unnaturally. I'm just saying she trod on shaky grounds with some male students, so perhaps you should broaden your focus."

"Sure," said Milo. "Give me some names."

"Someone I know—not Marty—talked to me in strict confidentiality. Someone with only thirdhand knowledge, so there'd be no point."

"School gossip?" said Milo.

"I'm sorry, that's all I can say."

"She was a cougar so she had to die?"

"Pardon?"

"You said no one should *have* to die unnaturally. That sounds as if she'd been sentenced."

Kenten massaged a freckled dome. "I thought I left that kind of parsing behind when I dropped out of law school. It was a figure of speech, Lieutenant. Look, I sympathize with Ms. Freeman and her family. I'm sure they're devastated. And I'm certain you'll eventually get to the bottom of it. But I'm here to tell you that the sooner you get away from chasing Marty, the sooner you'll succeed. He's a fine boy, I'd be proud to call him one of my own, and I've got six of my own, as well as nine grandchildren with two more on the way.

So I'd like to think I'm a pretty good judge of juvenile character and Marty's character is sterling. The same applies to his family, you'll never meet more upstanding, industrious people. I found out about Marty through Emilio. He works at my club and we've become friends."

Mistaking subservience for friendship, the way rich, delusional people do.

Milo said, "You've called us here for the sole purpose of offering character testimony?"

"Forgive me if I've wasted your time," said Kenten. "However, this isn't some situation where a friend of a friend asks me to write their offspring a letter to get them into Prep or Yale. I'm familiar with this boy's character in depth."

"You went to Yale?"

"Class of 'fifty-two, graduated at the bottom of my class, started law school, quit and went to Korea. You're ex-military, correct? Combat or ancillary?"

"I was a medic."

"That's combat," said Kenten. "I was ancillary. Monitoring inventory at one of the larger armories in Seoul. Taught me all about people, no need to get an M.B.A. after that."

"Glad it was a good experience for you, sir."

"Vietnam," said Kenten, "was a whole different ball of paraffin. My eldest, Eddie Junior, serviced helicopters, still won't talk about it. In any event, back to Marty: wonderful boy, bright, industrious, but for that blasted accident he'd be destined for stardom. Even with the injury, I'm holding out hope. The key is for him to take care of the shoulder, avoid undue stress. I'm afraid your chasing him doesn't help."

"Where's Marty now, Mr. Kenten?"

"Why are you after him?"

"I'd like an answer to my question, sir."

"What makes you think I know his whereabouts?"

"You're his mentor."

"And I'd be happy to mentor him now. Unfortunately, my efforts to reach him have failed, the poor boy's so frightened, who knows where he's gone?"

Kenten drank tea. "I'm surprised, Lieutenant."

"At what?"

"You didn't come back with the standard warning about aiding and abetting."

"*Are* you aiding and abetting, sir?"

Kenten laughed. "Hardly. I'm available to Emilio and Anna for support is all."

"For Marty, as well."

"Should he ask."

"If he does contact you, Mr. Kenten, you'll need to let me know."

"And you'll go straight to your boss."

"Pardon?" said Milo.

"No need to be coy, Lieutenant. We both know your boss's boy attends Prep and that raises the stakes. Needless to say, Marty or someone like him would be a much better suspect than a student from the right zip code."

"If you've got other students I should be looking at, Mr. Kenten, give me their names."

"If I did, I'd have already given them to you. Two things I do know: Marty's not involved and the chief's situation raises the risk of tunnel vision."

"The chief and everyone else in the department is interested in arresting the right offender for both cases."

"Both?"

"Yesterday, Ms. Freeman's boyfriend was beaten to death, his car stolen from his driveway. A young man was seen driving it away. I just returned from a dump site where the victim's car was found partially burned. All the contents had been removed except for a baseball cap that may have fallen off during the arson. Dark blue cap with what looks to be a gold *S*."

Kenten's cup held steady. So did his eyes. "That's your evidence? A baseball cap?"

"A South El Monte Eagles baseball cap."

"Marty hasn't pitched for them for over a year."

"It's not exactly a commonplace garment."

Kenten looked away. "I'm sure there's an explanation—anyone can buy a baseball cap."

"I'm sure your intentions were noble, sir, but from what I've heard, public school was a happier place for Marty than Prep. That would be good reason for him to hold on to a memento."

Silence.

"Sir, have you ever seen a cap like that in Marty's house?"

"I've never been to Marty's house."

"Has he been to yours?"

"I've had the entire family over for cookouts and such—we've got a fire pit, a game court, access to the beach, my grandchildren call it the Fun House. Marty hung out with my grandchildren. Does that tell you about my level of trust? There's no violence in the boy, Lieutenant."

"He ever show up wearing a hat like that? Blue with—"

"Never," Kenten snapped. "Never saw anything like that."

"We haven't latched on to him randomly, Mr. Kenten. Elise Freeman was frightened of him."

"That's ridiculous."

"Spoken like a mentor."

Kenten's blue eyes hardened. "Given your unique perspective

about me, I can understand your skepticism. But mark my words, Lieutenant: You won't solve your case—your cases—until you take off the blinders and stop pursuing Marty."

"Marty could help himself by showing up and submitting to an interview."

Kenten rose and rolled toward the door. "I've done my best to educate you. If I've frittered away your time, I'm truly regretful."

Milo said, "What did you mean by my 'unique perspective'?"

"Oh, come now, Lieutenant."

"I'm serious."

Kenten eyed him. "I'll take you at your word. What I meant was you need to be thinking about your boss's role in this investigation. Because of *my* involvement."

"How so, Mr. Kenten?"

"I was asked to serve on the Ad Hoc Public Safety Committee searching for a new police chief. I interviewed your boss and found him an interesting, capable man. But I had reservations about his judgment and his temperament. One example of his weaknesses in those areas was his pressing me to commit to hiring him early in the interview. Needless to say, I resisted, but apparently not with sufficient clarity, because he left that meeting convinced I supported him unconditionally. Nothing could've been further from the truth, though part of the blame may rest with me. I'm not one to confront, so he probably mistook lack of debate for assent. When it came time to vote on him—an allegedly confidential process—I was a dissenting voice. Since that time, he's convinced I sandbagged him."

Kenten plinked one elfin ear. "Lieutenant, don't tell me the moment he made the link between Marty and myself he didn't inform you of his version."

"Lieutenants and police chiefs don't meet regularly for tea, sir."

"That may be so, sir, but this particular chief meets with this particular lieutenant." Kenten took hold of the doorknob. Twisted, released, let his arms drop as if suddenly exhausted.

"Lieutenant Sturgis, I'm going to leave you with something to chew on: Your name came up during that first interview."

Milo blinked but remained impassive. "Did it?"

"Oh, yes," said Kenten. "He cited you as an example of what a tolerant fellow he was. I'm paraphrasing but his little speech went something like this: 'You know, Ed, there's a detective in the department named Sturgis, queerer than a second left shoe but does the job. Someone else would be put off by that lifestyle, but I keep my personal feelings of revulsion to myself as long as he continues to do the job. Send me a three-eyed, albino dwarf chimpanzee who can clear felonies, Ed, and I'll make sure it gets regular promotions.' "

Milo said, "That hasn't happened yet but we do have some knuckle-dragging primates in the department."

"Lieutenant, 'queerer than a second left shoe' is a verbatim quote. At the time, I wondered why he brought up the matter of homosexuality just to make a point. Years later, when I found out what he was saying about me, I figured it out. Not only does he think I'm insincere, he's convinced *I'm* gay. For the record, I'm not, though if I was I'd be comfortable with it. Any idea why he thinks that of me?"

"Why, sir?"

"I've donated substantial money to AIDS research, five million just at the U. Want to guess why I did that, Lieutenant?"

"You thought it was a good cause, sir."

"There are lots of good causes, Lieutenant. I prioritized AIDS because Major Andrew Jack Kenten, one of the finest fighter pilots the United States Air Force has ever produced, but more important a kid brother I raised after our parents died, was one of the first Americans to *die* of the plague. Your boss never took the time to learn that because *his* perspective makes it impossible for him to understand why anyone would operate outside a narrow range of selfish interest."

Kenten twisted the doorknob again. Smiled. "To be fair, I have been known to wear pastels from time to time."

"I see that, sir."

"Your boss can be an effective leader and he deserves some of the credit for the current drop in crime. Though we both know it's men and women such as yourself who do the actual work. Whatever his administrative virtues, he's wearing blinders on this case because for some reason, his son wants to attend Yale."

"For some reason?"

"I enjoyed my time there. But it's not where we get our education, Lieutenant, it's what we do with it. We both know the chief's primary goal is keeping the school out of the limelight until the letters come in."

"Marty Mendoza being a suspect could focus attention on the school."

"Not if he's no longer enrolled and is held up as an example of affirmative action gone wrong." Kenten's face flushed with anger. "To the people who run places like Prep, boys like Marty are serfs—hired help. Wrench a shoulder, good-bye."

"They hired Elise Freeman to tutor him."

"A formality and she knew it. That's why she shirked."

"Marty told you she shirked?"

"When I called to ask him how it was going, he said it wasn't going anywhere because she began sessions late, ended them early, and took phone calls throughout the hour. It was clear to Marty that she had no interest in him."

"Did she act out sexually?"

"Marty denied that, but he did say some of those calls were from male students and she was flirtatious."

"Marty denied after you asked him?"

"I asked him *after* he told me about the flirtatious calls," said Kenten. "I was wondering if he was veiling the truth to cover his own embarrassment."

"I've got a friend with a problem."

"Exactly."

"Flirtatious, how?"

"We didn't get into details, Lieutenant. I phoned Mary Jane Rollins, she said she'd look into it but I never got a follow-up and soon after Marty quit the sessions. But never once did he express anger toward her, Lieutenant. On the contrary, he laughed it off. To be frank, I think he was relieved."

"To be free of academic pressure."

"He's a bright boy, needs to have confidence beyond his ability to throw a baseball. If you allow another person's narrow self-interests to influence you, you'll be hindered, not helped."

Kenten flung the door open on office soundtrack. "Good luck to you."

The parking halfback handed the keys over. No more smile.

As we drove away, Milo said, "Talk about heavy-handed."

"Paying your bills with tax money can do that to you," I said.

"That reference to Yale, the clear implication was *Mess with me, I take it out on little Charlie.* Guy's way past overinvolved, Alex. Think there could be more than mentoring going on?"

"Another nosedive into yuck territory?"

"He does wear pastels." Smiling faintly.

"If Kenten's involved in something that sleazy and high-risk, why would he initiate a meeting and attract attention?"

"Because he can't imagine not getting his way. For all we know, Marty Mendoza's living a pampered life at Kenten's estate as we speak. His Graciousness tagged it as Paradise Cove but I looked it up and it's actually north of there, above Broad Beach. We're talking five-plus acres of oceanfront, one entry on PCH. Real easy to stash someone for a long time."

He got hold of Binchy again, ordered round-the-clock surveillance of the property's front gate, Sean alternating with Detective I Moses Reed and any "halfway intelligent" undercover officer they could find.

I said, "What about the Mendoza house?"

"That's mine. Rank has its privilege."

"El Monte outclasses Malibu?"

"I'm hoping the kid'll sneak back for some mama love. I get him away from the good life, he'll cave."

Spoken like a true hunter.

28

We met the next morning in an empty interview room. Milo and Moe Reed had been up all night. Despite clean living, the young detective looked beat. Milo's bear-on-the-prowl instincts kept him bright-eyed.

"First my show-and-tell, Moses, because it's brief: Martin's mommy showed up just after eight p.m., lugging a single bag of groceries."

I said, "Not cooking for a family?"

"For all I know it was a bag full of chocolate chip cookies for Marty. At ten twenty, Mr. M. arrives, still in his waiter's uniform, carrying what looks like doggie bags from the country club. No further action until seven a.m., when he leaves in a fresh uniform. I wager on him going to work and stick around to watch Missus. Seven forty-two, she drives to a day care center where a bunch of little kids greet her like the bestest grandma in the whole wide world. I phone the club, Mister's on the job."

"Hardworking folks going about their business," said Reed. "You could subpoena their phone records."

"I could if John Nguyen changed his mind about my having no grounds. How was your day at the beach, lad? I'm not seeing any tan."

"I'm one of those pink ones, Loo. Only place I could park was the land side of PCH ten yards up. What you see from there is a wall of hedges and big gates. I picked up from Sean after he trailed Kenten from the office to Mountain Crest, then home. By then it was close to six. Sean got photos of Kenten entering, guy wasn't exactly incognito, he tools around in a powder-blue Bentley Continental convertible, he's even got powder-blue caps on the wheels. It was me, I'd go black, charcoal at the lightest."

"Keep it assertive, huh?"

"We're talking five hundred sixty horses, Loo. Anyway, the top was down, no passengers, that model doesn't have much of a trunk."

"Muscle under the hood," said Milo, "and yet he paints it like a carousel pony. What does that say about him, Moses?"

Reed shifted his torso. His eyes darted to the left. "He likes to be noticed?"

"That must be it."

After Reed left, I said, "Carousel pony? You didn't really expect Reed to tag Kenten as gay."

"But you saw his eyes, that's what he was thinking, no? Interesting fellow, ol' Eddie. Either he's in serious denial or he really does have a thing for pastels. I made a few calls last night and the so-called gay community has nothing to say about him except they appreciate the AIDS money."

"So-called community?"

"Like we're a powder-blue monolith?"

His next call was thirty hours later, as I finished some court reports at home.

"Surveillance at Kenten's Xanadu and the Mendoza household has been as useful as a congressional subcommittee, same for drive-bys of Gisella's place. But as of twenty minutes ago, I am the proud recipient of my first bona fide tip on Elise. Anonymous, no call-back number, the clerk who wrote out the slip thinks the caller might've been male but she's not sure. For all I know, she screwed up the message but here it is: 'For the murdered teacher think May third, October eighth, November fifth.' "

I said, "Nothing like a little numerology to brighten the day."

"I already tried a bunch of historical websites and came up with zilch."

I copied down the dates.

"Freeman hasn't been publicized so this has to be someone familiar with the school. And please don't remind me that could include a prank by a preppie."

I said, "Do you find it interesting that it came in two days after you met with Kenten?"

"Pastel Eddie trying to divert me? Yeah, I thought about that and it would take his interest way past obsession. One of my plain-clothesers did get a little excited when a kid around Marty's age drove up to Kenten's gates this morning in a BMW ragtop. Unfortunately the tags traced to Garret Kenten, nineteen, address in Trancas Beach, probably a grandson. But that got me thinking. Kinda risky, not to mention sick, for Kenten to be shacking up with Marty when his young descendants have access to the property. On the other hand, Garret was in and out fast, left with the top down on the Beemer and a surfboard in back."

"Picking up gear at Grandpa's," I said.

"We'll keep watching both sites, maybe try to interview the Mendozas in a day or so. I've also got one borderline-interesting finding from the arson techs: Even accounting for incompetence, with the baseball cap found near the highest concentration of accelerant, it shoulda been totally toasted, not partially baked. Fire guys consider the fire wimpy. If you're gonna use accelerant, why not squirt rather than trickle? Toss in the open dump site and it's thought-provoking."

"The car was meant to be found, maybe with the hat in it? Marty Mendoza's being set up?"

"Eddie the K would sure love like that scenario. But it doesn't obscure the facts: Elise was scared of the kid, he's got psychological issues, and he rabbited. I need those two girls but Chavez got kicked out of custody."

"Chavez lives for weed," I said. "He's probably smoking up right now in that same apartment. That makes him arrestable at your convenience."

"Such faith in the goodness of human nature, from a scientist of the mind, no less."

"No comment," I said.

"You just made one."

Madame Internet's a seductress but she parcels out more tease than fun. Instead of logging on, I did it the old-fashioned way.

Staring at the dates on the phone tip until a headache came on and my blood screamed for coffee.

May 3

October 8

November 5

I finished a tall mug and half of another, brought the slip back to Robin's studio, explained what was going on.

She put down her chisel, studied. "Sorry, hon."

Blanche sighed.

I returned to my desk wondering if the tip really would boil down to a prank and I was wrestling with random numbers.

For argument's sake, assume a pattern.

Ignoring the dates, I studied the text.

That teacher. Something related to Elise Freeman's job.

Finals at Prep—someone's psychotic anger over a poor grade?

No, as a sub she wouldn't be administering any exams at all.

But her *side* job was preparing for a different type of test.

Two dates in the fall, one in late spring. I logged onto the Educational Testing Service website. October 8 was one of several scheduled dates for this year's SAT but May 3 and November 5 weren't.

Those who forget history are condemned to repeat it.

I pounded the keyboard like a chimp with a toy.

Both dates showed up on the previous year's calendar.

A second-grade teacher's voice sounded in my head.

You're such a thorough boy, Alex.

29

Milo loosened his tie, finished his fifth cup of coffee. Kept staring at the printout I'd brought him.

Finally: "What, Elise failed to boost one preppie's scores three separate times? Or a trio of preppies formed the We Hate Ms. Freeman Club and banded together to ice her?"

"Or she didn't fail," I said. "She succeeded but did it in an unorthodox manner."

"Such as?"

"Saving her client the hassle of actually taking the test."

"Sending in a ringer? What led you there?"

"Because that would be worth covering up. I searched for scandals involving stand-ins and found plenty. And those are the ones who got caught. The testing services are supposed to check handwriting samples, and I.D.'s are inspected at the door. But with a big crowd of test-takers and a ringer with a decent physical resemblance, you could pull it off. Also, sometimes the SAT's adminis-tered at Prep, but not on any of those dates."

"At Prep, no way a ringer could pass. Well, well, well."

"A test scam also fits with Elise's flexible moral boundaries and it could clarify the motive. Assuming the rape DVD was a hoax never put into action, she—probably in concert with Fidella—was no stranger to the concept of extortion. If the tip's righteous, it might also narrow your suspect profile: a rich kid pressured to get into a selective college, who'd failed to improve significantly with tutoring. That could be why her computer—and Fidella's—was taken. Her student records were in there."

"Rich kid with a gonzo bank account or his parents," he said. "Mr. and Mrs. Deep Pockets pony up for tutoring, then toss in a whole bunch more for someone to take the test for Junior because it's all about getting Junior into Harvard and Junior can't hack it on his own. The ringer aces the test, Junior buys himself a crimson sweater, everyone's over the moon. Then Elise hits 'em up for a serious sur-charge. But if it's only one kid, why three dates?"

"Once could've been the general SAT," I said, "the others the SAT IIs—achievement tests on specific subjects."

"We cover all your needs at the Academy of Scam."

"If we're talking big-time extortion, that could explain aban-doning the rape plot. This was so much easier and Elise would keep her job."

He got up, stretched, sat down. "With the stakes so high, how'd our tipster find out? And why be so cryptic?"

"Maybe a hardworking kid picked up on an unlikely score by another student and got resentful. Peer pressure would frown on snitching publicly, you'd be sentencing yourself to high school hell. And by exposing a scandal you'd be putting everyone at Prep at risk of taint, including yourself."

"I'm not really a rat, I'm just giving the cops a hint. They don't figure it out, it's their fault. Wonder what those ethical seminars they run at Prep would say about that."

He laughed. Turned serious. "Maybe Marty Mendoza's our tipster. He'd sure be p.o.'d watching some rich brat pay for a high score."

"Maybe," I said. "Though I'd think Marty would have less trouble being explicit. And something else: The basics of the scam could be right but the murder motive could be different. Not protection from blackmail, snuffing out the competition. Because the drive from Fidella's house to Sierra Madre runs right through Pasadena. And someone lives there who'd be a perfect ringer."

He stared at me. "Trey Franck."

"Brilliant, Prep alumnus, looks young enough to pass for a high school student, changes his hair color regularly."

"Not a hipster thing, a goddamn disguise. Does the grunt work and takes all the risk, gets tired of Elise and Fidella pocketing the big bucks."

"He's the one who directed you to Marty. We have only his word that Elise was scared of Marty. If that was a diversionary tactic, it worked."

"Oh, man." He shot up again, stomped into the hall, returned flushed. "I'm getting that itchy feeling, like I've been played. The whole Marty thing steered us away from Franck's relationship with Elise. All along you've been saying Elise's murder stank of calculation and brains. Franck's a chemical engineer, claims he hasn't worked with dry ice since he was a little kid but so what? Nothing adds fun to homicide better than a little nostalgia, right?"

"Franck as our bad guy also explains why Fidella got his brains bashed in. Franck had to finish both of them. Maybe he showed up at Fidella's house for a business discussion—now that Elise was gone, how would the scam continue. He didn't bring a weapon because he'd been there, knew Fidella had a pool cue. There is the matter of that alibi but he was up north for four days, could've had enough time by himself to fly down, do Elise, fly back. He was sleeping with her, may very well have a key to her house. And his presence wouldn't have alarmed her, she'd feel comfortable drinking in front of him."

"Then in goes the Oxy. So who are the two girls?"

"A couple of kids who'd do anything for a cute, older guy. For all we know, they're undergrads at Caltech. They could've even thought it was a prank. They're big on that, there: taking apart cars and reassembling them in dorm rooms, hacking into the Rose Bowl scoreboard."

He said, "The young guy driving away in the Vette could easily be Franck. And who better than a chemical engineer to orchestrate a controlled arson?"

"After ordering a South El Monte baseball cap that he leaves behind to set up favorite patsy Marty Mendoza."

"Evil," he said. "If there's something to the tip . . . okay, let's try to connect some dots, see if they lead to young Master Franck."

He phoned South El Monte High, talked to Jane Virgilio.

"Hi, it's Lieutenant Sturgis, again . . . no, not yet, but could you please check your student store and find out who bought an Eagles baseball cap within the last two months? Anyone who's not a team member . . . it's too complicated to explain right now, ma'am, and I'm really busy looking for Martin, so please check . . . yes, I know it's online but you must have access . . . yes, I'll be happy to wait."

After three minutes of toe-tapping, he gave a rocket-fueled thumbs-up. "Thank you *so* much, Ms. Virgilio, I'll be sure to tell the family you helped."

Grinning, he logged onto his PC. "Apart from players who lose theirs and the occasional alumnus, Eagle caps are a low-volume item, only one moved during the last sixty days. And get this, amigo: October twentieth."

"Twelve days after this year's SAT. Franck bought it himself?"

"I should be so lucky, but at least I've got a name: Brianna Blevins, address in North Hollywood. Which ain't that far from the ice place. If she turns out to be a voluptuous white girl, I'm gonna make her feel *real* uncomfortable. Yo Facebook!"

Brianna Blevins was nineteen years old, full-faced and prone to grinning vacantly, with gleaming black hair that hung past her waist and a pneumatic body showcased by a bikini shot that proclaimed *Less Is Not More.*

Not a student at Caltech; she'd graduated last year from North Hollywood High, was "looking for my place in the world."

Easy mark for someone with half Trey Franck's IQ. I wondered how the two of them had met.

If she did value the relationship with a Caltech genius, she wasn't advertising the fact. No shot or mention of Franck. But one of her frequently pictured friends was a pretty, slender girl with blond-tipped hair and overenthusiastic eye shadow.

Brianna's *BFF for sure and always, we party with our souls and dance to the same beat.*

Selma Arredondo.

Milo said, "Got to be La Flaca. Love this social networking."

Arredondo's page bore no reference to Franck, either.

He turned to the phone directories. No listings for either girl. "Maybe they still live at home, can't be too many Blevinses in North Hollywood . . . lucky me, only one: Harvey P."

No answer, canned voice-mail recording.

He left no message, searched for Arredondos in the Valley, found several, connected to most. No one knew Selma.

DMV coughed up driver's licenses for both girls, obtained three years ago when they were fresh-faced.

Brianna had racked up several moving violations in a Ford truck registered to Harvey Blevins.

Milo sang, "Til her Daddy takes the T-Bird away," found Selma's wheels:

Five-year-old black Honda.

"Chavez actually told the truth," he said. "It ain't quite enough to restore my faith in human nature, but maybe one tiny step forward."

Arredondo's address conformed to one of the no-answer numbers Milo had tried. He phoned it again. The only one without voice mail.

"That's why I don't play games of chance, bucko."

"Sal scored a jackpot and look what happened to him," I said.

"Let's pay Franck another visit. Don't wanna make him nervous so the cover story will be we found new evidence that implicates Marty Mendoza, e.g. the Corvette. Is there anything else he can tell us about the kid?"

"I wouldn't mention Fidella's murder. There'd be no reason for you to tell him."

"Makes sense. Same goes for bringing up Brianna and Selma. If Franck is connected to them, no sense giving them a heads-up. Any other suggestions?"

"Just be your usual master-thespian self."

He twirled the end of a nonexistent mustache. Punched the air again and clapped his hands. "Trey, my boy, I may be dumb but I can still nab your Einsteinian ass."

30

No answer at Trey Franck's apartment. The hallways of the dingy building echoed.

"Probably in the lab," said Milo. "Mixing up his potions or whatever chemical engineers do."

We made the drive to Caltech in three minutes. The chem-eng receptionist studied Milo's card. "Lieutenant? . . . one second."

She disappeared into an inner office. Her voice on the phone was a low buzz of anxiety. Moments later, a thin, white-bearded man in his fifties walked through the department's main door.

"Gentlemen? Norm Moon, I'm Trey Franck's dissertation advisor."

Milo held out a hand. "Professor."

Moon waved off the honorific as he shook. "You've located Trey? Please don't tell me something unfortunate has occurred."

"He's missing?" said Milo.

Moon tugged a beard hair. "You weren't aware, foolish of me

to assume. Then I suppose you're inquiring again about that tutor he worked for."

"Elise Freeman, Professor. Trey told you about that?"

"A few days ago, he seemed a bit distracted in the lab and I asked him why. He told me he'd just had a strange experience: interrogation by the police."

"We call it interviewing."

Moon smiled. "Be that as it may, Trey felt interrogated. As if you suspected him of something simply because he'd known the woman."

"Contacting a victim's acquaintances is pretty much routine."

"That would make sense," said Moon. "Nonetheless I'm sure most people don't enjoy the experience."

"How long has Trey been missing?"

"He's been absent from the lab for two days and we haven't been able to reach him. One of Trey's virtues is reliability. We're preparing an important paper so his participation is especially important."

"Perhaps," I said, "the pressure got to him."

"What pressure?"

"The paper added to his usual responsibilities."

"Hmm," said Moon. "No, I don't think so. Trey has never been the anxious type."

"Cool under fire. But the interview bothered him."

"He seemed more disappointed than anxious. That someone would think him capable of such violence."

"He described the murder as violent?"

Moon wet his lips with his tongue. "I don't believe we got into details—frankly that kind of thing doesn't interest me. I suppose he meant homicide, in general. Isn't the malicious dispatch of another human being always violent at the core?"

"When you and Trey traveled to Stanford were you together most of the time?"

"That sounds as if you're confirming an alibi."

I smiled.

Moon said, "Contrary to what you might think of academics, we do work hard. That was a work trip, our days were pretty much nine-to-five."

Milo said, "So Trey had evenings to himself."

"I'm his advisor, not his babysitter, I have no idea what he did at night. You might try Juliet Harshberger. She and Trey appear to be a bit of an item."

"You haven't contacted her?"

"I avoid meddling in my students' personal lives but I was contemplating doing just that."

"Where can we find Ms. Harshberger?"

"Most likely here, Lieutenant."

"In this department?"

"Here on campus. She's a grad student in biology."

"Thank you, Professor. Is there anything else you'd like us to know about Trey?"

Moon said, "Obviously I've enjoyed having him in my lab. He's smart and an excellent long-range thinker. In my field, problems often take years, even decades, to solve. Some of the brightest students fade when gratification slows."

"Trey on the other hand . . ."

"Is able to keep his eye on the core of the problem as well as the eventual goal." Moon stroked his beard. "You don't really think he was involved in murder?"

"Routine questions," said Milo. "Also, we like talking to smart people."

When we were out of earshot, I said, "Nothing like a careful planner."

"I was thinking the same thing."

In the biology office, two students studied the bulletin board as if it were a shrine.

Pinned to the cork were items for sale, birthday greetings to a professor, summer fellowship opportunities abroad, and a clipping about recent advances in computer simulation of fruit fly neural transmission.

Milo asked the receptionist where to find Juliet Harshberger.

"She's not here today."

"Any idea where we can find her?"

"No, sorry."

"Try her apartment," said one of the students, his eyes still on the board. Tall, dark, shaggy-haired, with poor posture, he giggled. "It'll be a high-probability endeavor because she's there more than she's here. Hell, maybe she'll even get her own lab there, never have to come in."

His companion, bespectacled, unshaven, stocky, raised an eyebrow.

The receptionist frowned. "Brian, is there something you need?"

Shaggy said, "No, Nadine, just spending a rare free moment searching for a potentially interesting way to spend July financed by someone else." To us: "*My* apartment's five rooms less than six, the walls start to close in."

The other student said, "Bitch, bitch, bitch."

Brian said, "And then you die, die, die."

The receptionist turned to us. "Anything else?"

Milo said, "Juliet Harshberger's address, please."

"I'm sorry, we're not supposed to."

Brian cackled and rattled off a street name and three digits.

Maliciously helpful but unnecessary. The girl on the veranda, snuggling up with Franck.

Nadine said, "Brian!"

Brian slapped his mouth. "Oops, silly me. Guess that slipped out because my prefrontal lobes are clogged from long nights of actually doing work."

"You're a prince," said his friend.

The receptionist said, "That was totally inappropriate."

Brian said, "So is coasting through grad school in the comfort of your six-room apartment with no serious obligations other than showing up to seminars while everyone else has to R.A. and T.A. and do mind-eroding scut."

Nadine flushed. "Brian, please—"

He stomped out, muttering, "Yeah, yeah, reality bites, big shocker." His friend looked at us, shrugged, followed.

Milo said, "Grumpy fellow."

Nadine said, "He just failed his orals."

When we caught up with Brian he was smoking a cigarette under an oak tree. The stocky boy had departed.

He sucked in a lungful of poison. "Once again, the gendarmerie."

Milo said, "Thanks for the info, Brian."

"Lucky for you, I'm an asshole."

"She's a rich girl, huh?"

"Her old man's Harshberger Petroleum Exploration. Nice *Texas* girl."

"Not smart enough to get in on her own?"

Brian ran a tongue inside his mouth. "Should I be fair or just spiteful?"

"Fair would be better."

"How about first telling me why the police are interested in her."

"It's in regard to her boyfriend."

"Sir Coiffure?"

"Pardon?"

"Her squeeze, the chemist. Changes his hairstyle every month. I figure he's researching dyes." Dry chuckle. "What'd *he* do?"

"He's a potential witness."

"To what?"

"Brian," said Milo, showing teeth, "I really need to be asking questions, not answering them. Juliet's not smart, huh?"

"She's plenty smart, but that isn't the point. Dr. Chang—my advisor—has never accepted more than one student a year and sometimes not even that. This year he took two."

"You and Juliet."

"After she applied months past the deadline. I'm on fellowship, she doesn't need one. Are you conceptualizing a causal thread?"

"So now you've got to carry her."

"It's not that she's increased my workload, Chang would be a slave driver anyway. But she's apparently exempt from everything the rest of us have to hassle with. Like I said, reality gnaws out huge chunks of raw flesh on a regular basis, but if she had a modicum of class she'd try to pull at least some of her damn weight."

"Six-room crib," said Milo. "Nice."

"Never been invited, but Chang was much impressed."

The Spanish-style building was even lovelier in daylight, trees perfectly barbered, shrubs glowing, sparkling beds of flowers a fauvist delight. A couple exited, arm in arm, white-haired, immaculately dressed, didn't stop to greet the petite girl on the veranda.

She wore the same Brown sweatshirt as when she'd put her head on Trey Franck's shoulder. The bench beneath her was stationary but she rocked back and forth, staring into the distance.

Like a whaler's wife waiting for a storm to disgorge her man.

She saw us coming. Kept rocking.

Milo's card caused her to burst out in tears.

◆

Juliet Harshberger's apartment was done up in authentic Deco-Moderne and fragrant with scented candles. Signed Cartier-Bresson prints hung on the wall along with an unsigned cubist painting. A long-haired white cat, so inert its occasional eyeblink seemed battery-driven, perched on a divan and ignored the proceedings.

Its mistress perched on the edge of a cream velvet chair trimmed in macassar ebony and continued to weep.

Milo's third tissue finally dried up the well.

"Ms. Harshberger—"

"I knew it would come to this. Trey was so scared, now you're going to tell me something horrid and nightmarishly permanent has taken place and I'll never be able to erase this terrible moment from my consciousness."

"We're not here to tell you anything bad. We'd just like to know where Trey is."

Juliet Harshberger's enormous pale green eyes stretched the limits of their sockets. She was five feet tall, probably less than a hundred pounds, with a pixie face dusted with buttermilk freckles under a mop of carefully layered mocha hair. Tiny pointy breasts fell short of filling her white cashmere sweater. Boyish hips were no more successful with razor-creased designer jeans.

Petite young woman easily able to pass as a high school student. I wondered if her bond with Franck extended to fraud.

She said, "You really don't know where he is? Well, neither do I and I'm worried sick. It's not like him to disappear."

Milo said, "What was he scared about?"

Her answer came too quickly. "I don't know."

We waited.

Juliet Harshberger said, "I don't *know*."

Milo said, "Where'd you do your undergrad work?"

That threw her but she murmured, "Brown."

So much for that rule.

"You went from there straight to Caltech?"

"I took a year off."

"Lab work?"

"I traveled. Why would you care?"

"I love to travel," Milo lied. "Where'd you go?"

"Europe, Southeast Asia." A beat. "Africa."

"World tour?"

Silence.

"Sounds nice."

"I *needed* to do it," she said. "Before the grind."

"Grad school's tough."

"Grad school at this place is . . ." Her eyes moistened again. "Everyone's a genius except me."

Milo said, "I'm betting you made summa at Brown."

Juliet Harshberger ground her teeth. "At Brown I was smart. At Caltech, I'm an inanimate object." Glance to the side. "Trey's a genius. He's been my lifeline."

"And now he's frightened. And missing."

She cried. He passed her another tissue. "What's going on, Juliet?"

"Just Julie."

"Tell me about Trey, Julie."

She shook her head. "I can't."

"What if he's in danger, Julie?"

"Please don't say that."

"I'm sure Trey told you about the murder."

Julie Harshberger reached for her cat. The animal rolled away, continued to feign sleep. "Omarine, you are *so* lazy."

"What did Trey tell you about the murder, Julie?"

"That you came to his place and interrogated him."

"When's the last time you saw him?"

"Then," she said. "Right after you left, he came here. The next day I didn't hear from him but sometimes he works late in the lab. It was only last night when I went by and he wasn't there for our dinner date. I was taking him to the Parkside Grill, it's my favorite. He hasn't been back since, nor has he come into the lab and his cell's not responding."

"What's he scared about, Julie?"

"I—I can't."

"We know about the SAT scam."

Her mouth dropped open.

Milo said, "Yeah, that was wrong but think about it: Trey was frightened enough to leave. So covering up and slowing us down could be hazardous to his health. When did he tell you about it, Julie?"

"A few months ago," she said. "It bothered him. *She* convinced him to go along with it."

"Elise Freeman."

"He said she would do anything for a quick buck."

"She hired Trey because he could pass for a high school student."

"Also, he was an alumnus."

"Of Windsor Prep."

Nod.

"That was important because . . ."

"All the students he sat in for were from there."

"Elise Freeman limited herself to Windsor Prep students."

"She told Trey it kept things simple. And she had plenty of business just from there."

"Lots of pressure to excel."

She grimaced. "I went to a place like that in Houston until I could no longer tolerate it and insisted I be sent to public school."

"Tough environment."

"Brutal, uncaring, selfish. Elise and some guy she hung out with exploited that."

"Some guy."

"Trey said he was pure sleaze, shake his hand and count your fingers."

I said, "How many SATs did Trey take for Prep students?"

"How would I know? I don't want to talk about it."

"Trey was okay talking about it."

"No, not really," she said. "We were discussing how insubstantial the world has become and he brought it up as an example."

"Of . . ."

"Something stupid and pointless. The test is a joke, there are tricks, it's really something you can figure out if you just pay attention."

"If you're as smart as Trey."

"My parents forced tutors on me from ninth grade on and they were useless. I understood that I needed to study specifically for the test, got 790 on the AP bio, 740 on the AP chem, 1490 on the SAT I. Back then it was out of 1600."

"Impressive."

"You think?" Her smile was unsettling. "My brother refused tutoring and got 1520."

I said, "Trey was a 1600 man."

"Of course."

"How much did Elise Freeman pay him?"

"I don't kn—oh, why not, she gave him five thousand per administration. She took more while he did all the work."

"How much more?"

"She'd never say, so he figured it was a lot . . . I hope he's okay."

Grabbing the cat, she stroked the animal hard enough to raise a startled mew. "Omarine, you're so warm . . . do you promise to help him if you find him?"

Milo said, "Of course."

"Then I'll tell you. It's not her he's afraid of. He's running from some kids."

"Kids he took the test for?"

"He's convinced they killed her to cover their tracks."

"Why?"

"He just said they're scary kids."

"What are their names, Julie?"

"He didn't *say*! I wish he did so I could *tell* you! I begged him, let's go to the police, my father knows people, I can make sure they do their job! He said, 'The less you know the better, Julie.' And now he's gone!" The cat jumped off her lap, curled in a far corner, and pretended to sleep.

Milo said, "Did he give you any details at all, Julie?"

"Rich kids," she said, as if it were a disease. "No surprise there."

I said, "Is there someplace Trey likes to go when he needs to think?"

"Here. I hold him, we listen to music, we both unwind."

"Did he ever mention the name Martin Mendoza?"

"No. Who's that?"

"Someone Trey talked about to us the first time."

"That name never came up. No names came up, he was trying to protect me." A small hand settled on a concave belly. "I'm feeling sick, I'll never be able to concentrate on my research."

"What's your topic?"

"Don't know yet, I'm somewhat of a searcher."

We made a second pass at Trey Franck's apartment, found the live-in manager's quarters on the top floor. The custodian of dinge was a forty-year-old physics student named Mario Scuzetti who didn't balk at unlocking Franck's flat.

"Sketchy tenant?" I said.

"We've had better," said Scuzetti. "As in paying rent in a timely fashion."

He stood outside the room as Milo scanned. Milo entered the bathroom, closed the door, emerged moments later. "Not here and nothing iffy, thanks."

Scuzetti said, "You find him, tell him to cough up last month's."

In the car, Milo removed a toilet-paper-wrapped wad from his pocket. "Left his toothbrush and toothpaste and hairbrush, which is kind of impulsive for a good planner."

"He probably wasn't thinking in terms of DNA analysis," I said. "You're not concerned about a warrantless search?"

"What search? I went in there concerned about the poor boy's safety because of what li'l Julie said plus everyone associated with the test scam dying unnaturally. Saw this material in plain sight and believed it might help us locate Mr. Franck, all in the interests of his personal safety."

He started the car. "Not to say DNA wouldn't be peachy but all I'm after now is a print I can match to the palm on Fidella's garage. Franck's smart and amoral. And you heard Moon: Franck had his evenings to himself, had plenty of time to fly in and out and do Elise. He knew we'd trace him through her phone records so he prepares himself, sics me on Marty Mendoza. That leaves him grace time to bash in Sal's head, after which he drives off in Sal's car, leaves it in plain sight with a hat that can be traced to Marty on the seat. And Julie just gave us the motive for all this mayhem: Franck's tired of doing all the work and being a junior partner in the scam. *Ergo* eliminate the middlemen. Everything fits, including his disappearance: He leaves personal things behind but skips out on the rent, because he's known for a while that he's gonna rabbit."

I said, "The cap being ordered soon after the October SAT test fits with serious premeditation. But since I'm your pal I'm going to point out a problem: If Franck's motive is to continue the scam, he'll need to be around."

"So he lays low, figures out a cover story, returns in time for the next round of SATs. Or, he got antsy because he felt we were getting too close. Given his skills, he can always find another prep school."

"Which leads me to another problem: Even if Franck's a psychopath, the smartest psychopaths avoid violence, not because they're repelled by it but because it's an inefficient strategy.

Franck's skills are portable, so why murder two people in order to eliminate them as business partners when he could set up shop elsewhere?"

"What a pal. So give me an alternative."

"Two murderous preppies covering their tracks."

"Given Franck's history, why would that be anything but another diversion?"

"It fits with both murders: Elise's was calculated, mean-spirited, a *Hah-hah look-at-me* piece of theater. Because she was in no position to resist. Sal, on the other hand, posed a great challenge, easier for two people to overpower him and bash him with a found object."

"Why wouldn't two homicidal kids bring a weapon, Alex? And covering up for someone taking your SAT is a better motive? If Elise and Sal—and Franck—went public, they'd be putting themselves in the crosshairs."

"It could be an excellent motive if you're a couple of indulged but intensely pressured brats waiting for the Crucial Letter when Elise Freeman lets you know she wants more dough or your future's blown to smithereens."

"Same problem, Alex: The scam comes to light, she's screwing herself."

"The fact that she considered the rape scam says she was willing to trade a bit of misery and exposure for the chance of big money. In both cases, she and Sal would figure the victims would settle quietly. Like any good cons, they timed the extortion to their prey's maximum vulnerability. And one more thing: The kids Franck sat in for didn't show up on Elise's doorstep randomly. Most likely, she was already tutoring them, but their scores just weren't edging high enough and they started freaking out. At the height of their anxiety, Elise says, 'You know, I've got a solution.'

And *that's* relevant because if they'd spent time at Elise's house they could be aware of *her* vulnerabilities: binge-drinking and poor judgment when it came to younger men."

"Party with Teach, spike her vodka with Oxy, then ice her. Lovely."

"For all we know, Fidella figured it out, was too greedy to refrain from putting on an additional squeeze. Unfortunately, he underestimated his victims."

"And Trey Franck misdirects us to Martin because . . ."

"Anything that keeps us away from the scam is in his best interest."

"Then li'l Julie blows it by being honest . . . I'll keep an open mind but my gut tells me Franck's an emotionally shallow little prick and he could still be the young guy seen driving away in Fidella's Vette. And need I remind you that Nosy Neighbor was pretty certain there was only one person in the car, not some deadly duo."

"Rich kids have their own cars," I said.

He rewrapped Franck's brushes. "I get a match to that palm print, it's no longer theoretical. Same for some juicy info from juicy Brianna Blevins, who I will locate even if it means an unprecedented level of sleep deprivation. Onward to North Hollywood, Jeeves."

"You're driving."

"I was speaking symbolically," he said. "Side effect of all the clever types I've had to contend with."

32

The Blevins residence was a pebble-roofed ranch house on a cul-de-sac north of Chandler Boulevard. Train tracks bisected the neighborhood, foisted on unwilling residents by transportation nannies on another futile quest to clear the freeways.

The house was neatly kept, as were its neighbors, but the lack of curbside trees gave the street a tentative feel. A spotless green Buick LeSabre sat in the driveway. A couple of sago palms sprouted from a lava rock bed below the picture window.

The man who came to the door wore a white shirt and gray tie, held a Palm Pilot in one hand, a stylus in the other. The furnishings behind him ran the gamut of green. The aroma of bacon had settled comfortably.

He poked the Palm, gave a befuddled look. Fifty or so, with the kind of bluish beard that never looks completely shaved and a salt-and-pepper brush cut. He screwed up his mouth as if yet another load of confusion had just been foisted onto his weary shoulders.

Milo's I.D. elicited a one-second examination. "Police? There was a burglary? Since the trains started running we're getting more unsavories, just like we worried about. But no serious problems. Yet."

"You're Mr. Blevins?"

"Harvey. What's up?"

"We'd like to talk to Brianna."

"*Now* what?"

"You've had problems with Brianna?"

"Maybe one day she'll settle down, get married, pump out a grandchild, and I'll understand why I became a parent in the first place." Blevins laughed, as if to scour bitterness from his voice. "Yes, she's given me problems. What the heck has she gone and done?"

Milo said, "We're looking at Brianna as a witness, not a suspect, Mr. Blevins, so if you could tell us where she is—"

"Don't know where she is, that's part of the problem. She's just like her mother, talk about genetics—here, come on in while I get my laptop."

We sat on a stiff green sofa as Blevins tucked his computer under his arm. "Excuse the mess."

The house was neater than a marine barracks at inspection. Despite the bacon perfume, the kitchen was spotless and a dishwasher hummed.

"Looks fine to me," said Milo.

"That's always Bri's excuse," said Blevins. " 'Looks fine to me, Dad, you want better, do it yourself.' "

"You're divorced from her mom?"

"Ten years ago but Glorietta's six feet under. Eight years, driving drunk. Luckily no one else got hurt."

I said, "By 'just like her mother' did you mean Brianna has a drinking problem?"

"She doesn't have one yet," said Blevins. "No teetotaler but she seems able to hold it, like I can. Due to my ex's issues, I did a lot of reading on the subject and it's a brain chemistry thing, luck of the draw."

"So her problems are—"

"She's got slut problems," said Blevins. "I know that sounds bad, a father shouldn't talk about his kid that way, but facts are facts. Even there, I can't blame her totally, it's also in the brain, Glorietta was a total round-heels, I didn't find out the extent until all these idiots show up at the funeral and start confessing to me. Classy, huh?"

His lower jaw swung from side to side. "It didn't bother me, we'd been divorced two years, but it did make me resolve to raise Bri the right way. Church, Girl Scouts, the works. For a while, it worked, she loved Sunday school, all the stories they told her. Then when she got to high school she fell in with the wrong crowd, started getting D's and F's. I took her to a bunch of therapists, they said it was a self-esteem issue. I had her tested, no learning disability, she's just one of those the best she can do is a C. So I guess she gave up."

"Started hanging with slackers."

"Slackers, sluts, kids bused in from the barrio or wherever, you name it."

"Was Selma Arredondo part of that crowd?"

Harvey Blevins's bushy eyebrows jiggled. "You know that one, huh? She get Bri in trouble?"

Milo said, "Her name came up as a friend of Brianna's."

"Some friend," said Blevins. "She comes in here, dressed in next to nothing, everything's bouncing and jiggling. Even Bri knows better than that. But what can you expect when they dance for a living?"

"Where do they dance?"

Harvey Blevins sat lower. "I don't like talking about it but every therapist said I need to be realistic, distance myself, finally let her take responsibility."

But he just sat there.

Milo repeated the question.

"What do you think, guys? I'm not talking ballet. We're talking a pole, okay?" He winced. "You wouldn't be asking all this if she didn't get herself into trouble. What's going on?"

"So far, nothing," said Milo.

Blevins peered at him skeptically.

"That's the truth, Mr. Blevins, and I'm sure it can all be cleared up once we talk to Bri. Where do she and Selma dance?"

"Don't know, don't want to know. They started doing it the second they turned eighteen and were legal. I tried to talk Bri into junior college. She said she'd never make as much money as she could doing . . . that. Everything nowadays is about money, right?"

Blevins checked his Palm Pilot. "Due at work soon."

"Where's that, sir?"

"Ref-Gem Motorworks, in Westchester. We build high-performance components for custom cars and boats. I'm on the paper end, assistant controller, reason I'm home at this time of day is with the economy they asked us to voluntarily cut our hours, so I'm down to thirty per week and they give me flex-time. Makes it harder on Bri 'cause I'm here more. She likes to be around when I'm not."

"So she lives here."

"When she chooses. The rest of the time? No idea."

"When's the last time you saw her?"

"That would have to be two—no, three days ago. She showed

up at eight in the morning just as I was leaving, big coincidence. Hello, good-bye, she usually comes in for food and clothes."

"Where does she work?"

"You call that work?" said Blevins. "All she'd tell me is gentleman's clubs. Like any gentleman would go there."

"Was Selma with her?"

"Selma dropped her off but didn't stick around, probably 'cause I was there, Selma knows how I feel about her."

"Bri doesn't drive?"

"She had a car but it got repo'd." Tight smile. "Guess *gentlemen* don't pay the bills."

"Do you have any idea where Selma lives?"

"Don't know, don't care."

"Who are Bri's other friends?"

"Her line of work, you don't have friends, you have oglers—oh, excuse me: *regulars.* That was a big deal to her, she kept trying to impress me with the fact she had *regulars.* I'm thinking great, some pervert has enough money to waste it on you. But I kept my mouth shut, what's the point?"

"Did she tell you anything about her regulars?"

"Rich, they're always rich, right? With the private jets and the platinum cards. I wanted to say, What, you found an old cassette of *Pretty Woman*?"

"What else besides rich?"

Blevins ticked off his fingers. "Rich, handsome, young, smart— goes to Stanford. Does that make sense? Stanford's up north, why would a smart person—any person fly down here *regularly* to watch pole dancing? Like there's no poles in Palo Alto."

"So we're talking one guy in particular."

"Two Stanford guys, one for her, one for Selma. Guess if you're going to fantasize, make it good."

"What else did she say about them?"

"It's actually relevant to something?" said Blevins.

"At this point, that's hard to say, sir. We collect as much information as we can, sift through."

"Doesn't sound too efficient."

"Sometimes it's the only way, Mr. Blevins. So what else did Bri tell you?"

"Two rich guys come in to watch her and Selma dance, soon they're taking her and Selma to Aspen, Vail, I forget which, some ski place. On a private jet, no less. This was months ago, it was summer, she tried to get money out of me for ski clothes. See what I mean? She can't even put together a logical fantasy."

Milo said, "Two guys, one jet."

"Maybe one owns it, the other gets to use it, maybe they're partners—hey, maybe you and I can *split* a private jet. What brand do you like? I'm a Buick guy, myself—guys, I really need to get to work."

We walked him to his car. Milo said, "Did Brianna ever put a name on these fantasy guys?"

"I'm glad you're getting it: fantasy. Like when after her mother died and she started wanting to be a princess. I told her, 'Look what happened to Diana.' "

"So no names."

"Actually, there was, something with a T. Trevor, Turner? Tristan, yeah Tristan. Like that's a real name. Right out of one of those trash paperbacks her mother used to read."

"Not Tremaine? Or Trey?"

Blevins thought. "Nope, Tristan. Like that opera—Tristan and Isabel."

"What about Tristan's friend?"

"If she told me his name I wasn't listening. When you see Bri, don't tell her I finked on her, it's tense enough."

He drove away and we got back in the unmarked. Milo put his cell on speaker and reached Moe Reed.

"Martin Mendoza's status as prime suspect has dropped, Moses, so no need for the watch on his parents, same for the Kenten estate. Unless you've picked up something interesting."

Reed said, "Early this morning, Officer Ramirez spotted Kenten's grandson entering again, another short visit, no surfboard. This time he had a passenger, but a white kid, not Mendoza."

"Two white boys in a nice car," said Milo. "I've got a lead on a couple of strip-joint enthusiasts claiming to be Stanford students." Milo filled in the details.

"Sure, Garret Kenten could fit."

"What did Garret's passenger look like?"

"They drove in and out fast, she couldn't even get a fix on hair color because he wore a baseball cap. But she says definitely Anglo."

"Blue cap with an *S* insignia?"

"She didn't specify. Want to hold?"

"Sure."

Moments later: "Tan, too far for any insignia, Loo. Brown shirt is the only other thing she can swear to."

"In my office is a Windsor Prep yearbook, Moses. Blue leather, fancy gold seal, it's right below the murder book. Go through it right now and look for any Tristans, starting with seniors. I'll wait."

"On the way, Loo."

A train whistle broke the silence, then faded west. A couple of ravens settled atop Harvey Blevins's house, pecked at gravel, dislodged a few pebbles and cackled in triumph.

Reed came back on. "Okay, got the book . . . here's the senior class . . . no Tristans . . . here's a Trist*ram*. Big dark-haired kid, kinda got that actor thing going on—the fake smile, you know?"

"Could he pass for twenty-one?"

"Oh, sure, easy. Want me to check Trist*ans* in the junior class?"

"Go."

Moments later: "Nope, just one Tristram, last name Wydette." Reed spelled the surname.

Milo and I looked at each other. The morning we'd met up with President Helfgott, he'd flown in on a Gulfstream borrowed from a Myron Wydette.

Milo said, "Fantasy springs to life."

"Pardon, Loo?"

"What does the book say about Young Master Tristram?"

"His extracurricular activities," said Reed. "Business club, foreign policy club, Model U.N., mock trial, varsity baseball, varsity golf—they've got a golf course?"

"Nine holes. I'm more interested in the Great American Pastime."

"Sir?" said Reed. "Oh. The hat in the car. Maybe he played baseball with Mendoza, developed a grudge?"

"Or he just knows a good scapegoat when he sees one. Moses, run him through every damn database you can find, then do a search pairing his name with Garret Kenten's. That comes up empty, go through the yearbook page by page to see if there's another male he's been photographed with consistently. If so, search that name also—and pair it with Garret, just to be safe. Sean in the shop today?"

"Still at the Mendoza house."

"At this hour?"

"Plainclotheser called in sick, Sean said he'd double-shift. Guy's got a bladder the size of Australia."

Milo said, "Don't rub it in, lad. One more thing: When you look into Tristram don't just count parking violations, look for consistent addresses on the citations, maybe it'll lead us to a strip joint or two or three. I *need* those girls."

"Done, Loo."

He got hold of Binchy, told him to get over to Harvey Blevins's house immediately, do his usual "eagle-eye."

"Thanks for the compliment, Loot."

"Thank me by producing."

We sped back to my house where Milo commandeered the computer.

Sometimes money intersects with fame. At a higher level, it can also purchase obscurity.

Keywording *myron wydette* produced only five hits and a single image.

The citations were a quintet of charity benefits with Myron and Annette Wydette's names embedded in lists of major donors.

American Cancer Society, the eye clinic at the U., Planned Parenthood, a pair of galas for Windsor Preparatory Academy.

Only the ophthalmology reference hinted at the source of Wydette's income: *Mr. and Mrs. M. Wydette and the Wydette Orchard Foundation.*

Muttering "peaches," Milo found a handful of references to a family fruit-growing concern founded by Myron's great-grandfather during Gold Rush days and sold a decade ago to Trident Agriculture, a publicly traded corporation. Myron Wydette's name remained on the board of directors but he didn't seem to be involved in day-to-day activities.

The solitary image was of a broad, ungainly-looking white-haired man with a benevolent, somewhat bleary-eyed frog-face, arm in arm with a tightly coiffed, tightly toned, tightly tucked brunette half a head taller.

Milo said, "Sounds like Tristram got his looks from Mommy."

Pairing *wydette* and *stanford* pulled up a three-year-old article in the university's magazine about a trio of incoming freshman, ostensibly picked at random. Annie Tranh was the granddaughter of Vietnamese boat people and a Westinghouse Science Award winner. Eric Robles-Scott was a biracial kid from Harlem who'd won a national competition in foreign languages by demonstrating proficiency in French, Swedish, and Gullah dialect.

Aidan Wydette of L.A. was the tenth member and fourth generation of his family to grace the Palo Alto campus.

Aidan's headshot revealed a dark-haired, thick-necked boy with an open, confident smile. Note was made of the Wydette clan's long history of contribution to higher education but no dollar amounts were mentioned and care was taken to list Aidan's qualifications: "outstanding scholar and athlete" at Windsor Preparatory Academy in Brentwood, National Merit Scholar, summer internship at a Washington, D.C., think tank where he'd co-authored a paper on fiscal policy in emerging democracies, followed by a summer at the sports section of *The New York Times*.

Achievements at Prep included "a full academic load," varsity letters in golf, hockey, and soccer, captain of the Model U.N. team and mock trial, co-captain of the business club, co-founder of a program donating unused restaurant food to the homeless.

Milo said, "Guess the Nobel comes in his sophomore year."

I said, "Three sports for him, only two for Tristram, Tristram serves on Model U.N. and mock trial, but Aidan's the captain of both teams."

"If Li'l Bro doesn't make National Merit, he's reduced to peasant status? Yeah, that would kick up the pressure."

"Merit scholarships are based on PSAT scores. Your percentile's high enough, you write a legible essay, you're in."

"Fake a score, get an award," he said. "Hell, maybe we're not just talking Tristram. For all we know *Aidan's* résumé got pumped up the old-fashioned way."

"Cheating as a way of life."

"You read the papers." His pocket jumped as his phone played a too-fast Bach prelude. No more "Für Elise." Did that mean something?

Moe Reed broke in. "Can't find a single link between Tristram Wydette and Garret Kenten, though Garret did graduate from Prep four years ago."

"He goes to college somewhere local?"

"There's no record he goes anywhere, the only thing that comes up under his name is a band. You'll love this: the Slackers. But there is a kid in the yearbook who's with Tristram in ten photos. Seven are from the baseball team, but there're also shots of the two of them horsing around on campus. To me they look like buds, Loo."

"What's this prince's name?"

"Quinn Glover. He doesn't have a record and neither does Tristram but your idea about parking was good because Tristram has piled up a lot of paper on or near Los Angeles Street, downtown. That's industrial but there used to be rave clubs in vacant buildings so maybe there're strip clubs."

"They bother enforcing parking there?"

"A while back there were complaints about drug deals so Central blocks off the area after six p.m. I guess once in a while they do enforce."

He read off the addresses on the citations. "One more thing, Loo. Quinn Glover's daddy is CEO of Trident Agriculture—that's the outfit Tristram's daddy sold his orchards to."

"Multigenerational ties that bind," said Milo. "Make up six-packs with each of these kids' faces. I'm gonna troll for a couple of pole dancers."

◆

The block was grubby, dim, lined with warehouses and industrial buildings, a good half of them vacant. Loose garbage specked the sidewalk. The air smelled oddly of raw pork and rubber cement. Signs every ten yards warned *No Parking 6 p.m. to 6 a.m.* No one in sight but for a few homeless men lolling or driving carts. Some of the drivers managed a straight line.

The Hungry Lion Gentleman's Lounge occupied a windowless maroon cube. A stretch of dirt and broken asphalt running behind the buildings served as parking. The space behind the club was empty. Posted hours on the gunmetal door out front said the merriment wouldn't start for another two hours.

A sign above the building featured a leering simba wearing a red paisley shirt and mirrored sunglasses and sporting a slicked-back mullet-mane. One manicured paw clutched a glass of something fizzy. The other held a wild-eyed, grinning, unclad blonde. The girl's expression said her ultimate life goal had been achieved.

Milo said, "King Kong was ambivalent, this critter's licking his chops. Hungry, indeed." He rapped the metal door, evoked a barely audible thud.

One of the cart-pushers rounded a corner, spotted us, and nearly overturned as he attempted a sharp U-turn. Contents shot out of the cart. We caught up as he stooped to reload cardboard boxes, newspapers, cans, bottles.

Milo bent to help him with the last few treasures.

"That's okay, Officer, I'm fine."

"Know anything about that club, friend?"

"I know to stay away, Officer."

"Bad influence, huh?"

"Bouncer getting upside your head is a bad influence, Officer. Used to be quiet around here, nice place to spend the night, then that place opened and it's like they own the whole street."

"Ever get close enough to see the girls?"

"The girls go in through the back."

"Same question, friend."

"Something happen there, Officer?"

"Still the same question."

The man said, "Sometimes the girls come out in front to smoke."

Milo produced Brianna Blevins's and Selma Arredondo's DMV photos. "That include these two?"

"These two," the homeless man echoed. "Big and little." Massaging his chest. "Yeah, they're always together."

"When's the last time you saw them?"

"The last time . . . hmm." Something changed in the man's eyes. Clearer, more purposeful. "I could sure use some breakfast, Officer."

"It's closer to dinnertime—what's your name, by the way?"

"I'm called L.A."

"Love your city?"

"It's for Loving Albert. My auntie who raised me called me that. She was a moral lady, would sure like me to have breakfast— I like breakfast anytime of day, Officer."

"Help me out, L.A., and you'll be breakfasting with the best of them. When's the last time you saw these two girls?"

"The last time . . . I'm thinking two nights ago, yeah, two, not last night, last night was the Ebony Princess contest, they had only black girls. Plenty of white guys coming in to watch, though."

"Two nights for sure or a guess?"

"For sure, Officer."

Milo gave him a twenty.

The guy stared at the bill. "I guess that could go two breakfasts."

"Who said anything about two?"

"My auntie was big on nutrition."

"Ever see these girls with the same customers consistently?"

"No, sir," said the man. "They with each other, always laughing, you know?"

"Know what?"

"I get the feeling they *like* each other." Three rapid winks caused the opposite side of his face to contract like a harried sea anemone. "Wonder which one gives and which one gets."

The twenty remained in his outstretched palm. Filthy palm but when he closed it over the money, he exposed trimmed nails. Go know.

"Twenty more, I could have three, four breakfasts, Officer."

Milo peeled off an additional ten.

"Another twenty would be nicer, but thank you, Officer."

"You lie to me, we're going out for a four-course dinner and you're picking up the tab, L.A."

"Whoa." Laughter. "That could clean out my 401(k)."

As we edged out of the downtown business district and got on Sixth Street, Milo said, "I'll be back when it opens, need to figure out a good watch-spot."

"Let's buy gold chains, return as gentlemen."

"Acrylic shirts I've already got—all that breakfast talk got me thinking Paul Revere."

"Little too early for a midnight munchie ride, Big Guy."

"I'm talking one by land, one by sea. As in surf and turf, as in the T-bone-fillet-langoustine combo at that place on Eighth."

I said, "Don't want my patriotism questioned."

We were well short of the steak house when Sean Binchy phoned in.

"Got Bri and Selma, Loot. Right in front of the father's house, I barely turned off my engine when they showed up."

Dropping names as if he and the strippers were old friends. Sean loves the world, an attitude unchanged by facing felonies daily.

Milo said, "Take 'em into custody."

"Already done, we'll be at the station in twenty. They've got interesting stories, Loot."

"About the murders?"

"No, nothing like that, just how they're thinking of turning religious, leaving the life."

"Tell 'em to hold off on repentance, Sean. I need 'em in full sinner-mode."

Brianna Blevins and Selma Arredondo wore white tank tops cut high enough to expose drum-tight midriffs, second-skin jeans, backless high-heeled sandals, oversized hoop earrings, gold-plated bangles cuffing their right wrists.

Both girls had eyebrow pierces, tongue studs, multiple holes in their ears. Selma sported a diamond between a perky mouth and a cute chin.

Brianna's visible tattoos were: a left forearm sleeve filled with roses and thorns, a barbed-wire biceps ring, a female devil's face in the hollow beneath her neck, *Love* inked in black gothic across one collarbone, *Devotion* stretching the length of the other.

Selma's neck was circled by a blue-and-red-ink necklace of yellow diamonds and red links "supporting" a pear-shaped black pearl that was a masterpiece of trompe l'oeil. Both of her arms were slave-braceleted three times. Chinese characters rose up from where cleavage would be if her breasts could produce such.

Milo asked her, "What does that say?"

"Something about life."

Cell phones confiscated and purses searched, the girls were placed in separate interview rooms and left to contemplate.

Fueled by adrenaline, detective room coffee, and a vending-machine roast beef sandwich that made him grumble about "turf that didn't deserve surf," Milo started with Brianna.

The girl, looking older than nineteen, eyes already running to crow's-feet, kept her eyes on the table.

"Hi, Bri. Me, again. And this is Alex."

"Uh-huh."

We sat down, crowding her. "Tell us about Tristram and Quinn, Bri."

"Don't know 'em."

"Actually, you do, Bri."

"I don't."

Milo showed her pictures. "Tristram Wydette and Quinn Glover, hot guys, I can see the attraction. Hot rich guys, Tristram drives that Jaguar, Quinn's got that yellow Hummer. They tip well for lap dances?"

The girl barely glanced at the images. "I still don't know 'em."

"Actually, you still do, Bri."

He gave her a few seconds to reconsider. When she remained mute and sullen, he scooted even closer. She looked over her shoulder, searching for room to escape. Saw blank wall and exhaled.

"Bri, we already know a lot, so you might as well help yourself. Let's start with you and Selma meeting Tristram and Quinn at the Hungry Lion, then partying together for months. We've got their credit card records, so we know when they started coming in, how much money they spent on you. We've got other sources, so we also know about the promises they made."

Pausing to give her a chance.

Bri Blevins shook her head.

"Promises of amazing stuff," he went on. "Like taking you guys on a private jet to Aspen. And all you had to do was be nice."

He let the last word sink in. The taut flesh sheathing Bri Blevins's scapulae turned rosy, bottoming the love-devotion message in rose.

She still had the capacity to blush.

Milo said, "We don't care about that kind of nice, Bri. The only nice that interests us is a favor you did for them on a certain night. Something you worked out with Gilberto Chavez. Know who that is?"

"No." Emphatic.

"He's a Spanish guy you paid to buy dry ice, out in Van Nuys."

False eyelashes quaked. The blush across her chest seeped out as if liposuctioned. "Remember that, Bri?"

No answer.

"Different kind of ice from what you're used to," said Milo. "We found that nice little chunk of meth in your purse. Selma said you're the one always bought, she just shared."

"That's a lie!"

"Your word against Selma's, Bri, and Selma's being helpful. But honestly, Bri, the dope's no big deal, I couldn't care less about that kind of ice. What I do care about is *dry* ice. 'Cause that was used for something bad, Bri. You know what I'm talking about."

The girl blinked, crossed her arms across her torso, and dropped her head. "Uh-uh."

"Actually, you do, Bri. And unfortunately for you and Selma, you also knew the dry ice was going to be used for something really bad. And guess how we know that?"

Shrug.

"We know because Selma told us, Bri. How else would we

know? You buy ice for some rich dudes, no problem. You buy ice knowing it's going to be used to kill someone, big problem, that's called accomplices before the fact. According to the law, that's the same as committing murder."

Bri Blevins looked up, tried to match his stare. Couldn't handle five seconds before she dropped her head to the table.

"Selma's already cooperating, Bri, and that's buying her a lot of goodwill. She may be your homegirl, Bri, but she's smart enough to realize that a life sentence for murder changes everything."

The girl's head shook from side to side. I'd heard moans like hers on the cancer ward.

Milo said, "It doesn't need to be bad, Bri. You've got one chance to tell us your side. After that, it's Selma being smart and you being stupid and ending up in the same situation as Tristram and Quinn. Up to you."

The head shaking rotated in a strange way, morphing to a nod.

"They're bad," she said.

"Tristram and Quinn."

"Yeah. Not the good kind of bad."

We've been partying like . . . months," said Brianna
Blevins.

"Where'd you meet them?"

"They came into the Lion, paid for lap dances, bought champagne, got into the VIP room."

"After that, then you started partying."

"Yeah."

"They party with anything besides meth?"

"Single malt," she said. "They always had bottles of it."

"Booze and ice," said Milo. "Then there was a different kind of
ice."

Brianna Blevins grinned.

"Something funny, Bri?"

Her smile died. "Not, it's just . . . when they asked us to buy it
we're like a different ice? Selma said it. Being funny."

"Did Tristram and Quinn laugh?"

"Um . . . uh-huh, they laughed all the time."

"Coupla happy guys."

"Why not? They had everything."

"What's everything, Bri?"

"Money, cars, they could do what they want. They're hot."

"And on top of all that, they had you and Selma for partying."

The girl's eyes drooped as her face turned ancient. "We knew we were like . . . a game, you know? They were going to Stamford College, said they'd take us but we knew that was bullshit."

"Stanford University in Palo Alto?"

"I guess."

"Tristram and Quinn promised to bring you and Selma to college."

She snorted. "Set us up in our own apartment. To be their mistresses. They liked that word. Mistresses. Like how kings and princes do it."

"Two fresh princes from Bel Air, huh?"

"Guess so."

"Did you believe the private-jet promise?"

"Probably not."

"But maybe a little at first," said Milo. "You were hoping."

"We thought it would be cool." Tears rolled down the girl's cheeks, tracked through thick foundation. "We were just a game. They showed us pictures. Of the place—Q's place, it's his family owns it. Up in the mountains, they walk out of the house, go skiing."

"Q being Quinn Glover."

"Uh-huh. Place was fiercely huge, they got a movie theater. We're like that would be cool. But no way, we knew they were lying."

"Same for the promise to set you up at Stanford."

"Stamford they'll meet girls like them, we're like stuck in a stupid apartment, can't dance, they're like you're our mistresses. No friggin' way."

"You're a smart girl, Bri."

"Not so smart. I'm here."

"Maybe we can clear that up. Let's talk about the day you paid Gilberto Chavez to buy dry ice."

"We didn't know him, we just found him."

"Where?"

"Walking on Saticoy. They said go there, there's always Mexicans need money."

"Selma take offense at that?"

"Huh? Why?"

"Selma's Mexican."

"Half, only her dad. She don't know him." She wiggled her fingers. "Could I have a smoke?"

"Not yet, Bri, but I can get you something to drink."

"Um . . . diet orange?"

"If we've got it. Second choice?"

"Diet Sprite."

He left the room. I smiled at her. She said, "I could really use a smoke. Is it like no smoking all the time?"

"He can be flexible."

"Oh."

Milo returned with a can of Diet 7UP, popped the tab. She sipped.

Milo said, "You found Gilberto Chavez walking on Saticoy."

"They surprised us. Tris and Q. We were gonna go to work then they called. They're like call in sick, we'll party all day. *We're* like no way, we'll get in deep shit with Leandro—that's who owns it. They're like fuck Leandro, we'll pay you boo-koo more than Leandro's gonna pay you, you say you got the flu, Leandro's gonna be cool 'cause you're the hottest dancers in the place."

Shy smile. One part of her brain still gloried in the flattery. "We're like no way. They're like we'll buy you dresses and shoes, four bottles of champagne next time, Leandro'll be chill."

"Was he?"

"Nope, he was pissed."

"So you didn't go to work. Then what?"

"Selma was already at my house 'cause my dad was gone, Tris and Q picked us up in a car, not the Jag, not the Hummer."

"What kind of car?"

"GMC Yukon."

"Color?"

"Black. They're like the Hummer's broken, this is a loaner. Except I saw an Avis label on the bumper."

Milo eyed the one-way glass. "Black Yukon from Avis, sharp eye, Bri. So where'd you guys go?"

"A hotel. They had it set up."

"Set up for . . ."

"Partying. Grey Goose, ice bucket, grapefruit juice, orange juice, pomegranate juice—oh, yeah, cookies and cakes . . . chips and guac, too."

"Which hotel?"

"Next to Universal Studios."

"The Sheraton?"

"That's it."

"Meth?"

"Mostly weed." Her eyes darted upward. "Yeah, some of that, too."

Milo said, "What else?"

"Oh, yeah, pills."

"What kind of pills?"

"Vitamin R, Trank."

"Ritalin and some sort of downer," he said. "Doing the old roller coaster, huh?"

"Head-surfing," she said. "It's like exercise, aerobics, you know?"

"R and Trank—aren't you leaving something out, Bri?"

Whispered answer, too soft to hear.

"What's that, Bri?"

"Ox."

"There you go," said Milo. "Who liked to party with Ox?"

"No one, they never had it before."

"But Tris and Q brought it that day."

"For later," she said. "For . . . when it's time to do the bitch."

"They didn't use a name, Bri, because you knew who they meant."

"No," she said. "They didn't use a name 'cause we didn't know a name. It was always 'the bitch.' "

"But you knew who they were talking about."

"The teacher," she said. "They talked about her all the time, we thought they were screwing around."

"About . . ."

"You know."

"I need to hear it from you."

"Doing her," she said.

"Killing her."

"Uh-huh."

"Why'd they want to kill her?"

"They were . . . they don't get mad, they're always laughing. More like . . . I dunno, like it was something they had to do."

"Why'd they have to kill the teacher, Bri?"

"She wanted to do *them.* Not the *same* do, do *them* like get it *on.*"

"The teacher wanted to have sex with Tris and Q."

"She was always showing herself."

"How?"

"Wearing no bra when they came over for lessons. Bending over, you know?"

"Tris and Q decided they had to kill Elise because she flirted with them?"

"They're like she's always horny, it's gross."

Milo sat back, stretched. Yawned theatrically. " 'Scuse me—by the way, Selma told us the real reason Tris and Q wanted to murder Elise. That's her name, by the way. Elise Freeman."

"What'd Selma say?"

"Guess."

"Um, Tris and Q were like we already paid her, now she wants more, the bitch."

"Keep going, Bri."

"They're like we paid her for taking a test—the SAT, that college one, so they could go to Stamford like everyone in their family. She did it for Tris's brother and Q's sister and other people, never bugged them but now she wants more, says she knows all the secrets. *That* pissed them off. It wasn't fair."

"I can see their point."

"Yeah. You pay, you play, except now she wants more, going to Tris and Q, not the parents like before, she's like you got your own money, take it outta your own money. They're like that's for partying. They're like she thinks we're vul-rable, we'll show her who's fuckin' vul-rable."

"How much extra was she asking?"

"They didn't say."

"How much did they pay her in the first place?"

"They didn't say that, either."

"So they killed her."

"It was also her being horny," she said. "Thinking she was hot when she was not. They said maybe we can do her if we close our eyes. Tie her up, DP her."

"That sounds kinda angry, Bri."

"No," she said. "They were laughing."

Milo rubbed an eye. "So they decided it was time to kill her."

"Uh-huh."

"How'd you feel about that?"

"I didn't know her."

"Okay . . . so now it's time to buy ice. Why?"

"To keep her cold," said Brianna Blevins, as if explaining to an idiot.

"Why'd they want to keep her cold?"

"They didn't want her to smell. Like if they had to take her somewhere. Then they said we'll do her here and use it anyway 'cause she thinks she's hot, now she's gonna get real cold. Then they laughed some more."

"How'd it go down?"

"They followed me back to my house and Selma and me got into Selma's car. They followed me and Selma to Fashion Square and bought us dresses and shoes and some jewelry from one of those carts. Then we went to Pizza Hut and ate. Then when it was starting to get dark, they followed us to Van Nuys and we cruised around and looked for a Mexican who needed money. We found a guy, he brought the ice to Selma's car."

"Then what?"

"That's it."

"Bri, if that was it, Elise Freeman would still be alive."

"Oh, that," she said. "They drove to her house."

"You did, too."

"We had the ice in Selma's car, they took it out with these gloves they had."

"Rubber gloves?"

"They said it was from the science class at school."

"Smart boys," said Milo.

"Not so smart they could take their own SAT."

"Good point, Bri."

"They do it at school, also," she said. "Cheat off smart kids, get the A's. Tris says it's preparing him for what he wants to do."

"Which is what?"

"Be president."

"Ah."

"He could do it, sir. He's hot, knows how to make good speeches."

"What about Q?"

"Q just wants to make money. He's gonna find some way to run like a charity so he looks like he likes poor people. Then he's gonna take the money."

"Okay . . . so now you're all at Elise's house—what time is it?"

"Dark," she said. "Tris calls her on the phone, he's like we're bringing all the money, also some Grey Goose—they took the Grey Goose from the hotel—we'll celebrate you getting the money and us going to Stamford."

"What'd Elise say?"

"Tris is like she's totally into it. He's like her voice is all drunk, already."

"Then what?"

"Then they go inside her house for . . . a long time."

"How long?"

"A long time, I dunno. Selma and me are getting bored. Then they come out laughing, say the bitch is *definitely* gonna be chill."

"How'd they actually kill her?"

She licked her lips. "Selma already told you."

"You need to tell me, Bri. For your sake."

"Okay . . . so here's what I'm gonna say: They're like we put Ox in the Grey Goose bottle, she got totally blasted, fell asleep, then they're like we put a towel over her nose and her mouth and she stopped breathing, she didn't even move, it was like going to sleep. Then they put ice in the bathtub, put her in it."

"So the ice was kind of a joke," said Milo. "For laughs."

"They're always laughing. Q called it a science project, said when he was little they did tricks in school with dry ice."

"Where were you and Selma when they were inside the house?"

"In Selma's car," she said. "We never went in, just like Selma told you."

"What were you doing in Selma's car?"

"Waiting. Getting bored. Okay, we smoked up a little. We were bored."

"Did it bother you?"

"What?"

"What Tris and Q were doing inside the house?"

"They told us later."

"You knew they were gonna kill her, Bri."

"Maybe they were kidding."

Milo smiled.

"Like I said, sir, I didn't know her."

Selma Arredondo sat with her arms folded across her flat chest. Exceptionally pretty girl even in station light, but hard-eyed and tight-mouthed and hostile. The sinew and bone and sharp angles of a carnivore that needs to consume its weight daily.

She said, "I'm not saying anything."

"Suit yourself, Selma." He headed for the door. "By the way, I've got a message from Bri: 'Homegirl, you're on your own.' "

Stab of fear. She covered with a smirk. "That's not Bri."

"How's this for a reality check, Selma: Tris and Q took you and Bri to Fashion Square before they killed Elise, bought you dresses, shoes, and jewelry. Then you got pizza at Pizza Hut, then you looked for a Mexican to buy ice. You knew what the ice was for and while it was happening, you and Bri smoke up in your—"

"Wait!" Black eyes flashed. "What do you want me to say?"

"The truth."

"Like what part of it?"

"All of it."

She stared. Smiled girlishly and tossed her hair. "Sure, why not?"

Milo said, "Let's talk about hats."

"Don't wear 'em."

"A baseball hat, Selma."

"Oh, that," she said. "That was Bri's idea. She said if it got left in the car, they could blame everything on the annoying kid."

"Because he was annoying."

"Yeah."

"You and Bri never met him."

"Nope."

"What did Tris and Q find so annoying about him?"

"Better than them at baseball."

"Both of them."

"Yup. It pissed them off."

"So why not frame him for a couple of murders."

"It sounded," she said, "like a real good idea."

35

Deputy D.A. John Nguyen left the observation room smiling. "Why can't you do this all the time?"

"Do what?"

"Make my life easy. Okay, Xerox the murder book for me and I'll have phone subpoenas on everyone activated within two hours, same for broad-based warrants for both families' houses in Bel Air as well the little monsters' desks and lockers at Prep. I'll also suggest to the Feds that Wydette Senior's plane was used to transport dope across state borders to Arizona, they can smooth it with the Aspen police for search of the mountain home. Anything else on your wish list?"

"Sounds good, John." Milo phoned Moe Reed and told him to copy the file.

Nguyen said, "You should be able to execute those warrants by tomorrow a.m."

"There may be a time lag between authorization and execution."

"What? This from Mr. I-Want-It-Yesterday."

"It's complicated, John."

"Seemed to me those bimbos just made it simple."

"On the contrary, John."

Milo carried the taped confessions back to his office. Moe Reed was just leaving with the murder book. His free hand waved a message slip.

"I was just going to look for you, Loo. This came in while I was copying."

Milo scanned the note. "You took this personally?"

"Came in on your cell, Loo. I copied pretty much verbatim."

Reed's meticulous cursive read: *I gave you SAT dates why didn't you do anything? Go after Tristram Wydette and Quinn Glover, everyone already knows.*

Reed said, "Young male. I tried to keep him on the line but he cut the connection."

" 'Everyone already knows.' "

"I took that to mean at the school, Loo. It's like those school shootings, right, Doc? Kids brag."

I nodded.

Milo said, "Nothing like being outside the goddamn loop. Okay, get the copy to John, you might still be able to catch him in the lot. Then stay on call."

Reed rotated his neck. "It's happening."

"Something is, Moses."

The chief listened.

    Milo finished.

The chief said nothing.

"Sir?"

"Do you feel physically confident, Sturgis? You're not exactly a gym rat."

"Confident of—"

"Your ability to kick two young bucks' asses if necessary?"

"Depends on—"

"What I'm getting at, Sturgis, is do you feel secure enough to go in there without a fucking army? I'd like to avoid some three-penny SWAT opera."

"If the school cooperates and doesn't alert them I think I can handle that."

"The school won't alert anyone because the school won't know."

"You want me to go in cold."

"Interesting choice of words."

"Yes, sir, it is."

"This has been a tough one, Sturgis. Lingered in all our minds."

"It has, sir."

"Fuck it," said the chief. "Just do what you need to do, but if there's a way to minimize disruption, that would be preferable."

"Thank you, sir."

"Just get it over with."

We sped past the allée of Chinese elms. Herb Walkowicz was out of his booth before we rolled to a stop.

He tipped his hat. "Now what, guys?"

Milo showed him the warrants.

"Whoa, and here I was gonna give you the song and dance about calling Rollins before I can unlock the gates."

Laughing, he fetched his key from the booth.

The first of Windsor Prep's sixteen acres was an immaculate concrete-and-brick lot stack-parked with gleaming vehicles. Milo and I searched for Tristram Wydette's Jaguar and Quinn Glover's Hummer, found neither.

"Means nothing," he said. "Kids like that can have access to all kinds of wheels." But he called Reed and Binchy, anyway, to make sure they stayed close to the Wydette estate on Bellagio Drive and the even larger Glover spread, a few blocks away on Nimes Road.

Reed said, "There's a guardhouse in front. First I thought it was a dummy inside, guy was so still. Then he moved his head. Once in ninety minutes. Talk about a fascinating job."

"I don't like surveillance, either, Moses."

"Pardon—no, I don't mind it."

"Then keep enjoying."

Beyond the parking area, a cluster of dun-colored, red-roofed Monterey Colonial buildings stood like chess pieces on a board of precision-mowed bluegrass. Monumental, perfectly positioned pines, floss trees, liquidambars, and redwoods were sculpted to symmetry. An adult female passed from one building to another. Then a male teacher in a tweed coat and khakis. A scatter of students studied on the lawn. No sound beyond breeze kissing leaves.

Off to the left, flags stood in barbered turf ringed by low white fencing. The nine-hole golf course.

"Poor darlings," said Milo. "They go to college, it's a step down."

All the buildings bore brass plaques. The largest was fronted by a cool, dim loggia and merited a double-wide slab: *Administration*.

Dr. Mary Jane Rollins's office was the prize beyond a hushed, green-carpeted, oak-paneled reception room overseen by a black woman in a red silk dress. *Sheila McBough* was stamped on her personal chunk of brass. The foundry loved this place.

Milo's card didn't impress her. "You don't have an appointment."

He said, "We have something better," and held out the warrant.

Before she finished scanning, he continued past her desk.

"You can't do that."

"That, madam, is an obvious misstatement."

Mary Jane Rollins's personal space was her secretary's office on steroids. The same honey-colored oak, green carpeting, enough carving and moldings to spell out *Authority*.

She was on the phone, said, "I'll have to call you back," and slammed down the receiver. "Now what?"

Milo told her.

Her initial reaction was the expected panic. Then she smirked. "Well, unfortunately for you, they're not here."

"Doctor—"

"It's a senior cut-day, Lieutenant. We have several, throughout the semester, prefer to bleed off tension on a regular basis rather than—"

"Where are their lockers, Doctor?"

"In the locker area."

"Show me. And bring your master key."

"What makes you think I have one?"

"You don't?"

"Your warrant says I need to answer personal questions?"

He showed her his badge. "This says if you don't cooperate, I'll cuff you and haul your educated but morally unschooled derriere off to jail."

She blanched. "I never—"

"Neither have I. Show me their lockers. *Now.*"

"This will not go unreported."

"Mercy me, pass the defibrillator."

As we left, Rollins told McBough, "Sheila, phone Dr. Helfgott immediately. There's a situation."

Milo said, "Sheila, don't phone anyone. There's a *situation.*"

The lockers lined two walls of a cavernous building labeled *Repository.* Oak, brass-fitted.

Milo said, "Open Wydette's and Glover's."

Rollins sniffed as she checked a list. "Calling me morally unschooled was unnecessary."

"I'm looking for two vicious murderers and all you care about is semantics."

"Not semantics," said Rollins. "I'm a good person. One day you may find yourself in special circumstances and react in a way that surprises you."

"Gee," he said. "That could never happen to me."

Both lockers were empty.

Rollins said, "So much for your evidence."

"Do you have any idea where I can find Tristram Wydette and Quinn Glover?"

Silence.

"Doctor, if you know where they are and you withhold that information, you'll go to jail on obstruction charges right now."

"I may go, but I won't stay long."

"Trust me, Dr. Rollins, you won't enjoy a single minute behind bars."

Her lips pursed.

Milo said, "A job's that important?"

"It's not a job, it's a calling."

"So was the Nazi SS."

"That is outrageous—oh, all right, seeing as cut-day leads into the weekend, they're where you'd expect them to be: embarking on a family *holiday*."

Her voice rose as the Briticism rolled off her tongue. Creepy ebullience.

"Both families?"

"I believe so."

"Where are they going?"

"I don't know."

"How do you know the families are traveling together?"

"I chitchatted with the boys yesterday. They were in excellent spirits and I find it difficult to believe—"

"What exactly did they tell you?"

"Tristram told me. They were going to use the plane. That it would be . . . wonderful. I believe his term was 'awesome.' "

"*The* plane."

"Mr. Wydette's Gulfstream Five," she said. "It's a marvel."

37

As I sped to Santa Monica Airport, Milo celled Reed. "Nothing, Loo."

"That's 'cause we may be too late, both families are scheduled to leave for the weekend. Check with the mannequin in the booth and don't take any bullshit. Tell Sean to find out what's happening at Wydette's place. If everyone's gone, we'll go ahead and search the houses and given the size, I'll need a small army, so get in touch with the lab and the duty sergeant and start recruiting."

Moments later Reed phoned back. "Mannequin's cooperative, ex–Rampart Division, hates the family 'cause they treat him like dirt. He's absolutely certain no one left today except Tristram, after Quinn Glover picked him up in his Hummer. That was an hour and a quarter ago, right before I arrived. They took luggage, Loo. A lot of it."

◆

The search warrant was extended to the Gulfstream by the time I reached Bundy Drive, takeoff to Aspen aborted by the tower at LAX as I turned onto Ocean Park. As far as the crew was aware, "unanticipated air-traffic buildup" was the reason.

I got buzzed through the gate at Diamond Aviation by mentioning Milo's name, drove onto the landing field, followed a porter in a golf cart to the G-V.

The plane's engines were running, as were those of two smaller jets. The noise level was at brain-puree.

When I reached the plane's left wing and stopped, the pilot looked down from the cockpit, curious, but not alarmed. Milo's badge-flash didn't change that. People who loft tons of metal in the air should take a low-key approach to life.

Milo motioned him out.

The engines switched off.

When they'd quieted to merely deafening, the door opened and the pilot lowered the foldout steps, descended two rungs, turned and shut the door.

Rock-jawed, the same man who'd flown Edgar Helfgott halfway around the globe and back on high school business. Rawboned, gray-haired, built like a runner.

Milo introduced himself, shouting to be heard.

The captain pointed several yards away and the three of us walked until we could hear our own voices.

The pilot said, "Rod Brewer. What can I do for you, sir?"

"I've got a search warrant for your plane and arrest warrants for Tristram Wydette and Quinn Glover. They inside?"

"Yes, sir."

"Who else is in there?"

"Captain Susan Curtis. Is she in danger?"

"Anything in the boys' demeanor worrying you?"

"Not really," said Brewer. "They're spoiled little bastards all caught up with their iPods and the shades are down. But with too much delay they might get curious. Mind if I tell Sue to lock the cockpit?"

"Good idea."

Brewer made the call, ended by instructing the co-pilot to answer any questions from the boys with "mechanical problems." To us: "Okay, what do I need to do?"

Milo said, "Where are they sitting?"

"First row on either side," said Brewer. "It's always that way. I can be flying over the Grand Canyon, they're into their own thing."

"The boys or the entire family?"

"Seems to be a genetic thing."

"Did you notice anything that can be construed as a weapon?"

"We've got silverware." Smiling. "Mrs. Wydette just upgraded to Christofle."

"Nothing else?"

"Everything's in the hold," said Brewer. "Except their iPods, *Hustler* magazine, and Silver Patrón. They're already half stoned, don't know if that works in your favor or the opposite."

"They get nasty when they're drunk?"

"Not really. Mostly they sleep."

"Parents allow them to drink?"

"When they're with their parents they drink Red Bull."

"How many times have they flown without their parents?"

"This is the first."

"But Daddy authorized the trip."

"Mommy."

"She say why the boys were flying to Aspen by themselves?"

"No one explains anything to me," said Brewer. "I'm furniture."

"Furniture who holds their lives in the balance."

"Lieutenant, people in their circumstances see the world differently. There's them, then there's everyone else."

"Okay, thanks. Pop that door, please."

"No prob," said Brewer. "Before you go in, you might want to check the hold. This is the first time they insisted on loading their own stuff."

The two duffels lay on the tarmac, black nylon, all-weather sturdy, stainless-steel fittings glinting in the untrammeled sun.

Milo had gloved up and unloaded them by himself, continued to sweat and pant.

Captain Rod Brewer watched him the way an anesthesiologist watches oxygen levels.

Milo touched one of the duffels. Patted it along the length, repeated the same for the other.

Arching his eyebrows, he unzipped.

Inside were layers of thick plastic sheeting, milky and opaque. Kneeling, he peered closely. Took out a pocketknife that he wiped with a sterile cloth.

Slicing carefully, he peeled back each layer.

Captain Rod Brewer said, "My God."

A face stared up at us.

Young, male, greenish-gray, slack-jawed. Flat, clouded cellophane disks where eyes had once functioned.

What the techies call a "defect" was visible in the center of the corpse's unlined forehead.

Entry wound, small and neat, probably a .22.

The body nested in a cloud of white pellets that began vaporizing the moment they impacted with warm air.

"What the hell is that, dry ice?" said Brewer.

"It sublimates," said Milo, wielding his blade and lengthening the slit.

The pilot blinked, looked away. An unflappable man but something had finally perturbed him and I knew what it was.

No normal-sized human being could fit into either of the duffels.

Milo finished peeling back the plastic. Stared.

Rod Brewer crossed himself.

The body had been severed just above the hips.

Not a clean job; the edges of the separation were ragged, bone ends had shredded like used firecrackers, exposed muscle resembled marbled steak, viscera had been frozen mid-action as they tumbled out of the torso, coalescing as horrid, olive-green sausage.

Something serrated and high-powered; my guess was a chain saw.

Milo stared, marched to the second duffel.

Solved the jigsaw puzzle that had once been Trey Franck.

The Gulfstream's cabin smelled of fresh flowers, apples, and tequila.

Tristram Wydette's long frame stretched the length of a brocade sofa on the plane's port side, a copy of *Hustler* tented over his face. Breathing slowly, evenly. One manicured hand brushed the carpet. Near his fingers sat a chrome-plated iPod.

Quinn Glover, larger and heavier in real life, with the bland good looks of a budding politico, sat with his feet up, wearing eyeshades, sucking from a bottle of Silver Patrón and bopping in time to whatever tune-buzz his gold-plated iPod was offering.

Both boys wore camouflage cargo pants and tight black T-shirts that showcased muscular builds. Combat boots and dirty white socks littered the aisle.

Uniformed for a mission.

Milo yanked Quinn up first, had him cuffed, belted into his chair, eyes and ears exposed, before his mouth could close.

Tristram remained asleep. Milo flipped him like a pancake, yanked out his earbuds.

Both boys gaped.

Milo said, "You guys watch a lot of TV?"

Blank stares.

"I'm sure you know the drill, but here goes: Tristram Wydette, you are under arrest for murder. You have the right to keep your stupid mouth shut, whether or not you talk really doesn't matter squat to me . . ."

The evolution of each boy's facial expression was as uniform as their getup: drowsy surprise morphing to cornered-animal shock, upgrading to terror, then tears.

Milo called for backup and we watched them sob.

Worth the price of admission.

CHAPTER

39

Battalion One: high-priced lawyers.

Battalion Two: high-priced publicists.

An attempt to curry favor at the *Times* because Myron Wydette played golf with the publisher backfired and the resulting self-righteous indignation was borderline slapstick. Wags insisted the real problem was Wydette cheated at the game and his greens buddy finally had enough.

The palm print found on Sal Fidella's garage matched Quinn Glover's hand. Faced with that addition to the mountain of eyewitness and forensic evidence, Quinn's legal commandos tried selling out Tristram Wydette in return for a lighter sentence, pushing the notion that Quinn was a weak-willed follower caught in the spell of Tristram Wydette's evil charisma.

Tristram, his former best friend claimed, had masterminded the whole thing because getting into Stanford was the most important thing in the world to him, he felt like the stupid kid in the family, Aidan was the brainiac.

When told that Aidan had also used Trey Franck as an SAT surrogate, the boy was genuinely surprised. "No shit. What was *his* problem?"

"You tell me, Quinn," said Milo.

"He always seemed smart to me."

"Maybe he just wasn't smart enough."

"Yeah. Sir. You're right." Laughter.

"Something funny, Quinn?"

"I guess he just fucked up. Sir. I guess we all did."

"That's a fair assessment."

"Assessment," said Quinn. "That's an SAT vocab word. 'The act or instance of evaluating.' "

"How do you assess your situation, Quinn?"

"It was T's idea, sir. I didn't like it, what could I do?"

"No choice at all."

"Exactly, sir. T thought of the dee-ice, T put her—Ms. Freeman—in it. He also bashed in that loser's head—we were gonna shoot him—*T* was gonna shoot him but we forgot the gun at T's house and we already drove all the way there so T said let's just do it."

"How'd it go down?"

"Loser came to the door, we—T pushed him in, saw the pool cue and bashed him."

Milo said, "There was no sign of a serious struggle, Quinn. That means Mr. Fidella was restrained."

"If you say so, sir."

"Be a lot easier for two big guys to restrain one middle-aged loser."

The boy's lawyer, silent and working his iPhone till now, said, "I'd prefer he doesn't answer that."

Milo didn't protest. "So T bashed in the loser's head. Then what?"

"Then T got into the Jag."

"And you drove away in the loser's Corvette."

The lawyer said, "I'd prefer if—"

"And I'd prefer not to waste my time, Mr. Neal. Grand Theft Auto is not your client's problem."

"It's not a matter of that, it's a matter of—"

Milo stood. Motioned to me to do the same.

"That's it?" said Quinn.

"According to Mr. Neal it is, son." To the attorney: "So far, I haven't heard anything of a 'forthcoming nature' and John Nguyen won't take kindly to that. Particularly in light of multiple victims, murder for gain, extreme depravity, lying in wait—"

"Fine," said Neal. "He drove the car."

We sat back down.

Milo said, "You drove off in Mr. Fidella's Corvette."

"Piece-of-shit wheels," said Quinn. "Made all sorts of noises." Smiling and hoping it caught on.

"Then what happened?"

Client glanced at counsel. Counsel nodded.

"We went to Tristram's house and stored it in the garage. His dad's got a huge garage, twenty cars in there."

"Then what?"

"Nothing until the next day, then Tristram took the Jag and I took the piece of shit, I almost thought it wouldn't make it."

"Make it where?"

"Pasadena."

"What's in Pasadena?"

"His place."

"Whose place?"

"Him. The nerd who took the test."

"Trey Franck."

"Yeah—yes, sir."

"Why'd you go there?"

"T said it was like his mom, she's crazy about being neat, doesn't matter if you leave a speck of cookie on the couch or you take a dump on it, she's going to freak out. So we had to go all the way."

"No sense leaving a speck of mess," said Milo.

"Exactly, sir. We had to be thorough."

"How'd it go down with Trey Franck?"

"The plan was we were going to knock on the door, say it was a friend or something, but right after we got there, he came out of the building and started walking. We drove up to him, it was dark, no one was around, so we jumped out and held him and cold-cocked him. He wimped out totally, like *out*."

"We?"

"T did the shooting."

"Who did the cold-cocking?"

Pause. "I guess that was me. But T held him and kicked him in the balls, by the time I hit him he was pretty much out of it. I didn't hit him that hard."

"What happened next?"

"T drove him and I followed in the Corvette."

"Where was Mr. Franck?"

"In the trunk of the Jag. T had him tied up with these plastic thingies."

A fact verified by traces of Trey Franck's saliva and blood in the rear compartment of the freshly vacuumed and detailed car.

"You were following in Sal Fidella's Corvette."

"Yes, sir."

"Where'd you go?"

"We drove to this place, T knew it 'cause his cousin has a ranch near there and his dad took him hiking and shooting up in the mountains there when he was little."

"Not recently?"

"No way," said Quinn Glover. "He doesn't talk to his dad, hates his dad, thinks his dad hates him."

"So you're at a spot T knew," said Milo.

"T pulls him out of the trunk."

"Was Franck conscious?"

"Guess so," said Quinn Glover. "He was making these whimpery sounds, all curled up. T rolls him on his back, says, 'Guess you're not so smart, motherfucker,' and shoots him right here."

Touching the center of a tan, unlined brow. "We tried to push the Vette down into the hole but it doesn't go, so T set it on fire and we booked."

"After putting a baseball cap on the seat."

"T's idea. Sir."

"What was the reason?"

"Blame it on someone else."

"Who?"

"Mexican dude, everyone knew he hated her."

"Hated who?"

"The bi—Ms. Freeman."

"How'd everyone know?"

"Dude told anyone who'd listen. She didn't like him, either."

"Elise Freeman complained about Martin Mendoza?"

"Yeah."

"To you, specifically?"

"When we came for tutoring, yeah," said Quinn Glover.

"How'd the topic of Martin Mendoza come up?"

"He was leaving and we were coming in, we said, 'You tutor

him?' 'Cause she was expensive, you know, and the dude didn't have money. She said, 'Unfortunately. Apparently my job description includes *those* people.' Or something like that. Sir."

"Which you took to mean?"

"She didn't like Mexicans."

"What'd you say to that?"

"Nothing," said the boy.

"But you thought of it later, when you and T decided to blame the murders on Martin."

"T's idea."

"What'd you do with Franck's body?"

"Wiped it off with some rags from the Jag, then put him back in the Jag."

"Then what?"

"You know."

"I know what?"

"You saw him, sir. What T did."

"T cut him up."

"Yes, sir."

"But the place you did it was your father's workshop, Quinn. All those tools he keeps back of your property for his woodworking."

"He makes birdhouses." Muttering.

"What's that, Quinn?"

"Nothing."

"What'd you just say, son?"

"Lame. Making those stupid birdcages."

"What use would a chain saw be for making birdcages?"

"That's for the trees," said Quinn Glover. "We have some land in Washington, lots of trees, he likes to run around with the chain saw and saw them down. Says it's his release. Then he turns them into birdcages."

"Guess your dad will need a new chain saw."

"Guess so."

Neal looked up. "Is this going to take a whole lot longer?"

Milo ignored him. "Back to something you just said, Quinn. When you saw Martin Mendoza. 'We were coming in for tutoring.' Are you telling me you and T had joint tutoring sessions with Ms. Freeman? 'Cause the records recovered from the laptop we found in T's bedroom at home don't back that up. Same for Mr. Fidella's computer recovered from your room—he had copies of all Ms. Freeman's files."

Quinn Glover licked his lips.

Milo said, "You had individual sessions."

"Yes, sir."

"So maybe it was you who had that conversation with Ms. Freeman about Martin, not both of you."

The lawyer said, "Don't answer that."

We stood again.

"Oh, c'mon, Lieutenant. You need to balance what he's given you with what he hasn't."

"I need to?" said Milo.

"You know what I mean, Lieutenant."

"You're a lawyer, Mr. Neal. That means no one—including yourself—knows what you mean. Bye."

"This is inappropriate and . . . impetuous!"

"There you go," said Milo. "Two SAT words for the price of one."

As details of the cheating scandal hit the national news, the Educational Testing Service announced a comprehensive review of all exams administered to Windsor Prep students over the past five years.

Sal Fidella's computer files showed he'd contemplated finding additional blackmail victims after Elise's death. The files Tristram and Quinn had added concentrated on porn, tunes, photos from exotic car and motorcycle sites. Email correspondence between the boys indicated they viewed their murder spree with hilarity, wondered what it would feel like to *do a girl.*

like bri and selma?

yeah they'd be softer but you'd probably need a new blade anyway

John Nguyen said, "No deal, no way. I've got a bisected corpse, if anything's a death penalty case this is it."

No one gets executed in California, but prosecutors collect lethal-injection sentences like baseball cards.

In the end, a deal was cut. Guilty pleas to first-degree murder and life sentences, but with the possibility of parole because both killers were young, had no prior criminal record, and were potentially "redeemable."

Milo said, "Coupons are redeemable."

One file that didn't show up on either Elise's computer or Fidella's was an indication of where four years of SAT scam money had gone. With fees of fifteen thousand a pop and the possibility that Trey Franck, wearing a variety of wigs, had gamed the system over two dozen times during a three-year period, the total was significant.

One day after the plea bargain hit the news, Dr. Will Kham called Milo from Cottage Hospital in Santa Barbara and asked for an appointment. We met him at Café Moghul, where Milo was making up for lost time with a mountain of lamb.

Kham wore a dark blue suit and a matching shirt and tie, entered the restaurant furtively.

A physician, but his black bag today was a wheeled carry-on.

Out of it came a sheaf of papers. Eighteen months of investment records from a Citibank subsidiary in Santa Barbara.

Nine hundred and eighteen thousand dollars joint-accounted to Kham and Elise Freeman's sister, Sandra Stuehr.

Milo kept eating as he read. When he turned the last page, he said, "Value stocks and corporate bonds, you guys haven't done too badly, considering."

"I want out," said Kham. "I can tell you exactly what's mine and what's hers."

"Tell me about it, Doc."

"The figures will speak for themselves."

"Tell me anyway."

Not a talkative man, but after some struggle, Kham got the story out.

He and Sandra had planned to be married, though the scandal had changed everything, no way would his family tolerate that kind of thing. And he'd been having doubts, himself.

"Too rushed. The fact that she was so eager was starting to concern me."

A year ago, Sandra had insisted on a joint account to "prove the strength of their relationship."

Kham had contributed five hundred and twenty thousand, Sandra a bit over three hundred thousand. Investments purchased at the bottom of the meltdown by Kham had added nearly a hundred in profit.

"Looking back," said Kham, "I know she used me to launder the money. Because prior to that, she'd been claiming financial hardship, her ex was withholding all sorts of assets from her. All of a sudden, she presented me with a cashier's check for three oh nine. When I asked her where it came from, she said savings and changed the subject. Back then, I was love-stupid so I let it go. But

I held on to the receipt—it's in here. Drawn on a bank in Studio City. When I heard about what her sister had done, I figured you should know."

"We should, Doc. Thanks very much."

"Thank me," said Kham, "by helping me get my five twenty back. She can keep the interest, it's dirty money, I don't want any part of it."

"Sounds like your parents raised you right."

"So they'd say, Lieutenant."

40

A week after Tristram Wydette and Quinn Glover bargained for their lives, the police chief gave a press conference describing the arrest as "the product of meticulous investigation and precisely the type of corruption I'm committed to eradicating."

Among the cadre of suits surrounding him was Captain Stanley Creighton. Milo was nowhere to be seen.

I called and asked him about it.

"If I wanted to be an actor, I would've learned to wait tables."

The following morning, at eight a.m., an aide to the chief got through to my private line and asked me to "confer" with her boss in three hours.

"At his house, Dr. Delaware, if you don't mind."

"Not at all."

"Great, I'll give you the address."

I already had it, but no sense editing her script.

When she hung up, I gave Milo another call.

He said, "Rick and I are going over travel stuff. We were thinking Hawaii, but maybe the Atlantic deserves us. Ever been to the Bahamas?"

"Never. My travel plans extend to Agoura. Want to drive together?"

"I would if I was invited, Alex."

"Oh."

"Guess I'm the lucky one."

"I wonder what he wants."

"Maybe he'll sweeten the job offer."

"There ain't enough sugar in Hawaii," I said. "Same goes for whatever they grow in the Bahamas. Okay, keep you posted."

"Here's my post: John says Tristram's lawyers are panicking for a quick transfer to Corcoran."

"That's a tough place. County Jail décor doesn't cut it?"

"Getting the shit beat out of you by some resident County gangbangers doesn't fit young T's lifestyle. The fervent hope is isolation with the snitches and the child molesters and the white-collar mopes will help."

"There you go," I said. "Everything's about connections."

In the daylight, the chief's spread was scragglier but more appealing. Like the set of an old western movie.

Hot day in Agoura, despite impending autumn. He sat in the same rocker, wearing a black suit, white shirt, and red tie that had to be cooking him. The three metal folding chairs to his left soaked up full, punishing sun.

Three young men occupied the chairs: a husky Latino kid with his arm in a sling wearing a South El Monte High letterman's jacket, a smallish but muscular guy, slightly older, in cutoffs and a Zuma Jay T-shirt, and a beanpole with a humongous Adam's apple, awkward mannerisms, and fuzzy red hair protruding from a beige Huntington Gardens cap.

I bypassed the chief and walked up to Cutoff. "You're Garret Kenten?"

"Yes, sir."

"Good to meet you."

"Same here."

"Impressive and entertaining, Doctor," said the chief. "One day you can take the show to Vegas."

Charlie removed his cap. "Da-ad."

"Sorry, son." Different voice. Subdued, embarrassed, unsure. I'd heard it from countless parents of adolescents.

"Forgive me, Dr. Delaware. As you can imagine, it's been a bit challenging around here."

"Shouldn't be, Dad," said Charlie. "Seeing as we did the *allegedly* right thing."

Garret Kenten high-fived him.

Martin Mendoza smiled.

I shook his left hand, continued to Charlie.

The chief said, "Please sit down, Dr. Delaware. No sense drawing this out. Garret and Charlie have been hiding Martin Mendoza since shortly after Elise Freeman's murder. Technically, when Marty was a fugitive, that was illegal. But given how things have unfolded, I'm sure you recognize the need for discretion."

"Of course," I said. To the trio: "Good work, guys."

"No big deal," said Garret Kenten.

Marty Mendoza said, "To me it was, dude."

"The fugitive," said Garret. "We should've filmed it."

Charlie hadn't taken his eyes off me. "It was a clear matter of right and wrong, unsullied by those inane moral dilemmas they keep tossing at us so they can feel good about themselves. As if theoretical situations are relevant."

Garret Kenten said, "What matters to me is my grandfather doesn't get hassled." Talking to me but looking sidelong at the chief.

The chief said, "That'll be no problem."

"I know you can't stand him, sir, but you need to forget about that."

"Your grandfather and I—we've had our differences. He's obviously a good man but there are . . . differences."

"I don't care about that, sir. I just don't want you to hassle him."

"No problem."

Charlie said, "No reason for there to be, Dad."

His father glared. Pulled at his mustache. "Not a single hair on your grampa's head will be touched."

Garret grinned. "Good, he doesn't have too many left."

Marty laughed. Charlie remained serious.

"We had to do it," he said. "We don't deserve credit because there was no other logical choice. They made explicit threats against him."

The chief said, "Son, there's no need to get into—"

"They hated Marty because they're insubstantial posers and his abilities threatened them. It was a matter of life and death."

Marty said, "Maybe not that bad. At least I got to learn surfing."

Garret said, "You learned to flop on your ass."

I said, "So you stayed in Malibu."

"Yes, but not at my grandfather's estate because we knew . . . we just figured it wasn't a good idea. My grandfather rents me my own place in Trancas, I'm taking a couple of years off to do a documentary on surfing. Probably come to nothing, but I'll give it a try then maybe head to UC Santa Cruz." To Marty: "At least you're neat, dude."

"Like you'd know the difference."

I said, "Nice setup. You even got him his own surfboard."

All three boys stared.

"Your grandfather's house was under surveillance, Garret. You were seen bringing a board out and the following day you left with a guy in a beige cap."

Garret Kenten said, "Whoa."

Charlie shrugged.

The chief said, "Okay, everyone got to share feelings, now go inside, guys, I need to talk to the doctor alone."

Martin Mendoza stood but the other two hesitated.

"Don't push it," said the chief.

Garret and Charlie flanked Marty. As they turned to leave, I walked up to him. "I'm glad you're okay."

He said, "History class there was all that talk about good Germans saving Jews. I wasn't sure I believed it."

The three of them trudged to the house.

The chief said, "You know what I'm going to ask you now."

"Not really."

"This mess, every single application from Prep is being looked at like a slice of freeze-dried dogshit. Charlie earned his way into Yale. I want you to write him a letter of recommendation and make it good."

"How does he feel about that?"

"Look, Doctor, anything from his teachers and that asshole Helfgott's gonna be poison. You, on the other hand, still stand for truth, justice, and all that good stuff. And you've got that professorship at the med school, they like that kind of thing."

"Be happy to do it," I said. "After I talk to Charlie."

"About what?"

"For me to write a good letter, I need to know him."

"I'll tell you what you need to know: 4.0 GPA and he takes the hardest classes—honors, APs. His extracurricular activities are off the chart, I'm talking a broad range of—"

"Not that," I said.

"Then what?" he barked.

"I want to know *him*. Not his circus tricks."

CHAPTER

41

Charlie slouched out of the house with the look of every other teenager pushed into doing something he despised.

I said, "Let's walk."

"Why?"

"I feel like it and you're too young to have sore feet."

"Whatever."

We began circling the motor court. He jammed spidery hands into his pockets, stared at the ground.

"You know what your dad wants."

"Emphasis on 'your dad.' As opposed to what I want."

"That's why I'm talking to you."

"He's utterly obsessed."

"With you?"

"With me getting into some weenie emporium."

"He said you chose Yale."

"That's like saying I hate cheese and someone says your choice is Gruyère or Cheddar."

"You couldn't care less."

"No," he said, "if I said that, I'd be just another phony cretin. Sure, I care. I've been conditioned to care."

Two steps. "Sometimes I think about going to junior college. Just to show them how stupid the whole thing is."

"That would be something," I said.

"Where'd you go to school?"

"The U."

"No pressure from your parents?"

"The Ivies weren't in my universe. I was just glad to get the hell away from Missouri."

"What's wrong with Missouri?"

"Absolutely nothing."

He stared at me. "Oh. Anyway, don't feel you have to do anything that contradicts your principles."

"Writing a letter for you doesn't," I said. "On the contrary."

"You don't even know me."

"I know enough."

"Whatever—if I say don't write it, you won't?"

"Not a comma."

"He doesn't take well to being told no."

"I've told him no before."

Brown eyes widened. "In what context?"

I said, "He's been bugging me for years to give up my practice and work for the department. Keeps tossing more money and better titles my way."

"Yeah, that's his style. So what, you shine him on because you don't like him?"

"I could deal with him, Charlie, but the money still sucks and always will and, more important, I prize my independence. You can relate to that."

His look turned sour. *Don't Patronize Me.*

I said, "Don't get all sensitive, I'm stating a fact. No need for me to kiss your ass."

The follow-up look, saucer-eyed and confused, said *Who Is This Space Alien?*

We walked a bit more before he said, "It's utterly absurd, his thinking I deserve a prize. I just did what was necessary."

"Were you and Marty friends?"

"I don't have any friends," he said. "Neither did he, at Prep."

"Common enemy's as good a reason as any for rapport."

First smile of the day. "True . . . he used to sit by himself, a couple of times I went over and talked to him. He was polite but didn't have much to say. After he hurt his shoulder he wasn't much for any kind of sociability, I could see he wanted to be alone, so I stayed away. But then I heard some of *their* clique trash-talking about Marty killing Ms. F., I knew I had to do something. Planting lies is so typical. They live to deceive."

"T and Q," I said.

"They take no responsibility and the system feeds their narcissism."

"Finding scapegoats."

"Finding and tossing them over cliffs. That's the original concept. Of scapegoat, I mean. It's from the Old Testament, used to be literal. When the community deteriorated to utter corruption, they picked two goats. One was designated godly, the other was the Azazel and they tossed it over to atone for everyone's sins." Huffing. "As if."

"They teach Bible at Prep?"

"Oh, sure." He snickered. "Between agonizing analysis of Malcolm X and *Catcher in the Rye* there isn't much time left for *ancient* texts. No, I've been known to read on my own. Even when I should be studying for the SAT."

I said, "You like the Old Testament."

"Old, New, the Prophets, the Gospels, the Quran, the Bhagavad Gita. The truth is, all religions promote kindness as well as incredible brutality."

I said, "So T and Q's clique had pinned Ms. Freeman on Martin. Think they believed it?"

"Who knows? Are they even capable of belief?"

"They talked about it openly?"

"No way," he said. "But one time I was being my usual asocial loser self and walking near the back of the campus—right at the back, there's a dense, kind of foresty area where no one goes, which is precisely why I do, I need peace and quiet so I can read what I want to, cut myself off from all the—anyway, I was back there. Reading Job, actually, and for the first time I heard someone else. It was T, smoking weed. Then Q joined him and he lit up. I said, *Great, there goes my last refuge.* I thought of leaving but didn't want them to see my—I just didn't want to deal with them. So I stayed, I was behind some thick bushes, it's a place I always go, just me and the beetles, once in a while there's a squirrel. They had no idea. I had no interest whatsoever in anything they had to say but they were close by and talking loud enough for me to hear. Then some of their clique joined them and they all started talking about it."

"Ms. Freeman."

"Yes. No one was exactly grieving. Mostly because they're superficial. But in T's case and Q's, there was anger. 'Ding dong the bitch is dead,' that kind of thing. Then T started going off on Marty, blaming him for it, saying he was going to call in an anonymous tip to the police and name Marty. Everyone thought that was a great idea. Then everyone lit up and the air started stinking of weed and I wanted out of there but I waited until they were gone, then took out my cell and texted Garret and he called his grandfather and he called the Mendozas. They decided they needed to keep Marty safe until it became clear if those threats were real. Mrs. Mendoza packed up a suitcase and drove Marty to Garret's."

"You texted Garret first because you and he are friends."

"I already told you: The concept of friendship is alien to me. I knew him from surfing. He surfs at County Line and I do, too, because the waves are usually good and I can just drive over the canyon from here." Second smile of the day. "Bet you didn't see me as a surfer. I can't play ball worth shit and I spaz out in basketball but on a board my balance is pretty good."

"You're full of surprises, Charlie."

"Going to put that in your letter?"

"Am I writing a letter?"

"Far as I'm concerned, there's no need. The entire process is utterly absurd, not to mention corrupt and despicable. Look where it led."

"Bad people can turn anything rotten."

"The *system's* rotten," he said. "The haves keep getting more, the have-nots keep getting ripped off. Don't think I'm a socialist or an anarchist—any kind of ist. Those systems inevitably sink into corruption, as well. I just work at seeing things the way they are."

We walked some more.

I said, "What made you decide T and Q might be guilty themselves?"

"My long-term analysis of their personalities plus the anger—rage, really—that I heard in their voices when they were discussing Ms. Freeman. It all made sense, when you knew about the SAT scam."

"Did everyone at Prep know?"

"I can't speak for everyone, but anyone with a brain in their head had to know. T getting a 1580? Q pulling 1520? That's about as likely as me dating a supermodel."

"So you suspected them, but didn't want to go to your father."

"He's the last person I'd go to. All he'd care about is how it impacted my application."

"Instead you called in those anonymous tips."

Silence. "That was cowardly, wasn't it?"

"The first one was kind of abstract, Charlie. Three dates."

"Abstract as in useless," he said. "No one figured it out."

"We did," I said. "And it led to everything else that followed. Your spelling it out on the second tip was a nice boost."

"We couldn't hide Marty forever and no one was getting anywhere. I knew I'd been too oblique the first time. How'd you know it was me?"

"The second time you phoned Lieutenant Sturgis's cell directly. Only insiders have that. As in your dad. More important, that phone registers caller I.D."

He slapped his forehead. "Oh, brilliant. Put that in the letter: Charlie has trouble with basic logic."

"If you feel like flogging yourself, that's fine. But the truth is you did the right thing and you were the only one at Prep who did."

"Big deal, it was too little, too late." He rotated a finger. "Whoopee-doo."

"Okay," I said. "Good luck."

"That's it?"

"Unless there's something else you want to say."

"No, I guess not . . . are you going to write the letter?"

"If you want me to."

"Can I think about that?"

"When's the application deadline?"

"Couple of weeks."

"Give me a day or two's notice."

"Okay." Shooting out a spindly, dry hand. "Sorry if I'm being a butt. Things are just weird and all."

The merest hint of shrink-talk would necessitate teenage sarcasm.

I said, "You'll get over it."

CHAPTER

42

One week later, I received an email, posted at two a.m.

dr delaware, it's me, you probably won't see this until tomorrow. if you still think it's appropriate, you can do it. either way, it's okay. thanks.

In late December, I received a follow-up, also sent during the early-morning hours:

dr delaware, it's me. due to profound and alarming lack of judgment on the part of the yale admissions committee, i got in. i'm deferring for at least a year, going to try a seminary in ohio. there was some turmoil which was to be expected. but i'm holding fast.

ABOUT THE AUTHOR

JONATHAN KELLERMAN is one of the world's most popular authors. He has brought his expertise as a clinical psychologist to more than thirty bestselling crime novels, including the Alex Delaware series, *The Butcher's Theater, Billy Straight, The Conspiracy Club, Twisted,* and *True Detectives.* With his wife, the novelist Faye Kellerman, he co-authored the bestsellers *Double Homicide* and *Capital Crimes.* He is the author of numerous essays, short stories, scientific articles, two children's books, and three volumes of psychology, including *Savage Spawn: Reflections on Violent Children,* as well as the lavishly illustrated *With Strings Attached: The Art and Beauty of Vintage Guitars.* He has won the Goldwyn, Edgar, and Anthony awards and has been nominated for a Shamus Award. Jonathan and Faye Kellerman live in California and New Mexico. Their four children include the novelists Jesse Kellerman and Aliza Kellerman.

www.jonathankellerman.com

ABOUT THE TYPE

This book was set in Simoncini Garamond, a typeface designed by Francesco Simoncini based on the style of Garamond that was created by the French printer Jean Jannon after the original models of Claude Garamond.